A former journalist, Helen Muir has written five previous novels, as well as books for children. She lives in Primrose Hill, London.

Critical acclaim for Helen Muir:

'[*The Belles Lettres of Alexandra Bonaparte* is] artful and funny . . . Helen Muir is quite as serious as she is deft and skilful'
Martin Seymour-Smith, Financial Times
(*The Belles lettres of Alexandra Bonaparte*)

'In a world where we have to suffer fools every day, Muir would have us laugh uproariously at their foibles and, even in the most mundane situations, see life's beauty and brilliance.'
Jill Harley, Sunday Times
(*Nothing For You Love*)

'Many Men and Talking Wives is that rare thing, a funny novel by a woman writer . . . short, wry, idiosyncratic . . . its nose for what's funny is very sharp'
Hermione Lee, Observer
(*Many Men and Talking Wives*)

CONSEQUENCES

Helen Muir

POCKET BOOKS

LONDON · SYDNEY · NEW YORK · TOKYO · SINGAPORE · TORONTO

First published in Great Britain by Simon & Schuster Ltd, 1994
First published in Great Britain by Pocket Books, 1995
An imprint of Simon & Schuster Ltd
A Paramount Communications Company

Simon & Schuster Ltd
West Garden Place
Kendal Street
London W2 2AQ

Simon & Schuster of Australia Pty Ltd
Sydney

A CIP catalogue record for this book is available from the
British Library.

ISBN 0-671-85228-0

Typeset by Hewer Text Composition Services, Edinburgh
Printed and bound in Great Britain
by HarperCollins Manufacturing

With love to Michael,
Julian and Natalie

Love is either the shrinking remnant of something which was once enormous; or else it is part of something which will grow in the future into something enormous. But in the present it does not satisfy . It gives much less than one expects.

Anton Chekhov

1

She Said to Him

You said you were going to ring me. I've been very worried about you after what happened and what you told me. I thought you might need a break. I've been given two theatre tickets . . .

'Four one five oh.'

'Hello? Who . . . who is that?'

'Len Derbyshire.'

'Hello Leonard! I looked in the book and guessed this might be your number. How are you? It's Ruth.'

'Who?'

'Ruth Bly. We met six weeks ago at that singles club.'

'Oh . . . hullo.'

'Hello. I wondered how you were. You . . . you said you were going to ring me but you haven't. You sound a bit muffled at your end. Can you hear me? Have you got somebody there?'

'I was sleeping.'

'Lucky you. You know it's nearly lunchtime, I suppose? Is that your narcolepsy? You told me you had to take naps all day. I expect I'm disturbing you. I was only going to say hello.'

'Ah. Hullo . . . thank you.'

'I . . . um . . . I haven't been back to another evening at the Melstar Hotel. Have you?'

'I told you, my company's in the middle of collapsing. I'm sorry, Ruth . . . I meant to ring you but I'm up to my neck in lawyers and trouble. It's been fairly depressing.'

'Poor you. This is why I phoned. I was awfully worried

about your company after what you told me. I thought you might need a break from it all and somebody at work has just given me tickets for a new play on Friday. It's called *Corner Boy*, about Wardour Street. Have you heard of it?'

'Er, Friday . . . the theatre, ah . . . I never go to plays if I can help it.'

'But I thought you said you'd won an award for your film about men and women?'

'Four films of mine have won Academy Awards.'

'Leonard, really, I don't believe you never . . . are you yawning? You are, aren't you?'

'I can't sit through a play.'

'Oh, never mind. Look, sorry. Forget it.'

'No, well . . .'

'Just forget I suggested it. It was only a thought. Go back to sleep.'

'But I always drop off at plays.'

'Okay, fine. I only thought you might like to be keeping up to date in your world.'

'I'm not particularly worried about keeping up to date in my world, as you call it. I tend to believe I'm ahead. On Friday I have to give a talk at the National Film Theatre. You could come to that if you want to?'

'Oh, lovely. Well, yes, great . . . that's fixed then. I'm longing to hear more about your work. Smashing.'

'I'll leave a ticket for you at the box office. We can meet in the bar afterwards.'

'Okay. Fine.'

'Bye, then.'

'Wait . . . Leonard? Are you still there? How's Tania?'

'Who?'

'Leonard! Tania was at the singles club. You were dancing with her. You are incredible! I've never met anybody in such an intellectual dream. You only half-killed the poor woman.'

'Tania . . . yes, don't remind me. Serve her right. I knew something terrible was going to happen.'

2

He Said to Her

I can't dance. Don't ask me. I've got too many problems and I want to go home.

'The point is, Len,' Joy Sadler had remarked in her old-fashioned Kensington voice as they were driving past Harrods on their way to the Melstar Hotel off Cromwell Road, 'marriage is a state of mind. I mean it's like going into business, isn't it? If you decide to do it, you look for someone and you *just* get on with it.'

Joy was a big woman with an amiable English rose countenance and a glorious smile which revealed a good deal of her gum. She and Len Derbyshire had been friends for years, since her divorce from Roly, but love had not found a way with them.

'I can't dance,' he'd repeated for the third time. An uneasy latecomer to the driving test, he peered out into the evening traffic with anxious aggression. The car, bought at an auction a long time ago, had an abnormally high front bumper and rakish headlights. Its floor seemed to Joy to be thin and draughty, with things banging about rather disturbingly beneath it.

'You told me you danced when you went deep-sea diving and in the merchant navy.'

'Yes, that was in brothels.'

'Well, what of it?'

'Hardly dancing, was it. I was pulling their clothes off and doing Mickey Mouse drawings on their breasts. This is a formal affair.'

'Don't be silly. It's not formal.' Joy gave her head a little shake which flicked her hair from her face. 'And it doesn't matter these days about knowing steps. Dance if you want to. My accountant says they have foxtrots and such things occasionally in between the disco stuff. He danced and danced at the Melstar after his own marriage broke up.'

'Is your accountant a ballroom dancer?'

'Well, he knew enough to get round the room. He met all kinds of women . . . divorced forty year olds and girls of twenty. He was in such a euphoric state he even started listening to pop music. Unfortunately, he's a recluse now. But don't worry about the dancing, there won't be much ballroom anyway. It'll be pelvic twitching and limb spasms on the spot, don't you think, like a disco. Shuffle your feet and rock about a bit with your fists up as if you're winding wool. No, I've got it, imagine you're boxing your way out of a swarm of midges. That's exactly what people look like. I've seen them on television.'

Len slowed for lights and yawned. 'At least I can talk to women. I know how to keep them entertained.' He smiled in a mysterious, superior manner. 'I ask them riddles and they tell me their dreams.'

Joy Sadler gave a scornful laugh. 'Good Lord, women don't want riddles. They can't abide them. Women never ever tell each other jokes. Well, actually, yes, Jewish women do but nobody else does.'

'You're talking tripe; all women enjoy jokeyness. They're intrigued by the really confident, off-beat approach.' He suddenly shot away from the lights and overtook four cars in a reckless manner to emphasise his decisive train of thought. 'You've got to help them unleash their fantasies about themselves, that's the secret. I used to be able to pick them up like anything when I was young and then I never knew what to do with them. I couldn't do anything because I hadn't got any money. I just had to leave them wondering.'

4

Joy was staring out of the car window, considering south-west London and the odd fact that the men accompanying women were all walking along on the inside of the pavement as if deliberately making up for their years on the outside. Or maybe the modern woman automatically seized the outer position? She'd noticed it was the women these days who draped their arms round men. That wouldn't come naturally to her. She'd need the man to put his arms round first. She'd heard all Len's theories before and was scarcely listening to him. 'Aren't we nearly there? Isn't this exciting? What sort of woman are you hoping to meet?'

'I'm not hoping to meet anyone.'

'But don't you secretly want someone to change your life?'

He darted an exasperated sideways glance at her. 'That's the last thing I want – my life changed. Oh, well, yes, I suppose it could work if someone happened to slot in . . . if our neuroses were complementary . . . you know what I mean?

'Of course I'd welcome a partner who understood my work, but there's really no room in my life for another person in this recession. Dealing with my computer company going bankrupt is a total nightmare. I've run out of money. I've run out of energy. I would never dream of coming to a place like this to meet women. It's your idea. You wanted me to come with you.'

Joy's face creased radiantly into affectionate smiles. 'I know. You are good. How one values the old friendships at our age.' She jerked up in her seat and pointed. 'Look, it's there . . . Melstar Hotel! God, what are we letting ourselves in for?'

They found a place to park and Joy Sadler, mother of three grown-up boys and grandmother-to-be, banged the car door and sailed ahead into the singles gathering at the Melstar Hotel with a straight back and hope in her heart. Len Derbyshire followed her. Outwardly, his face was bathed in social acquiescence. Inwardly, he expected nothing. At best boredom. At worst an embarrassing debacle of some sort. His jaw clenched as he stifled more yawns. He felt infinitely depressed. He hoped he'd be able to stay awake.

The Melstar Hotel was an unpretentious functional place, fairly recently renovated, with much chrome and garish carpeting. The singles evening was already half-heartedly underway when they arrived. Disco music was blaring, coloured lights swirled on the ceiling but the place was not yet jumping. The singles were arrayed about the room in desultory groups. A few were dancing. Others stood or sat alone.

Joy stared about, her enthusiasm for re-marriage immediately dwindling as her eye fell upon what appeared to be a sheepish cluster of bank clerks. Once, she reflected, this room would have been called the ballroom and available only to those with partners. Now, it was re-christened Conference Room and full of people without partners. She could see what her accountant had meant. They were all ages. Some, probably the new members, were dressed rather formally. The regulars of both sexes seemed to be in a uniform of pants, T-shirts and pumps. All members, except them, were meant to be graduates and over thirty. And all, she thought scornfully, were bound to be nutters like Len and herself, who were making a ridiculous mess of their lives. She caught the smiling, somewhat foxy eye of a ginger-haired man in a blazer and turned quickly to Len. 'Shall we get a drink?'

'I'll go,' he said amiably, 'What d'you want?'

'White wine, please. Len, look! That ginger man is staring at us.'

'Well, you've asked for it.'

She watched Len weave his way through the dancing to queue patiently at the bar. He was not a man who thrust in front to attract instant service. She admired him because he wasn't, and was then irritated.

CONSEQUENCES

Two slim, youngish, collected-looking women in boardroom clothes – lawyers, perhaps, or administrators – were
casting interested glances his way while they kept a conversation going beside him. Len's looks intrigued women before
they realised what was coming to them. From his father,
who was a gipsy, he'd inherited the dark curls and tough
brooding air of the fairground. Joy could imagine those liquid
brown eyes resting impassively on endless pairs of giggling,
squealing girls, as he lolled at the controls of the Big Wheel
or the Divebomber, and lazily gave their spinning airborne
chairs an extra mischievous twist. That was half of him. The
other half was all ideas and eccentric rumpled teddiness. He
was larger than life and he was not really equipped for the
everyday existence that most people have to put up with. That
was why he couldn't get on with women properly. Women
want practicality.

Relationships were not so much a question of matching
intellect, Joy reflected, more a matter of matching pace. Len's
energy came in such manic bursts. He could see five films in
a day. He could set out to lunch hundreds of miles away at a
moment's notice but, if there was a setback in his work, he
took to his bed and lay sleeping like a mute mothball with
the covers pulled over his head. He was a sort of sexual
monk. He could never have gone to work on a commuter
train and spent the hours between nine and five behaving
normally. Now, one of the collected women was leaning over
to speak to him and then they all laughed, like public relations
people, making much of nothing. Joy felt a wave of envy. How
easy it was for men! But she wished he would meet someone.
She turned back to the dancing, found herself a seat and sat
waiting, tapping her foot tentatively to the music.

Beside her an appealing, fresh-faced tweedy man, probably
young enough to be her son, was telling an attentive female
listener all about himself.

'Since my wife died, I'm getting used to being on my own
with the animals. Taffy, the labrador, sleeps in the kitchen

7

beside the Aga but Digby, he's a big tabby, comes in and out of the bedroom window all night. He swings up the clematis trellis onto the garage roof and hauls himself in from there. The more beastly the weather, the more trampling he does across my face before he settles. Sometimes he brings a baby rabbit in with the head bitten off, so he can have a dreadful midnight orgy under the bed.'

'Ohhh . . .' exclaimed his rapt-faced listener and then they both laughed. In her mind's eye the girl was already happily embracing the nocturnal tramplings of Digby as part of her impending friendship and marriage with his owner.

Joy silently echoed her approval, visualising a pleasant suburban cottage with sagging animal-ridden chairs. There couldn't be much wrong with a man who called his cat Digby. That had to be one of the drawbacks of computer dating systems. Lack of idiosyncratic specification. A potential partner might have all the right general qualifications on paper. He might be tall enough, clever enough, but statements like 'interested in the arts' could mean anything. It could mean he carried a purse. Whereas a small well-worded disclosure about Digby's filthy habits might easily be the clincher.

The dance floor was filling up as people began to make hesitant moves towards one another. A disc jockey started introducing the music and making announcements. Half the room was dancing now. Several lone women were on the floor doing their own thing. Joy looked again for Len but he was still, oh God, nodding and smiling at the two boardroom beauties while she was left here like an ancient wallflower, dying for a drink.

He was so slow about getting drinks because he only drank fruit juice himself. She suddenly felt much too old and annoyed for a singles club. If Len didn't dance with her, she hadn't the courage to get up and dance on her own and nobody else was going to ask her. Men had not come to the Melstar Hotel looking for a twelve stone fifty-year-old with painful knees and bags under the eyes like a hen. What was more to the point, though, she didn't like the look of most of them either. Sourly she studied them all and notched off examples of their unsuitability as they performed in front of her. Why had she and Len come to this awful place?

By George, look at that; *there* was a real posturing humourless horror with a button nose and he was wearing blob shoes. God, what a turn-off. Odd how shoes could be a deciding factor. Was he planning to walk through rivers? So many beards too. Smelling, if one got close enough, of fusty drawers in bed and breakfast houses. That prancing dope in bright blue, piloting his partner to the bar, was obviously about to ask her what her poison was. Better to be alone for ever than have to listen to that. And the bad news about the pursed-up, pedantic little midget in the dark suit and specs, who was being bumped into by everybody, was only too likely to be halitosis. Those pinched unsmiling rosebud lips invariably concealed rancid caverns of dubious teeth. Before she married she used to think she was not looking for a man she could live with but the one she could not live without. Now, living with anyone, in any circumstances, seemed far-fetched. Glory to God, what was this? She mused disbelievingly on a glamorous blonde, a gangling figure in grey lamé and red Theda Bara lipstick, who was stepping to the floor to dance with a beguiling little Chinese beauty many years her junior. The blonde was a bit over the top, wasn't she? Her bosom was poking out like two King Cones. Was that hair a wig? She looked outrageous. Joy was smiling as she met the darting eye of the ginger man. He reacted immediately.

He bowed in front of her. 'May I have the pleasure?' Looking terrifically straight-backed and solid and buttoned-up in his blazer, he was positively bouncing on the balls of his feet.

'Oh,' she responded in a high gratified voice, 'I'd love to, thank you. I must warn you, I haven't danced for years.'

His head went back in rather a theatrical manner and he stretched out an arm to help her up. 'I'm Clive.'

'And my name is Joy Sadler.' She took his hand and he led the way into the middle of the dancing.

'Clive, just a minute. I ought to tell Len, the friend I came with, or he'll wonder where I am.' She pushed through the jigging bodies to the bar where Len Derbyshire was at last attempting to excuse himself from his new acquaintances.

'Joy, I'm sorry! Come and meet . . .'

With a little explanatory wave, and a smile which included them all, she stopped and called from where she was. 'I'm going to dance. I shan't be long.'

'Right, Leonard, you can stay and talk to us then.' One of the thin women laughed and laid a jokily possessive hand on his arm.

As Joy rejoined Clive, some sensational music started up with a lot of trumpets and a loud, wild throbbing beat. She felt such a thrill she couldn't stop herself beaming like a mad woman. She forgot her hurting knees and threw herself into her own abandoned breathless dance.

He was a most accomplished dancer. Poised, imaginative and energetic despite the portly body on dainty feet. When the music stopped she was surprised to spot a wedding ring on his finger. An odd accessory to flaunt in a singles club and usually the badge of a womaniser in her experience. Still, the ageing single, like herself, moved in mysterious ways and she didn't want to start noticing off-putting things. The dancing was heaven. Their partnership was perfect. She didn't care what his marital status was. All she wanted to do was dance on with Clive, through the night and for evermore, even if her face was purple, her heart pounding and he a womaniser.

'Clive, this is glorious. I love it. You know, I feel people of our age have been starved of dancing. Well, I mean I have. Not you.'

'We must see if we can remedy that, mustn't we?' He spoke, she thought, with a little knowing smirk of power. He had a common nose. At eighteen she would probably have found the smirking commonness quite an excitement.

Between dancing bouts, while they were having a rest, he told her about the flat he'd bought in Motspur Park because his wife was leaving him to marry a social worker. Thanks to her chain smoking and seven cats, this upheaval didn't seem to bother him. What mattered to him more immediately was the finding, or forcing, of conversational openings for his succession of puns. Exuberant manly laughter followed his own jokes, somehow conveying that meeting a woman of true mind was the inspiration for his dazzling wit and Joy laughed with him because the evening was having a giddying effect.

He went on swinging her hand until the music started again then he swung her onto the floor. 'I'm game if you are, as the peacock said to his mate?'

'This peacock wants to go on and on.'

'You must come over to Motspur Park one evening when my new lounge suite has been installed. I'll take you to dins at my super local restaurant. I'm a bit of a foodie. Are you a foodie?'

'Only a nursery foodie.'

'Ours is nouvelle cuisine. Better than anything in South Ken, and the waiters can't do enough for me.'

'How lovely,' she replied, her heart sinking. But pleased to be asked, to have an invitation from anyone at her age, she dabbed surreptitiously at a rivulet of sweat on her cheek.

'What do you do, Joyce?'

'Actually, Clive, it's not Joyce. It never was. It's just Joy.'

'Sure. Joy.' He gave a little consenting salute with his finger. 'Now tell me about yourself. You look to me like a feisty lady who's been doing something interesting with her life.'

'Library indexes. I used to visit architects' offices. It was convenient working the hours I wanted, you see, while my boys were growing up. Recently I've been looking after a friend's sports shop and trying to write.'

'Got yourself a nice little racket! Yes, I know the urge to scribble. I'm a people watcher myself but then I've had to be.'

'You're a psychologist?'

'Not a psychologist.' He swung onto his toes, 'A surveyor.'

She nodded encouragingly. 'Oh?'

'Yes, being in the property world, I tended to see a side to people they might normally try to conceal. Buying or selling houses seems to bring out their worst. I'm speaking in the past tense here because I've just taken early retirement but I've always thought there was a best seller ticking over in my head if I could find time to put pen to paper.'

'Well, how wonderful. You'll find it now.'

'Not while I'm involved with CSCWS, I won't.'

She leant forward to hear better. 'What?'

'Our Crossed Swords Society.'

'I'm sorry . . . what did you say?'

'Our Civil War Society. Haven't you heard of us? We were on television last year. They filmed our performance of the Battle of Marston Moor.'

'Roundheads and Cavaliers? You don't dress up, do you? Clive, you cannot mean you actually fight?'

He beamed at her, enjoying himself. 'Certainly. And very authentic it is too. We all feel sick with nerves beforehand until the blood lust takes over. Once the adrenalin is flowing we can't stop fighting.'

'Good Lord! How dreadful!' She laughed in wonderment. 'I'm aghast. And which are you?'

'A Loyalist, of course. When you come over to Motspur Park, you'll see my battle trophies. I've got all sorts of relics. And some day you really should come and see us re-enact a battle. It's a superb spectacle, I can assure you.'

'Yes, I'd be most interested. I hope my nerves would stand it!'

Clive swivelled to look at Len across the room. 'And

your friend . . . he's an old friend, is he? What does he do?

'Oh Len,' Joy's voice rose with enthusiasm, 'He's immensely talented. An imaginative genius. His work has won all kinds of prizes. At the moment he's doing some amazing animation experiments on the computer at Imperial College. I'm hoping he's getting off with one of those nubile women he's chatting to.'

'He seems to be getting on all right.'

'I know. But he gets them interested and then he never develops it. Women can't put up with him. Come and meet him.' She gave Clive another of her radiant girlish smiles. 'Then we can do some more dancing.'

Len Derbyshire was in the middle of a lengthy description of his work. His two companions were listening with solemn expressions of intense concentration but their eyes were a bit too wide open and sparkling as if they were receiving some love chat on their way to bed.

'Len,' Joy said, still hand in hand with Clive, 'This is Clive Pownall. I'm afraid I don't know anybody else's name,' she added, smiling at the other two.

'These ladies have been kindly keeping me company,' Len replied, 'Susan, Suzanne . . . er, Meaks, isn't it? And Ruth Bly.'

Suzanne Meaks, the less attractive of the pair, had obviously hung back to let her sexually superior friend take possession of their desirable male find. In her early thirties, Ruth Bly conformed to most recent generations of professional women with her steady serious gaze and anorexic body. Women whose degrees entitled them to something. She had a radiant skin. Her shortish hair was a thick fizz of dappled squiggles, and she made intelligent, blunt, fairly unsmiling conversation, a bit like her short, pale, unpainted nails, Joy thought. It could have been reserve but she had the feeling that Ruth had decided if she withheld the smiles she would be treated with more respect. To Joy, who had always considered herself anybody's equal, and more, behaviour of this kind was simply a mystery.

'All right, girls,' Clive's lively cyclopian eye embraced them warmly, 'Now, what are we drinking?'

Joy smiled. 'Clive, thank you. I have my wine.'

'I'd like a spritzer,' Ruth said.

'Just fizzy water, please,' murmured Suzanne.

They all took turns to buy drinks after that. Joy led the conversation with a laughing description of how she'd bludgeoned Len into coming to a singles evening and the talk was carried along easily enough by the mood of the moment and the music. The others had not been before either.

Joy and Clive did some more dancing then he danced with Suzanne and Joy was a bit taken aback when she overheard him inviting her to go and see his new flat when his lounge suite had been installed. She tried not to let herself feel crestfallen. She wasn't really. After all, a man who wore a womaniser's wedding ring and talked of lounge suites, was hardly worth getting upset over. Clive Pownall of Motspur Park was by no means first prize in life's lottery.

'Let's get Len dancing!' She could hear herself beginning to squawk from the noise, a dry throat and some sudden coquettish smoking she was doing from a packet of ten cigarettes she'd bought on impulse. 'I want him to dance. He danced in the navy.' The effects of drink were making her forget about Len's low mood and his dancing discomfiture.

'Where did you say he danced?' Clive enquired.

'In Middle Eastern brothels,' she shouted, 'In the merchant navy.' She blew out a long thin trail of smoke, wondering which would perturb the fastidious Clive more, fags or VD-ridden brothels. 'He drew Mickey Mouses on his partners' breasts while they were dancing.'

'*Mice*? Oh how revolting!' Ruth backed away, hands across chest, protesting shrilly. 'Now a nice landscape,' she added, giggling at Len, 'a few flowers and trees, would be more acceptable.'

'I never had a refusal.' He barely stifled another long-suffering yawn. 'How's *her* dancing then?' he asked Clive, gesturing at Joy.

'Ah, yes . . . yes,' Clive's head was nodding fast to show how highly he rated her as a disco partner, 'Joyce is just the sort of fun doll I like.'

'Fun doll?' Len made an odd sound and stared, delighted. 'Fun doll. Is she? I've never thought of *Joyce* in that way, I must admit.'

Joy knew she oughtn't to go on laughing like a hyena. The evening was becoming absurd. Clive was looking awkward, very ginger and furry, and Ruth and Suzanne were looking disapproving. 'Well, I can only say I'm frightfully flattered to be described as a fun doll,' she declared defiantly. 'How wonderful and, since I am a fun doll, my suggestion is that we all go and dance. We can stay in a ring together or we can dance on our own. Do come. Let's go now. Don't waste this music. The evening's nearly over.'

Len sighed. 'I'll regret this.'

A frenzied drumming began as they moved in a group onto the dance floor, making stiff self-conscious movements at first while they watched each other. Only Clive was worth watching. When Len took his first ungainly steps, Ruth and Suzanne laughed openly. Looking most conspicuous, he was shifting from foot to foot, heavily and carefully, like a pantomime bear in wet cement, hands up like paws. They stayed in a ring, facing and turning, meeting eyes and smiling. The music was irresistible. The Melstar Hotel was jumping.

When the tape changed next time, so did the dancing. It went into ballroom, with a foxtrot.

'Oh,' Joy said, in a rapturous voice. 'Listen to this! How I adore these old tunes. D'you know, I've kept all my parents' seventy-eights. I can't bear to part with them.'

*I took one look at you
That's all I had to do
And then my heart stood still*

She remembered the band playing it at somebody's twenty-first the night she met Roly. Her heart had stood still. Now, for an instant, she was caught off-guard and a wave of nostalgia turned without warning into an illogical sense of loss for Roly and a type of existence she'd never even had with him. In a grim flash, a sort of sudden waking horror, she gazed about at all the alien people in the Cromwell Road singles club, trying not to panic at where she'd ended up. 'Oh God . . .' she was saying in her head, as the satisfactorily-matched Melstar couples closed up to put their arms round each other, touching cheeks for the first time, 'Omigod'.

'Joy?' murmured Clive Pownall, holding out his arms for her to dance.

Suzanne tactfully withdrew to a seat.

Len looked on as the dancing started then he too made for the chairs. 'No . . .'

'Yes,' said Ruth Bly, hauling him back.

His ballroom dancing was even more awkward. He'd never learned the steps properly in his life and he was too exhausted to concentrate now. He was bulky, he trod on her toes, and they banged into other people because the evening was coming to an end and the floor was crowded.

'I don't think I can go any further, Ruth,' he announced, after a few minutes. 'I'm going to fall asleep.'

'Thanks. I'm sorry dancing with me is such a pain.'

'It's not that. I have narcolepsy.'

'Narcolepsy?'

'I can't stay awake,' he informed her ungraciously, yawning like a tiger. 'I've got too many problems at the moment.'

'Oh, same here,' she replied, relieved. 'I'm often dead on my feet. My job's pretty demanding.' Pleased to have him to herself at last, she started to talk and was dismayed when Joy Sadler's beaming face appeared alongside them.

'Excuse me, Ruth. Naughty of me to interrupt but I must just go once round the room with Len. I promise to hand him back. Here's Clive dying to dance with you.'

Ruth's small laugh was not one of amusement. As Clive swept her away, Joy and Len stayed still, carefully preparing themselves to move off. Joy was positioning his arms and showing him the steps when the big glamorous blonde with the King Cone bust came swirling by, elaborately convulsed at the spectacle.

'Slow, slow, quick – quick, slow!' she called out in a deepish upper class voice, stooping over her partner in a thin curve of grey lamé and exaggerating the steps on her long thin legs.

'We can't all be ballroom champions!' Joy called back. 'What an extraordinary woman,' she added, sotto voce, but Len wasn't paying attention.

'Joy, let's sit down, can we?'

'No, no, we're fine. Quick, listen, I only wanted to find out what we ought to do about going home?'

'You'd like Clive to take you?'

'Good Lord, no.'

'Well, give him a chance. You said you wanted to meet someone and he seems a successful dependable guy. Is he in the Army?'

'He's a Cavalier. No, no, I don't want to go with him. I meant what about you and Ruth Bly?'

He made an exasperated sound, lost the rhythmic thread and trod on her foot. 'Sorry . . . but how many times must I tell you . . . I can't cope with a woman at the moment. Ruth's very nice but she's not my type. She wouldn't put up with somebody like me and she's got her own car anyway.'

Joy leant forward and mouthed into his ear. 'She's keen as mustard.'

He laughed and twirled her under his arm. 'That's what I can't cope with. Women always like me at first but Ruth's a yuppie, and she's only thirty-two, you know. She books her own swimming lane at the Barbican. I bet you've never done that. Okay, maybe I'll ring her someday when I haven't got so many problems to deal with. She's . . .'

'Shhh . . . be careful. Here they come.'

With a purposeful smile, Ruth leant out of Clive's arms and tapped Joy on the shoulder. 'Clive would like you back,' she declared briskly, as she re-claimed Len.

'What it is to be popular!' the larger-than-life blonde commented, dancing by again. Next time she overtook she joked with Ruth about the secret of Len's success while he went on smiling his vague good-humoured smile and steered them into another embarrassing dodgem bump.

'Let's be honest, it's not his dancing, is it!' The blonde woman skipped out of their way and performed a few adroit charleston steps. 'I betcha it's his two lovely black eyes?'

Ruth laughed happily. 'Leonard's a real gipsy, you know,' she volunteered with a possessive air.

On her third time round, King Cone, looking mischievous, dumped her own partner and placed a bold, red-nailed finger on Ruth's neck. ''Scuse me, darlin',' she said.

Ruth was aggrieved. To say Len was aggrieved is not to grasp his state of gloom. He was worn out, in despair about his bankrupt company, his heart was in his boots. With a dreadful deadpan expression of resignation, he put his arms about his unwelcome partner, tipped his head back and pushed her forward into a waltz. He couldn't see. She was six feet three.

'Tania Galway-Lamb.'

'Hi, Tania,' he responded heavily. He was staring ahead, his head swinging from side to side as he tried to steer a clear course.

'*If you will come to the ball, you will be queen of them all!*' Joy hovered alongside, with Clive, singing loudly to them.

Tania laughed. 'Isn't she naughty, Leonard! Queen of them all! Push off, you two!'

Of course Len didn't know all the words of these old musical comedy tunes as Joy, and probably Tania, did. His youth had been spent on ships and docks, not at decorous little middle class dances. He wasn't put off by oddity, being fairly odd himself. But he was put off by Tania's height, the wide smiling up-tilted carmine mouth and the outsize personality. She looked like a sort of towering femme fatale. Leaning towering.

'Are you going to tell my fortune?' she demanded.

He gave an aggravated grunt. 'I loathe all that gipsy stuff. I want to forget it.' But then, trying to play his part, he dragged up some dancing dialogue from the brothels of thirty years ago in the Middle East and Liverpool. 'You must be a Scorpio,' he said.

'How do you know?'

'I can tell by your earrings.'

Tania was grinning at him, exuding party spirit. 'Do sapphires have something to do with it?' she enquired in her furry burnt-ochre voice. 'How fascinating. Do tell me. I am a Scorpio.'

Len stared past her, negotiating a corner and kicked her toe. Pinpointing the right star sign had been luck. With the strain of having nothing more to say, he fought a whopping yawn which flared his nostrils and showed his clenched teeth like a horse.

'Anything wrong?' she asked, eyes watering from the kick.

'I'm a narcoleptic.'

Tania Galway-Lamb, a hearty, straightforward personality, did not have a wide vocabulary. Certainly narcoleptic was not one of the words in it. Her mind raced with possible meanings, starting with biting. Was it a warning about female clothing? An underwear fetish? Narca . . . naked . . . maniac . . . fits? Nark . . . nick . . . did this chap violate dead bodies? Bite women? Kill? Narcol . . . cotic . . . peddling, pushing, addi . . . HIV positive? Galway-Lamb stumbled.

Len Derbyshire moved ahead, fighting an intense attack of nervous drowsiness, as his partner's ankle twisted on its high heel. With a swirl of grey lamé and a long flash of thin leg, the oppressive glamourpuss crashed beneath him, flat on her back. Derbyshire appeared to dance on, in the crush stepping on the body and being unable to get off it. Tania's anguished roar of rage and pain was brutally stifled by a shoe on her throat and fourteen stone of muscled ex-docker on top of it.

Stumbling himself, Derbyshire regained his balance, turned back to help and swayed anew at the sight of his partner. Other people stopped dancing, stared and scattered into little frozen groups. 'Look out! Someone's hurt.'

'Give her air!'

'Is it serious?'

'Get the manager.'

Galway-Lamb's beautiful young Chinese friend, the one who had been dancing with her, pushed her way through the stationary couples and crouched down. 'Tony?' she said, gently, patting her face.

Len was looking down but he had to force his head up again and close his eyes. His partner's eyes were closed too. To his horror, her face was bruising black already and swelling. The red mouth was squashed out of shape like a clown's, the lipstick smudged into a blob of blood on the cheekbone. She'd passed out.

He crouched beside the Chinese girl, anxiety giving his speech an off-handed wooden quality. 'I knew this dancing would end in tears, but she asked for it.' He was fighting a monumental urge to lie down beside the huge wounded tart and sleep for ever. 'By the way, her name's Tania. She might think you're talking to somebody else.'

'You stupid swine,' the Chinese girl snapped, 'I saw what you did. Go and get me some water.'

'It was an accident. How could I help it?'

'There's no need to go on stamping on someone when

they're lying on the floor. Oh, Jesus, hurry, will you. Just get the water.'

Len glanced over his shoulder at the people behind him and waved towards the bar. 'Cold water, please . . . hurry!' He turned back to the girl. 'I'm going to get an ambulance.'

'No, don't,' she said sharply.

'What d'you mean?'

'Just don't, that's all. Leave her alone.'

Joy crouched beside them, checking rapidly for herself that the woman was still breathing. 'Listen, she can't stay here, that's obvious. She needs attention.' She stood up to clap for silence. 'Can you all be quiet please! QUIET PLEASE! There's been an accident. Is anybody a doctor?'

'Shh . . . shush . . . it's an accident . . . listen!' People hushed each other and moved forward to hear.

'Any doctors?' Joy repeated.

'Who is it?' asked Suzanne.

'What's happened?' Ruth demanded. 'Is she all right?'

The Chinese girl swivelled bitterly and gestured at Len. 'All right? Hardly. She's only unconscious, if you call that all right. This bloody dickhead knocked her down and jumped all over her.'

Clive patted her arm. 'Now, come on, calm down. That's not . . .'

'I'm a doctor,' a young man announced, coming forward with his case. As he knelt and reached for the pulse, his patient groaned and one blackened eye half opened, 'narcoclepto . . . maniac,' the deep voice murmured and the eye closed again.

The evening broke up then. The manager came and a stretcher was produced. Clive issued more invitations to Motspur Park. There was a general exodus. People collected their coats and went. While Len waited for Joy in the hall, he could hear the Chinese girl talking at the reception desk.

'A double room for to-night, please. My mother, Mrs. Tania Galway-Lamb, has been trampled underfoot in the

Singles Club. Horrible, isn't it? Some epileptic weirdo flung her to the ground in the middle of a waltz and kicked her windpipe. She ought to sue him. A doctor's examining her now.'

By the time Joy reappeared, bringing Ruth and Suzanne with her, Len had sunk into a merciful oblivion. He was asleep in an armchair.

Smiling sympathetically, Joy lowered her voice: 'Poor Len, that dance with Tania has finished him off. Now, don't you two wait any longer. He and I will have to stay to hear that all is well, and then we'll go ourselves.'

Ruth hesitated, reluctant to leave without giving Leonard Derbyshire her telephone number but unable to think of a good enough excuse for detaining Suzanne. 'No, no . . . we . . .'

'Do go,' Joy urged. 'I'll say goodbye to Len for you. We must all meet soon and do some more dancing.'

'I'll leave him a note.' Ruth opened her bag to find pen and paper.

'Don't bother about me,' Suzanne said. 'I can easily pick up a cab.'

Night night – thanks for a marvellous evening, Ruth wrote and added her telephone number. *P.S. I'd love to hear the end of the Tania drama.*

As she poked the message into Len's pocket, he made a sudden grab for her hand with his eyes still closed. Opening them, he smiled at her. 'I thought you were a pickpocket.'

'I wanted to say goodbye.'

He read her note and stuffed it back in his pocket. 'I'll give you a ring.'

A few minutes later, after she and Suzanne had left the Melstar, the doctor came down the stairs.

'How is Tania?' Joy called, getting up to greet him.

'Fairly comfortable,' he replied. 'Sleeping now. I've given him something for shock. It's mainly bruising as far as I can tell, but it's probably a good idea to get an x-ray.'

'You did say "him"?' Joy demanded. 'Of course, he's a man. That's it! I knew it!'

The doctor winked discreetly as he moved towards the swing doors. 'Our Mrs. Galway-Lamb is a captain in the Life Guards. She's expected on duty on Horse Guards Parade to-morrow morning.'

3

She Said

*If I marry Leonard Derbyshire, we can give
dinner parties and invite the Sweetings. Then
I'd be able not to give a damn about Sweetie.
The Sweetings can come to our wedding. The
Sweetings can stay at our house in France and
sit in our box at the opera.*

Ruth Bly worked on a periodical called *Plain Speaking* which
came out monthly and had overtones of *Country Life*, the *Church
Times* and *This England*. There were articles on country pursuits
and antiques, social gossip and some plain speaking to the
General Synod on inflammatory questions such as homosexual
or divorced priests, the ordination of women and whether God
exists. There was also the question of the editor's local parson
who passed wind at the altar at Sunday Communion which
he found equally disturbing. He was attacking such flippancy
in the presence of the Host in a critical piece containing other
examples of anti-social behaviour, hoping the man might see
it and mend his ways.

Ruth had her own little column, called *Without Prejudice*,
in which she raised and discussed legal rights on aspects of
neighbourly nuisance, for the voice of the magazine was not so
much that of the plain man as that, say, of the decent people
of St. Annes-on-Sea or the wife of a retired Guildford bank
manager, who would sometimes be moved to write a poem
and send it in. Occasionally the editor would dash off a few
lines of verse himself to fill up a corner, and certain readers
cut them out – though probably not the Guildford poet.

CONSEQUENCES

I reach a hand to you, my friend,
As you give yours to me.
For without the hand of friendship
How drear the world would be!

The editor had rather lost his own belief in friendship
since he'd been stabbed in the back and paid off by *The
Times*. With his flamboyant manner of dressing, white wavy
snow-rinsed hair, lordly bearing and beautiful voice, Conroy
Sweeting (Sweetie he was called at the Beefsteak and the
Cavalry and Guards Club and in the office) presented an
intimidating and unexpectedly racy figure to the average
reader, if he chanced to meet one, which was only rarely.
Ruth Bly had been in love with him for two years while his
wife, an old war correspondent called Marigold Belper, went
on trailing round the world because there were always wars
going on somewhere and war was in her blood.

She was in the office now, messing about and getting
Sweetie's secretary to do things. Tweaking a scarf from
the coat rack, she draped it round her neck. A life of
travel had given her a curious freedom with other people's
possessions. The alice band she was wearing was the result
of an absent-minded snatch in the *Plain Speaking* ladies'
cloakroom.

'Oh, you've got Arnold Pope coming to see you,' she
commented, glancing through her husband's diary. 'He used
to write off and on about music for *The Times*, didn't he?'

Conroy Sweeting jumped. 'Not that old fool again. He's
not coming here, is he?'

'Yes, he is,' his secretary said, wondering how on earth to
reclaim her precious silk scarf.

'To see me? Oh, God, why?'

'He wants to discuss his article. You told him it gave you
food for thought.'

'Where is it?'

'You put it in your drawer.'

'Oh hell.' Sweeting swung back in his chair, opened his desk drawer and peered in at the mess, fingers pressing into his temples. 'Can you get me out of it?'

'I can't,' she answered. 'He'll be here in a minute.'

'Sweetie, doesn't Arnold Pope live near Oxford? I've heard he puts on rather splendid recitals for the great and the good at his house in Buscot.'

'I mistrust a man who wears a freshly cut rose in his buttonhole.'

'He gives fabulous parties.'

The editor looked at his watch. 'Sorry, darling, got to go. I'll see you later. Make my apologies to Arnold, will you.'

Avoiding the lifts, he descended by the back stairs and turned out of the building to go for a walk. He was already absorbed in mapping out a piece he was going to write for *Plain Speaking* on heroes, and he put his thoughts together as he strolled round the block. Oblivious of the scurrying stream of office workers and shoppers on the pavement beside him, he went round once, pleasantly assembling martyrs, soldiers and political leaders of the past. Next time round he listed heroes of the present. A sorry string of self-interested deadbeats. People who had got away with something. He walked with his head up and back, his eyes scanning the heavens, as he turned and decorated the phrase, snatched at the half-remembered quotation. Then a girl drove a pram into the back of his leg and he trod in a pile of rotting hamburger and sick. He cut short his walk.

Forgetting Arnold Pope in his anxiety to get away from the street and back to his desk, he also forgot stealth. Omitting to use the back stairs, he stalked into the building by the front entrance and stepped into the lift. On the fourth floor, he stepped out, exchanged a quick word and some gaily reverberating laughs with the golf correspondent, then he strode along the corridor eager to get started on his article. He stopped, appalled, and froze.

There, locked in discourse, right in front of his office, were his wife and Arnold Pope. Marigold was leaning forward, blinking earnestly.

'Sweetie found your piece most cogent.'

'Yes, I'm about to have a word with him about it.'

'I'm the bearer of bad news, I'm afraid. Sweetie's frantically busy. He sends his apologies.'

'Has he been held up?'

'He's been called away.'

Pope's face fell. 'Oh, that's rather a disappointment for me. I came up from the country specially.'

'He had to go, Arnold. It was terribly important,' she said, putting her hand on his arm. 'Now, tell me, what are you *doing*?'

Down on his luck and doing precious little, Arnold Pope searched for words then he rallied and plucked the red rose from his buttonhole. 'Dear lady,' he replied, presenting it to her with a playful smile, 'What am I *not* doing?'

Conroy Sweeting slid into the nearest doorway, which happened to be Ruth Bly's little room. She was sitting at her computer terminal, staring morosely at the screen and wishing Leonard Derbyshire would ring.

'Hi,' she said, surprised and pleased to see Sweetie.

He put his finger to his lips and whispered, 'Busy, Roo? Would you like a swim?'

'Right now?'

'Right now. Have we got our bathers here?'

She nodded and got up to get them from the bottom drawer of the filing cabinet. She always kept two costumes in the office in case the editor had time to swim. Sometimes they managed it at the end of a working day but it was usually when Marigold was at a war. Ruth held out the smart navy trunks which she had bought for Sweetie herself. 'Here.'

'You bring them. Book us a swimming lane, will you. I've got to go down the back stairs,' he murmured, peering round the door. 'And can you ring Jock? Tell him to bring the car to the Hope Street entrance.'

Sweeting had insisted on a chauffeur being written into his contract with *Plain Speaking* because the offices had recently been moved to Kingsbury and he'd never driven a car himself. The owners of the magazine had departed from the normal practice with their editors and provided him with a chauffeur-driven BMW, hoping they were getting a colourful controversial journalist who might help to raise the falling circulation figures and save *Plain Speaking* from extinction. They relished his reputation as a renowned party-goer because it got *Plain Speaking* talked about. Something that had not happened for a very long time.

Ruth enjoyed the parties as much as Sweetie did. Being on his arm took her into a sparkling circle of writers, philosophers and celebrities to which she would hardly have had access in her own circumstances. She could invite anybody to her dinner table in Hornsey, providing she called it Highgate and Conroy Sweeting was coming. She no longer experienced that hesitant reserve, that silent faintly calculating stare which questioned her status and social worth. She'd quite often invited people in the past who never asked her back. That didn't happen these days. As Sweetie's girlfriend, she was accepted.

She sat beside him in the car now on the way to the Barbican pool, heartened that he'd had a sudden spontaneous urge to go swimming with her in the middle of the afternoon even though Marigold was around. 'What were you being so mysterious about, going down the back stairs and doing all that whispering?'

'I didn't want to see Arnold Pope.'

'D'you mean to say we are only going swimming because you didn't want to see Arnold Pope?'

A flicker of irritation crossed his face before he smiled. 'I don't have to see Arnold Pope *or* go swimming,' he said. 'Come on, darling, it's good for us. We both need a bit of exercise now and then.' He leant back and folded his arms so that he could poke his fingers out and touch her without Jock, the chauffeur, noticing anything. 'We do, don't we, Roo?'

She folded her arms too and the chauffeur noted in the driving mirror that they were holding hands in their usual clandestine fashion.

Ruth was really hooked on their Barbican swims. She treasured these little shared rituals which had developed with Sweetie, and she basked in the health club's sleekly pampering aura. Members were greeted with warm towels by the glowing track-suited receptionist as they staggered from their problems at work into an even more competitive and intensely public atmosphere. They could lift weights, "climb" a moving treadmill staircase or run on the running track. There were saunas, jacuzzis and the latest share prices. Ruth and Sweetie always had a swimming lane to themselves, while round the sides of the flower bedecked pool the real fitness fanatics pedalled furiously on exercise bicycles.

Most people observed each other furtively on the monitor screens but Sweetie behaved as if he were the only person there. Ruth enjoyed watching him in the water. She liked to see him standing on the side at the deep end before he dived in. His long thin touching vulnerable thighs had always excited her. She wondered if others were as moved by them as she was. His dive was adequate. But dashingly adequate. *Former Times Home Affairs Man Takes Plunge.* Then he did a lovely, strong loose methodical crawl up and down the bath, not stopping for ten lengths. Her own swimming went in frenzied spurts. Fast for one length as she tried to thrash past him – being nearly half his age – then floating inertly on her back while she recovered. She swam alongside him now.

'You're not going back to the office, are you? I've got to go home and do something about my hair. Jock's still here, isn't he?'

He seized her buttocks under the water. 'He can drop you somewhere if you like but I'll need him myself now to take me to one or two places.'

'You do remember it's the party for the Bergson water-colours at Agnew's to-night?'

'Marigold's here. I'll have to take her.'

'Oh, Sweetie, no.'

'She wants to go.'

'Why didn't you tell me?'

'Sorry darling, I thought I had. Well . . . you come. Why don't you?'

'I don't want to be left bundling off into the night on my own, thank you.' She sighed with exasperation. Her face was creased with disappointment. 'I suppose that means you can't come to the Freemans' silver wedding lunch at Grosvenor House on Sunday?'

'I'll be in the country. No gentleman is seen in an hotel on a Sunday.'

She swam away from him in case she made a scene. She was used to the last minute cancellations but they were becoming harder to bear, not easier. She was getting no further with Sweetie. He wouldn't leave Marigold and she didn't know what to do.

Leaving Sweetie probably meant leaving her job, losing her brilliant social life and returning to a vista of uneventful evenings with girlfriends interrupted by occasional outings with decent bores, or depressed destitutes who went droning on about their money troubles with their ex-wives. They wouldn't be in the same league as Sweetie who was not decent but was never boring.

She saw him climb out of the water and turn to wait for her to follow but she pretended she hadn't seen him and swam away again, doing a slow thoughtful breaststroke.

Leonard Derbyshire wasn't boring either and at least he wasn't married. He was a gipsy who had done everything for himself the hard way and ended up winning just about all the awards in the animation industry. Even Conroy Sweeting could hardly put talent like that in the shade. But Leonard had seemed endearingly natural on the platform at the National Film Theatre, answering questions from that respectful audience who had come to see some of his old films. He'd looked earthily professorial, striding about with his battered old briefcase, greeting people and talking shop. He was so funny and modest or, if he wasn't modest, unlike Sweetie, the conceit didn't show. Actually he was adorable. And his latest film about a little man in hell being browbeaten into political correctness by health experts was a marvel of wit and perception. If she married Leonard, they could give glorious dinner parties to which the Sweetings would be graciously invited and she would be able not to give a damn. She turned her head to see where Sweetie was but he'd gone off to get dressed. She let herself float gently to the steps. The Sweetings could come to their wedding. The Sweetings could stay in their house in France or sit in their box at the opera. Yes, Leonard Derbyshire would have the lifestyle, as the winner of Academy Awards, to which she had become accustomed. She was determined not to lose it again.

The only thing wrong with Leonard was his name. Len was a name for old-fashioned old burglars or dubious acupuncturists. Of course there was a certain dash to the awfulness of it, a bit like having a dog called Rover. But being Mrs. Len Derbyshire was really more than she could cope with, however brilliant he was. She would insist upon re-christening him for social and domestic purposes when the opportunity presented itself.

As she dried herself her satisfying reverie was punctured suddenly by some awkward doubts, and she had to admit that if they were going to be married, they had not exactly got off to a flying start. He hadn't telephoned her since she'd been to his talk and it had been at her suggestion that they'd had an Indian meal together afterwards. He'd been insistent that he hadn't gone to the Melstar Hotel looking for a permanent relationship. He said he was only escorting Joy Sadler because she'd pushed him into it but he had promised to ring. Perhaps he had rung when she was out? Perhaps he was still too drained from the horrors of his computer company going bankrupt? It could even be that he was waiting now for her to invite him?

When Sweetie dumped her, after a quick drink, to go off to Agnews with Marigold, she was in exactly the right mood to do so. She phoned Leonard as soon as she got home. He sounded rather pleased to hear from her again and they fixed a day. She started at once to plan the menu.

Doing things properly was important to Ruth because she took herself very seriously. She hadn't the confidence to be casual. She wanted to impress and she wanted her friends to be impressive. She felt she had a special position to maintain because of her background and she worked hard to keep up any links with the past. Her job now, running her nuisance column at *Plain Speaking*, was respectable enough but her opinion of herself remained low. If people treated her casually, even to the point of brutality, she had to win them to her as the ones worth knowing.

Her mother, Patrice Gleason, had been quite a well-known ballet dancer. She had lived long enough for Ruth to have vivid memories of her exotic presence, her friends from the company and her admirers outside it. Her parents had divorced when she was five so she could remember a string of lovers trailing in her mother's wake. These smiling men – smiling one minute and sullen the next – had played games with her, given her sips of champagne and showered her with toys. When one gave up, another always took his place, so that the presents and attention never stopped until her mother died of cancer when Ruth was nine.

Conroy Sweeting had been one of Patrice's admirers. The link was discovered when Ruth applied for a job on *Plain Speaking*.

Sweetie couldn't stop staring at her during the interview. Sometimes he even forgot what he was about to say. 'Do forgive me. You remind me so much of someone I used to know. She's dead now, of course. She was a ballet dancer.'

'Patrice Gleason?' Ruth smiled. 'She was my mother.'

'Patrice was the most beautiful girl I ever saw,' he said. 'You look so very like her.'

So Ruth knew she was going to get the job because she looked like her mother. Sweetie couldn't leave her alone at first. He took her out and showed her off and gave her a column of her own. He thought he was going to love her as much as he'd loved Patrice. He took Ruth to the same places, and told her their secret jokes, trying to recapture the laughing excitement of those days when he was young. He didn't want to hear what a poor little waif Ruth had become after her mother had died. He'd listen silently with a pitying disapproving face as if it was her fault that she was badly treated.

Ruth was sent off to boarding school because her father had already married again and had a new ready-made family of two step-sons, a bit older than she was, and his own little girl, Melanie. Ruth wasn't by any means automatically embraced for the holidays. Sometimes they only wanted her to come to them for a specific period and then she had to spend the rest of the time at her school. She sensed in due course that her arrival created some sort of trouble but she couldn't understand why. The boys, Jason and Shaun, were kind to her but Melanie seemed to expect all the attention and she either got it or made a fuss. Ruth expected it too but didn't get it and a tantrum didn't work for her. Her step-mother resented Patrice Gleason's glamorous reputation and she didn't want Ruth shining more than Melanie. She didn't treat her as the other children's equal and her father, weakly, didn't stand up for her. Quietly, Ruth adored him all the more, convinced that it was her own fault. If she could be a more perfect daughter, he would become a more loving father who wanted to keep her by his side.

Ruth knew she was as pretty as her mother had been but she was without her ability to shine. She was sensible. She couldn't dance and she lacked *dash*. When she won a cup at school for helpfulness and tidyness, she'd thought Patrice would be as proud as she was. But she overheard her laughing about it. 'How typical of my poor little Roo. What an unglamorous prize!'

It was Ruth who tried to make a proper home for her mother and herself. She'd envied her friends who had ordinary secure families that sat round the table together at routine mealtimes with their own secret language of nicknames and old jokes. Of course they invited her to tea and included her in outings, but her own mother was never there to invite them back. She and Patrice always seemed to be eating pieces of toast in the air and passing each other on the way in or out of the house. The excitements made up for the lack of homeliness but then these were suddenly taken away. She never stopped missing that life with her mother and she didn't intend to go on through life with her nose pressed against the glass when she was surely entitled to a place on the inside.

'I remember you as a child,' Sweetie had told her. 'You were a solemn little thing. I took you to have lunch at the Cavalry Club once while your mother was doing some shopping. You saw some pictures of the Blues and Royals in action then you absolutely refused to eat whatever it was for lunch because you said you could smell the gunpowder in it.'

On the day Leonard was coming to dinner with Ruth, Sweetie went racing at Sandown without Marigold. But Jock was driving them both on to spend a long weekend with Lord Troughton at Delver Castle. Ruth left the office early, relieved there was no need for any explanation of what she was doing. She thought it most unlikely that Sweetie would bother to ring later. After the hairdressers, and already running late, she took a cab home weighed down by her bags of shopping. The meal was going to be a substantial affair with lots of accessories.

Although Bosworth Crescent was a rundown and undistinguished road, it was wide with tall old trees and fairly peaceful because of the sleeping policemen. However, the state of her second floor flat was a source of pride and pleasure to her and fortunately ready just in time for Leonard Derbyshire's appearance on the scene. The furnishing of it had used up most of the money from an unexpected legacy she received on the death of a great-uncle.

Wanting it to be suitable for Sweetie's friends, she'd attacked the decoration in a frenzy, scouring places tirelessly to get things right. The exact shade of ivory Japanese silk for the blinds, a two-thousand-pound handmade French bed of wondrous comfort, a specially commissioned stained glass window and all the little details like old door knobs, brass taps, and special strawberry tiles from Provence. Having central heating installed, tungsten lighting, then black slate laid in the hall, were the final inconveniences. Now the effort had proved worthwhile. The flat was dazzling. People gasped as she'd meant them to.

Her spacious sitting room, in the modern manner, was bare. There were two sofas, a limed oak dining table which folded into a narrow strip against the wall, prints by Richard Long and Baselitz, a large vivid abstract by nobody in particular and a Turkish wall hanging in brilliant harmony with two Heriz rugs on the polished floor. The tops of two occasional tables were hand-painted and, naturally, she was not without that necessity for the lone young woman in two rooms – a cellular phone. She positioned it carefully as part of the scenario for Leonard's perusal, forgetting Sweetie's possible call, then she made a hasty re-arrangement on the bookshelves, stuffing *Women Who Love Too Much* out of sight and placing a life of Wittgenstein to the fore. If the flat had an unlived-in air, that was because she had purchased it only fourteen months before and was out more nights than she was in. In any case, she was a great tidier and cleaner, not someone to use a cup and saucer and leave them sitting on the draining board unwashed.

The kitchen was part of the sitting room but cleverly

designed and she didn't object to cooking in front of guests. In fact, as she was confident about her cooking, she actually enjoyed it. Her new kitchen equipment gave her great pleasure. She went on adding to her store of little bowls and jugs, her precious china and glass, and she really used such outré objects as the fish kettle, the espresso machine and the fondue set. When Marigold Belper was at home, and she couldn't see Sweetie, she often spent evenings experimenting with recipes using lavish ingredients, which she put into the freezer. She wasn't taking any risks with Leonard though. He was having avocado mousse followed by lamb kebabs. The pudding was raspberry pavlova because he'd mentioned a passion for meringue. Raspberry pavlova was his current favourite. Whenever he passed a Marks and Spencer, he'd told her, he bought three or four at a time. He could wolf a whole pavlova at one go.

She set the table across the French windows. In the centre of it pinks floated in a shallow glass and ivory napkins matched the silken blinds. Her balcony was filled with tiered troughs of pinks, geraniums, busy lizzies and stocks. The scent was strong on the evening air as she stood back with satisfaction. They would be eating by candlelight.

At eight o'clock she opened a bottle of red wine. She went to the mirror again to see herself as Leonard Derbyshire was going to see her. Her legs were bare. They looked long and brown and appetising against her brief white skirt. Her baggy black T-shirt had a loose wide neck. It had cost a fortune. In her flushed excited state, her hair fluffed with electricity, she reminded herself of an old photograph she'd seen of Zelda Fitzgerald and she hoped Leonard might share this fleeting impression. She was smiling at herself in the glass. Smiling at the thought of him. Then she put the rice on. At eight-thirty she looked at her watch and felt the first twinge of doubt.

Where was he? No, it wasn't late. Not for somebody like Leonard. He'd be coming in a minute. She did some washing up then added to the salad.

Ten to nine. Leonard was late now. He must have got lost. He was so vague. What if he'd fallen asleep somewhere? As she put the rice in the oven, she heard a taxi stop outside.

The cab started up again. No Leonard. Ten o'clock came. She sat on the edge of the sofa nibbling at a piece of pitta bread. She picked up the phone and put it down. Why didn't he ring? He might still be coming if he'd been held up somewhere. He might be having a quick nap at the wheel of the car. He said he'd fallen asleep once standing on a railway platform and look what he'd done to that Tania at the singles club. Ten minutes more and then she'd ring the police.

His narcolepsy couldn't have made him forget the day, could it? It could if he had no interest in coming in the first place; better not deceive herself. Something more interesting must have arisen. She went to the window and stayed watching in case he came round the corner. She took deep breaths to calm herself.

She remembered there were two or three determined-looking women hanging about waiting for him after his talk at the National Film Theatre. He'd lolloped benevolently right through them except for one dramatic little foreign dame, posing dourly in a bucket hat like a Bulgarian. She'd pinned him down and informed him intensely that she wanted to go home with him to discuss his work. Was he with her?

But Leonard hadn't even bought her a drink. He could afford to behave like that because women would always be running after him, as she was, picking up the things falling out of his briefcase, listening to his problems and then putting their arms round him.

She got up and started to clear the table. That was that then. He wasn't coming.

The bastard.

4

She Said

*If I had to go and live in Motspur Park I think
my heart would break. I'd much rather slide into
cosy baghood in familiar surroundings.*

'Darling, don't eat up all the paté,' Joy grumbled at her
youngest son, Matthew, who was lounging about the kitchen,
picking at things, while she prepared the supper. 'Claire and
Jill will be arriving soon. Are you going to eat with us?'

'You're joking. I'm eating now.'

'No, I can't stand it . . . all this mess. I'm trying to write
something and you've put paté on my papers.'

'What's it about?'

'I'm not telling you. Oh well, all right, what do you want
to eat? I can put an Ocean Pie in the oven for you but it will
take forty minutes.'

'Thanks, Mum, but I've got to go. I'll eat later with Tod.
I just want to make some calls about my stall for Saturday.
I'll do them in your bedroom.'

'I'd better make some toast for you to have with the paté,
then. I'll have to give Claire and Jill something else.'

Matthew had left home a year ago, aged twenty. He was
expelled from school for using the headmaster's car and
had firmly vetoed any suggestions that he should make
further attempts to get to a university. He told Joy that
the universities had nothing to teach him which could be
of any use when the White Revolution came – an event, he
prophesied, that was close at hand.

Matthew shared a flat with his girlfriend, Tod, and four

others in Stoke Newington but he still stored most of his stock with Joy for his weekend stall at Camden Market, and borrowed her car whenever she'd lend it. She counted herself fortunate to see so much of him although the more one saw of one's children, she sometimes thought, the more worried one became. Christopher, the eldest, was in the States teaching English at Cornell and about to be a father. Guy market-gardened in Worcestershire. Seeing much less of them, she tended to hear only the good news and precious little about any of their problems. Matthew had already been knifed by a street gang and had recently announced he was a Rastafarian. His clothes were gaudy and she simply had to try not to see the dreadlocks he was cultivating lest she burst a blood vessel.

'Matt, try not to be too long on the phone, darling,' she called upstairs, furtively pouring herself another drink. 'I'm expecting Chris to ring at any moment to say the baby's arrived!'

Claire and Jill appeared only minutes after Matthew left. Jill brought her Yorkshire terrier, Poppy, and Claire, who was rich, brought three Harrod's bags of jumble for Joy's animal charities.

'That wasn't Matt we saw, was it?' Jill enquired in a tone of humorous incredulity. 'With dreadlocks?'

'Yes, he's a Rastafarian,' Joy replied, evenly as she could. Claire stopped dead. 'Oh Joy, I *am* sorry.'

'My goodness, how difficult for you,' Jill echoed sympathetically.

'It is a bit difficult,' Joy agreed. 'He's writing tracts all the time about the White Revolution which he tries to get me to buy to hand out to my friends.'

'Why not a black revolution?' Jill asked.

'I don't know. I honestly can't remember. I think he means the whites are going to get their comeuppance.' She reached out to take the bottles of wine they had brought for her. 'Thank you . . . thank you, both of you. Hullo, Poppy

39

dog! Now, let me take your coats. We'll eat in the kitchen, shall we?'

They always ate in the kitchen. Their meetings were a regular ritual which had been going on for years. Joy and Jill had been at school together. Jill and Claire had giggled together in their first jobs in an advertising agency until they were separated by their exasperated boss.

Nothing had changed except that Jill's hair, once dark, was now fair. Their suppers never varied. Whichever house they went to, they slumped into the same chairs. Claire by the heat because of her birdlike bones. Jill, with Poppy and her mending, by the open window. They had the same food. It was either a free range chicken because Joy and Jill were against factory farming, or fish pie from Marks and Spencer with three vegetables. To-night it was fish pie.

'This is awfully good, Joy,' Jill said as she tasted her first forkful.

'*Awfully* good,' echoed Claire.

They always said "This is awfully good, So and So" to the one who'd done the cooking, imitating the deep military voice of Claire's husband who used to say that to her when they first met before he grew critical.

Claire, being thin, ate like a bird. Joy and Jill, who were not thin, ate like beasts as they'd been doing ever since school. In those days they'd organised midnight feasts, with indoor fireworks and deep breaths of BO, in the stifling depths of the Sunday dress cupboard on E landing. Both of them still pined for suet pudding and spotted dick.

Through the years the three of them had shared friends, clothes and men. Opinions on events were exchanged in their almost daily telephone calls. Claire was married but childless, and Jill was divorced like Joy. She had one newly qualified solicitor daughter who had never put a foot wrong. And she had a married lover who was always taking his wife away on extended holidays which the other two had to agree with her was hardly an aphrodisiac.

'Christopher rang earlier,' Joy said, standing up to pour more Cape Country Chardonnay into their glasses. 'He says the baby's coming any minute. I'm waiting for the call now.'

The faces of the other two lit up with pleasure for her. 'What an excitement!' Claire responded. 'Grandmotherdom! How absolutely marvellous. I do hope it arrives while we're here so we can all celebrate together.'

Jill was smiling too. 'It's all too much! You're having everything at once . . . grandmotherhood, true love . . .'

'Clive?' Joy interjected quickly. 'Oh, not true love, you know.'

'But he's the demon dancer?'

'Yes, we've danced and danced,' Joy said laughing. 'He thinks I'm a fun doll. We've been to Stringfellow's. We went to a dinner dance in a Surrey hotel, and danced in a huge converted cinema place in Kentish Town with the most heavenly deafening music. Isn't it hilarious? I don't know what I'm thinking of. I hope I don't meet my own son somewhere. Everybody is so young and they take it so seriously.'

'Is Clive lovely?' Claire demanded.

'Lovely, no. But he's nice and I think he's committed himself to our regular meetings. At least I'm not waiting for phone calls,' Joy admitted, rather proud of her latter day conquest. 'What is nice about him is that's he's masculine and attentive. He's straightforward and jovial and dependable. Anyway, I expect you'll meet him soon,' she added, hoping they wouldn't. 'He isn't a husk, even though he's chosen to take early retirement. But, of course, he's from a different way of life.'

'If you had to live in Motspur Park,' Claire demanded, 'would your heart break?'

'Mm. Yes, it might. I think I'd much rather slide into cosy baghood in familiar surroundings. His flat has black walls with fearsome weapons all over them. I have nightmares

41

when I'm sleeping there that I'm going to wake up with a dagger in my throat.'

'Is it blissful sex?' Jill asked, wistfully.

Joy made a high strangled noise and closed her eyes. 'It's so painful, I can't tell you. I expect it's because I haven't done anything for so long.'

'Have you tried Slippery Elm?' Jill answered incoming letters for a tabloid agony aunt. 'That's what I recommend to Demented of Birkenhead.'

'What a foul name . . . it's a helpful cream, is it, or do you eat it? Oh, my God, what we come to, don't we?'

And over the pudding they lapsed happily into one of the interminable discussions with which they so amused themselves each time, cackling like witches. About the menopause, husks they had known, their waning hopes of finding the perfect relationship and their doubts of meeting its demands, in their middle-aged state of mind, if they ever did.

'Is HRT our only hope?' Joy asked Jill.

'Well, I know doctors who have advised patients it's either that or lose their husbands,' she replied. 'A reader who wrote in to us last week had been told she had to choose between the risk of cancer and the risk to her marriage.'

'Outrageous,' Joy commented, opening another bottle of wine. 'Makes one positively yearn for battleaxedom.'

Jill and Claire exchanged smiles. 'Hark at the barker!' Jill said. 'You know, I suspect that if women don't have the habit of a long partnership already, without hormone replacement therapy they lose interest in men. They start studying the natterjack toad or collecting cats.'

Claire added, 'Anything's better than having someone who says "Well goodnight to you!" at ten o'clock and then goes into his own room and shuts the door. That's what I've got.'

'Yes, but you said he sometimes gets it up.'

'No, no, never gets it *up*. Occasionally a half-hearted attempt is made after I've ranted at him, but what goes in feels more like . . . you know, in my mind it's a tropical fish.'

As Joy and Jill gave little shrieks of dismay, the phone rang. 'Chris!' they chorused.

'Len here,' said Len Derbyshire.

'Fun doll speaking.'

'Hullo, fun doll.'

'Len, I'm afraid it's difficult to talk at the moment. I've got Jill and Claire here.'

'I like Claire. Can I come round?'

'No. You'll only ogle her and monopolise the conversation.'

'I wanted to ask you something.'

'Yes?'

'What's the name of that girl Ruth? We met her at the singles evening.'

'Um . . . um, I remember . . . Bly. Ruth Bly.'

'That's it. Bly. Where does she work?'

'*Plain Speaking*.'

'Of course. Thanks. I think I forgot to go to dinner with her. I've got to ring.'

'Len! You mean you didn't turn up?'

'I forgot all about it.'

'You'd better tell her you had a near-fatal attack of narcolepsy. Poor Ruth. I liked her.'

'I like her too. It's just that I suspect she's into smart dinner parties and all that, and it's not my scene.'

'Well, you shouldn't make an arrangement in the first place,' Joy said crossly, watching Jill's sewing slip from her hand as she fell asleep with a pleasant listening expression still on her face. 'You'll have to shift yourself a bit if you want her.'

'I don't want her.'

'Any word of Tania?'

'Tania? I don't want a word from him either. He might want to do some more dancing with me.'

'Clive and I have been dancing.'

'You are a fun doll.'

'Yes I am. For the time being.'

'What's going to happen there?'

'Only dancing, twinkletoes, and more dancing.'

Joy nodded at Jill as she put the phone down. 'Our Lady's dropped off,' she said to Claire. Usually two out of three dozed during the evening. On more than one occasion they had turned on the television for something special and then all three of them had fallen asleep.

Jill woke again as Poppy jumped up and yapped at the window, responding to another dog that had started to bark outside.

Joy stared into the darkness as she shut the window. 'There's a poor dog over the road,' she said. 'Three foul men have moved into a room opposite and their dog is turned out into the street or shut on the balcony. I'll have to go and ring their bell if they don't open the door. I've had to do it about ten times already. I must say I do pine for a dog myself, but it's so difficult with the shop and everything and going off to stay with Christopher and Guy. Okay, calm down Poppy dog. You come with me. I've got some bits for you.'

'Lucky Poppy,' Jill said, and closed her eyes.

The other two went on chatting. 'Wait until Ruth sees Len's little dolls' purse with flowers on it,' Claire reminded Joy, amused.

'I know, he cannot resist anything from an Oxfam shop,' she replied. 'But I should have thought the floral purse was the least of her worries where Len's concerned.'

'How's his narcolepsy?' Jill asked, in a far away voice. 'D'you think I've got it too?'

'His is psychological. Yours is fatigue,' Joy answered crisply as the phone rang again. 'Hallo? Chris? Yes . . . no! Is she all right? And the baby? It's a boy!' she said, breaking off to tell the others.

'Ohhh . . .' said Claire and Jill together looking just as thrilled as the grandmother. 'Send our love. Congratulations!' And they both raised their glasses to her.

5

He Said

Jelly please. Jelly is what I like for Breakfast.

Ruth made sure that Conroy Sweeting was to be out of town when she next saw Leonard. On that day Sweetie was taking part in a religious programme in Manchester called *Hear Our Prayer*, a debate entitled *Adultery: Marital Compost or Moral Decay?* She hoped he wouldn't ring her while she and Leonard were having dinner.

When Leonard arrived with an armful of ill-wrapped flowers and two packets of grape juice, it crossed her mind that he had just robbed a crematorium. With his battered leather jacket and dark unfathomable eyes, he looked quite capable of it.

'They're beautiful,' she murmured, smiling, as she took them from him. 'I am impressed.'

'That's the idea. I had to make amends for my gaffe over dinner. Sorry I messed up your arrangements. I've been completely knackered recently. I've been with my solicitors all day today about my company.' He glanced about without comment as if her superb flat was just as he'd expected it to be. When he saw the balcony, lit up and ablaze with reds and pinks, he exclaimed with pleasure. 'Fantastic! I want to do something like that on my roof but my cat digs up the plants as fast as I put them in.' As he took off his coat and tossed it over the back of a sofa, the telephone rang.

It was Sweetie.

'Oh, hi,' she said.

'Is that Miss Bly?' She knew from the thick silly voice that he'd been having a rollicking good dinner with someone. 'I want to talk to Miss Bly.'

She smiled at Leonard. 'This is she.' She rapped out the words humorously. 'Did the programme go well?'

'It went very well. I told all those religious listeners that adultery was extremely good for their health.'

'Actually, you've rung at a bad moment for me. I've got a friend here.'

'Is it a hen feast? It's whatsit, is it? Suzanne, your febrile red-headed . . .'

Ruth cut him short, wishing the phone had been in the bedroom. 'Sweetie, listen, I can't . . .'

'Ring me back, darling. Room 221.'

'If I can.' She turned her back on Leonard and took some large awkward steps into the kitchen, holding the phone at her ear. 'I'm in the middle of cooking.' She picked up a wooden spoon and poked about in a pan.

'I've had rather a vile day. I want to talk to you.'

'Sweetie, sorry, I'll explain in the morning, but . . .'

'Carry on,' Len Derbyshire urged in a loud voice. 'Finish your conversation.'

Embarrassed, she shook her head, making a little 'one-minute' sign to him with her finger.

'Hullo?' Sweetie said. 'Roo, are you still there?'

'Mm, but I've got to go.'

'I want to kiss you. D'you know what I want to do to you?'

'Mmm . . .' she repeated, enjoying a new sensation of not needing him so much.

'Nighty night. God bless, my darling.'

'G'bless,' she muttered, snapping the aerial down. 'That was my boss,' she explained to Len, 'The editor.'

'A sweetie?'

'Everybody calls him Sweetie.' With an expression of jaunty innocence she poured their drinks, juice for Leonard and wine for herself, and resumed the meal preparation wondering whether to reveal that something had been going on with Sweetie in the past. 'It's Conroy Sweeting. He was at *The Times*. D'you know him?'

'No. Did he say he knew me?'

She laughed. 'I haven't mentioned you yet. He's in Manchester today. I must introduce you.'

'*The Times* interviewed me last year. I've had some really helpful write-ups from them about my work.'

'Not from Sweetie,' she said, lighting the long red candles on the dinner table. 'He was Home Affairs. He used to do stuff on prison reform and that kind of thing before he became editor of *Plain Speaking*. Now he writes on God and ethics and makes up little verses about blue skies and everlasting sorrow which old ladies paste into scrap books. He's so brilliant.' She gave a grim little headshake. 'He's wasted. He writes like an angel.'

'Thank God, I don't believe in God.'

'Neither does Sweetie. Neither do I, but I've noticed that men seem to cling to the structure of their religion even when they don't believe in it. That's why they're not susceptible to heresy, I suppose, in the way women are.'

'I have sometimes wondered if I'm God,' Leonard said.

In her amusement Ruth barged into the table and banged the dishes down. 'What makes me doubt it,' she answered, 'is your dancing. I can see that a divine clumsiness might seem an appropriate way of humbling oneself in dancing circles, but is it right to maim the innocent?'

He nodded slowly. 'It's either the dancing or an earth-quake. Anyway, I don't call Tania Galway-Lamb innocent. A guy messing about in tart trotters is hardly innocent, is he? He knew we were bound to have an accident and it could have been a lot worse. I might have broken my back on top of my company going bankrupt.' He pulled his chair up to the table and tucked his napkin into the neck of his red sweater to tackle the avocado mousse. 'Joy's keen on religion, you know. She goes to church. I bet she's a heretic. She'll be weeding

47

out the bits of doctrine which suit her and ignoring the rest. By the way, she thinks your column is splendid.'

'Oh, thank her. Have you ever read *Plain Speaking*?'

'I read it when I go to my dentist. I'm going to write in to your column with one of my insurmountable problems. Did you say you had a legal qualification?'

'I was only a legal executive. After university I worked in a solicitor's office for a time while I was deciding what to do. It means I know how to do legal research and that's why Sweetie gave me my column. I think I'm quite well organised in my present job.'

'Then you won't need my book on how to organise your life.'

'Is there one? I'll buy a copy.'

'I'm in the middle of it. I've been working on it for years.'

'Are you a good organiser of yourself?'

'I'm totally organised. I had to be because I went away to sea when I was sixteen. But being an able seaman for four years meant I had plenty of time to study, so I read virtually all the major writers then.'

'Of course,' she said, touched, 'that was when you did the Mickey Mouse drawings in brothels.'

'Yes, I still read comics. I only read comics now, and computer magazines. But I've always worked to a plan. I had to teach myself certain things in order to communicate my ideas.' His smile was brazen and unblinking. 'My plan was to change the world.'

'Mm . . . oh, yes!' She laughed again, not knowing whether he could be serious, and passed him the bread basket. 'Do you cook?'

'Frozen pies in the microwave. I can't cook.'

She helped him to kebabs with a small shaft of satisfaction. She watched him eat, imagining the gourmet recipes which would secure his dependence on her. Looking more vulnerable and uncared for with his napkin at his neck, he gave himself up to eating. He ate hungrily, taking huge mouthfuls, reaching out for more bread, more rice. 'You are a good cook, aren't you?' he kept saying. These were the manners of a man uninterested in food (except for cream cakes), who was used to eating alone. If she hadn't been already half in love, and determined to make it wholly, she might have been put off.

Leonard's talk, coupled with his eating, reminded her of descriptions of Dr. Johnson's large, wild performances at the dinner table. This was a performance too. Leonard held forth, making genially provocative pronouncements, while his disturbing dark eyes gleamed like a gipsy's, full of wisdom and sometimes, she thought uneasily, a sort of lurking contempt. He was a disconcerting mixture of Dr. Johnson and Stanley Kowalski from *A Streetcar Named Desire,* she decided, seeing Leonard, elemental side up, beneath her new grey duvet cover. 'Do finish the salad,' she said.

By the time he'd obliged her, conversationally he seemed to have dried up. He stifled a yawn and more than once, Ruth suspected, his eyes were closing. A Johnsonian gloom descended upon him as if he was now forced to contemplate the reality of the present again and depressed by it. She was tempted to make a Thrale-like attempt to rouse him by laughingly enquiring whether he agreed with Dr. Johnson that a man is better pleased after a good dinner than when his wife talks Greek. But she didn't dare mention Dr. Johnson's name in the middle of this display of neanderthal eating or even utter the word wife when she was so precipitately planning to be his and she no longer felt like laughing anyway.

An awkward moment came when she produced her raspberry pavlova. Leonard seemed embarrassed, rather than pleased, that he'd revealed his craving for meringue and that she'd acted upon it.

After that stiffness she felt they went completely out of communication, and she didn't know what to say to get them back into it again. He wasn't asking her any questions. She couldn't tell whether this was out of delicacy, self-absorption or lack of interest. With a slightly sinking heart, she saw that she would have to enquire again about his failing computer company, and she experienced a sudden surge of longing for Sweetie, who was gossipy. His Tory dinner-party flippancy, and lightness of social touch, Leonard would probably despise even if he envied it. He droned, when she got him going again, in a serious, somewhat hectoring style about visual images and she had to listen, nodding, with her best clever woman's enraptured face on although she was not in the mood for hearing how she had to learn to visualise ideas because the written word was going out of date. She wanted to hear how he visualised their relationship.

'Books are finished,' he summed up, rocking backwards to her consternation in her precious Windsor chair and straining the legs. 'Mickey Mouse is the image of the twentieth century.'

'Oh, come . . .'

'In a million years they'll dig up the remains of a Disney theme park and discover who it was we worshipped. Mickey Mouse and Coca Cola are what will be remembered from this century.'

'Well, I sincerely hope they find the frozen bodies of a few Middle Eastern brothel dancers with mice gods on their bosoms. But, surely, Leonard, we haven't sunk . . .'

'Len.'

'If you insist.'

'Len is my name.'

'Oh, well, I like Leonard better, that's all. Anyway, I was only going to accuse you of hypocrisy . . . promoting the visual image with the written word and making a fortune from it with all your Academy Awards.'

'Should have made a fortune. I haven't, though. I had to sell those scripts for nothing to get myself launched. D'you know, I'm the first person in my family to have a passport and a bank account? I'm the first one to eat yoghurt. Yes, I did expect to be a millionaire by this age. That was part of my plan as well.' He shrugged, with a helpless winning little smile, and reached for the remains of the pudding. 'Can I finish it off?'

'Oh, please.'

He ate it in the air straight from the dish. 'Of course, I've made money at various times in my life, mainly in advertising, I suppose, but I've been too reckless with it, putting it all into schemes that went nowhere, like my diving school. Ironic, isn't it? I'm about the best known name in the animation world for my adventurousness, and I'm the one still on the dole.'

Ruth looked faintly, politely puzzled, unable to take his situation seriously. 'But you'll make money again,' she said, 'with your reputation.'

'Other people have salaries. They don't take risks. But if the recession hadn't hit my company, it would have survived.' He could see her incomprehension and seemed suddenly weary of the subject. 'Never mind, I don't want to keep on talking about myself.'

'I like listening.'

'I'm boring myself. Look, I want to hear something about you now.' He yawned, put his head in his hand and rubbed his forehead. 'You talk.'

'What about?'

'Talk about anything,' he muttered vaguely and then his eyes closed.

She waited, pouring more wine for herself, until they opened again.

'Can I sleep on your sofa, Ruth? I can't drive when I'm in this state. I've passed the point of no return.'

'Is it a narcoleptic attack?'

'What ... yuh ... oahhh, yes. Yes, it is.' His yawns seemed to spread and affect his entire body. 'I won't disturb you in the morning. I'll be gone by the time you wake up.'

She got up and tested the sofa for comfort. 'Come and lie down now. I'll go and get some bedclothes for you.'

Happily, she produced sheets and blankets. She presented him with the new blue toothbrush she had selected for herself the day before. Then she started to make up a bed for him on the sofa while he was taking off his socks and shoes, shirt and trousers and going to the bathroom.

'There, it's ready for you.' Her back was still to him. 'What do you like for breakfast?'

Too sleepy for proper washing, he settled himself at once on the sofa, shifting and twisting like a dog bedding down, until he'd made a comfortable hollow in the cushions. 'This is great, Ruth. It's a perfect bed. Thank you.'

'Breakfast?' she repeated, in a jolly mothering voice, deliberately keeping her eyes away from the dark hairiness of his muscled chest. 'What do you like?'

He smiled dreamily, falling into his vulnerable teddy-needs-looking-after role. 'Jelly please,' he mumbled, his face disappearing into a cushion. 'Jelly is what I like for breakfast.' He hauled a piece of blanket up to cover his bare shoulder and went to sleep.

While she cleared the dishes, Ruth searched her cupboard for a jelly. She found a red one she'd been keeping for her half-sister Melanie's little girl, Cora, and added a tin of blackberries. As she boiled the kettle then stirred the torn-up jelly squares, she hummed quietly to herself and shivered slightly with nervous excitement. It had begun. If he was staying, it must have begun. She wanted him and, given time, she was going to have him. It was her turn for the star from the top of the Christmas tree. This time she had to make it work out. She would nurture him through his depression over the company. She wasn't going to lose him.

When she'd had a bath, she pattered back into the sitting room in her white bath robe to have another look at him, still with the excited elated feeling that he was staying and starting to be hers. As she pulled up the blanket to cover him properly, his eyes opened. Again they seemed to her to glitter like a gipsy's with old wondrous sexual secrets as if he knew exactly what was in her head. He reached out and drew her towards him.

'You smell gorgeous.' He touched her lips gently with the most fleeting of kisses. 'Sorry, sorry. I'm dead. Sleep well.'

Dismissed, she went to the door. 'I hope you'll be all right in here, Leonard.'

'*Len*.'

'Not Len. It's a burglar's name. But you're not really a Leonard either. I'm thinking of my own name for you, but I haven't got it yet.' She switched off the lights, went into her bedroom, stopped and came back. 'You know you look like a Leo to me. You're not a birthday Leo, are you, born in August?'

No answer.

She didn't like to step into the room again. 'Leo suits you perfectly,' she added, suspended on one leg outside the door with her arms spread like wings to keep her balance. 'Can I call you Leo instead of Len?'

Silence.

'Lee . . . o?'

He gave a faint snore and turned over.

She waited, lying in bed listening, hoping he might wake up refreshed and come bounding in to her.

At three o'clock in the morning, Sweetie rang.

Horrified, she darted into the other room and snatched the telephone. 'Yes?' she said in a sharp voice.

'You didn't ring me.'

'I couldn't. Sorry. Now I'm asleep. I can't talk to you.'

'Wake up, then. I can't sleep.'

'I can't help that, can I?' she answered, pleased that for once it was he who was suffering.

'You realise you've kept me awake and waiting after a dreadfully exhausting day.'

'Is that your boss?' Len enquired, looking at his watch.

'What's that noise?' Sweetie demanded, 'Is somebody there?'

53

She took a deep breath. 'Yes.'

'Hasn't she got a home to go to? Can't you get rid of her?'

'It's a bloke. He's asleep on the sofa. He's a narcoleptic.'

There was a puzzled critical silence. 'That sounds bogus to me. I'd steer clear of him if I were you.'

'It isn't bogus.' Ruth turned to look at Leo, who was lying waiting with his hands clasped behind his head, and smiled. 'If you can't sleep, why not take a pill?' she suggested to Sweetie in a jocular voice.

His tone changed instantly from petulant lover to cold irritated editor. 'Because I have something to discuss with you.'

'Surely not in the middle of the night? Can't it wait?'

'It can't wait, I'm afraid. No.'

'It's three o'clock in the morning. What's it about?'

'Your work.'

'My work . . . *what?*'

'Your piece on street rubbish.'

'Oh, Sweetie, please . . .'

'My dear girl, we can all get stale.'

'You think it's stale, do you?'

'There's been criticism in some quarters recently. I've defended you. But give your column more thought instead of losing sleep over lame dog narcoleptics. That's my advice to you. *Without Prejudice* needs livening up.'

'Does it?' In that instant, all the festering hurts and frustrations of life with Conroy Sweeting flared into an explosion. If her job was to become impossible as well, she had nothing to lose except Leo. 'Stuff it then,' she said, meeting his eyes and feeling exhilarated. 'I'm leaving *Plain Speaking*. If you don't like my column, you can get somebody else.' She cut the call off.

Len's quiet voice came from the depths of the sofa. 'I wish I'd told my bosses to stuff it. I am impressed.'

Ruth stood bemused, pulling at her lower lip with her fingers and trying to collect her thoughts. 'Urrrm . . .'

'What did he want? The sweetie?'

'He said he wanted to talk about my column.'

He glanced at his watch again. 'A workaholic, is he, or an hysteric?'

'He's a bastard.'

'And you were going to introduce me? Is he in love with you?'

'We've had an affair,' she admitted, regretting the timing of her revelation. 'Anyway, he's married. His wife is a war correspondent called Marigold Belper. She's often away so they lead their own lives.'

'Marigold Belper?' Leo made an astonished noise down his nose and propped himself up on his arm. 'She used to go to the Arts Club. She must be old as the hills by now. Is she still thieving?'

She nodded, preoccupied. 'Yah, she steals things from the office. Oh God, what a mess. But I've known for ages I had to leave that job. *Plain Speaking* is losing readers anyway. I didn't mean to go so suddenly, though . . . still, I suppose it must be for the best. I couldn't go on as things were.' Her voice trailed off. She felt she'd said too much as it was. She went back to bed and lay awake in a turmoil, wanting Leo, half-wishing he wasn't there so she could ring Sweetie in Manchester to put things right, and wondering if it was true that the management had found fault with her column.

At four o'clock Leonard got up and went to the lavatory. He padded back to the sitting room, flopped onto the sofa, coughed three times with an open mouth like a dog with a bone stuck then he switched the light off. A few minutes later he was up again switching it on. She heard him taking books from the shelves, then she heard him give a long sigh.

'Are you all right?'

'Ah, that's good,' he said, sounding relieved. 'So you can't sleep either?'

'But you've had several hours of sleep,' she couldn't help

pointing out as he wandered into her room in his floral underpants looking distinctly refreshed.

'I was wondering whether I ought to go home?'

'But I've made jelly for breakfast.'

'Did you? Did I suggest it? I always make jelly if I have time. Are we having breakfast now?'

'You lie here,' she said, getting out of bed herself. 'It's more comfortable than the sofa. I'll make tea.'

He lay with his hands clasped behind his head, stretched out on top of the duvet. 'I don't want tea. Come back here. I'll massage your back for you. It'll soothe you after all your office dramas.'

A wave of excitement fanned through her body as she obeyed.

He pulled up her nightdress (a present from Sweetie from Rome), and climbed across so that he was kneeling astride her. He began to rub silently, with long sweeping strokes all the way down her back and onto her thighs.

'Is that what you like?'

'Mm . . . gorgeous.' Her face was pressed into the pillow but she was imagining the blackly covered chest and the thoughtful street-wise dark eyes, as if he'd seen everything there was to see and would do it to her if he wanted to.

'So you and the sweetie met in the stationery cupboard on quiet afternoons. Was that it?'

'You are joking! At the Ritz, more like. We went about in a perfectly open manner. Marigold knew, I expect. It wasn't publicly acknowledged, that's all.'

'Unsatisfactory for you.' He stopped massaging and she could sense him examining her slender body of which she was rather proud. 'And now you've lost your job because of me.' His voice was dreamily detached. He pushed her hair up over her head and stroked her neck with his fingertips but somehow Sweetie had come between them again and spoilt the atmosphere. Leo's depressed mood was almost tangible. 'If I made love to you,' he said, 'I'd feel as if I was crushing a child.' He pulled down her nightdress and covered her up. He patted her behind in a friendly fashion. 'I'd better go. I've done enough damage to you. I should keep out of your life with all my problems.' He swung his legs over the side of the bed. 'It was very kind of you to make me such a splendid dinner.'

She made herself sound buoyant. 'We've got to have our jelly.'

They had it, at five o'clock in the morning, sitting side by side in bed, both of them trying to hide their low moods.

'Presented with all the flair of the Ritz,' Leo said in a hearty appreciative voice as if he could see how crestfallen she was that things had not advanced more between them. 'I knew you'd make good jelly. You were born to run a house and give dinner parties, weren't you . . . the manor house, of course. I'm only surprised you're not already doing it.'

'Would you rather a woman made good jelly or talked Greek?'

'You have to be careful with Greek. Orchid means testicle.' He poked a spoonful of jelly into her mouth. 'One for the sweetie.'

'*Sweetie*! Bad cess to that sod,' she said ferociously, scowling because he was suggesting she should be in a manor house with someone else. 'Don't go on about Sweetie. I'd like to spit this all over him.'

'Well, one for the Leo, then,' he replied mildly and held out the spoon.

'Are you a real Leo?'

'Yes.'

'I knew it.'

They both laughed and suddenly the communication came back.

'Next time the Ritz breakfast will be fondant surprise,' she said.

'Yes, fondant surprise at the Ritz.'

6

He Said

*Her mission in life is dinner parties. She wants
to find somebody and be a couple, and go to
other couples and invite them back. No love story
will ever be unfolding with Ruth Bly.*

'You did get in touch with Ruth Bly, didn't you?'

'Yes. She's a very good cook. She says I'm a Leo.'

'You are a Leo. It suits you.'

'But she calls me Leo instead of Len.'

'How sweet. Yes, I think I'll call you Leo too. I like it. But
if she's giving you pet names, does this mean a love story is
unfolding?'

'Fun doll, how can I convince you? No love story will ever
be unfolding with Ruth Bly. Her mission in life is dinner
parties. She wants to find somebody and be a couple, and
go to other couples and invite them back. She wants to be
taken out to dinner every week. I can count on my fingers
the times I've taken a woman out to dinner in the way she
was expecting.'

'She obviously likes you, though.'

'She rings me. She's temporarily romanticising my gipsy
past, as they all do. She's beautiful, isn't she? And I like
her, but she does not interest me. So why should I dance
attendance on her? I've promised to take her to some jazz
films and that will be it. Our expectations are different, you
see. I want to change the world. She wants people to admire
her new curtains.'

'Your loftiness is so shocking. You haven't a hope of getting on with a woman. You don't listen. You're either talking about yourself or lecturing them.'

'Quite the contrary. If I find a woman interesting, I'm listening hard all the time for anything I can pick up and respond to.'

'Yes, I know; you'd respond if she asked you to show her how to work her computer.'

'Women like to be told what to do. That's what Ruth wants.'

'D'you know what Professor Tonks of the Slade said? He said "Women do what they are told; if they don't you will generally find they are a bit cracked". Well, you certainly can't say Ruth is cracked. She's terribly sensible.'

'Too sensible. That's the trouble.'

'And I suppose you haven't heard anything of Tania Galway-Lamb?'

'No, of course I haven't. Why should I? In any case, she doesn't know where I live.'

'You don't think we ought to ask how her face is?'

'Good God, no.'

'I feel so curious about it. I mean, fancy her being a captain in the Guards. How extraordinary.'

'I don't want to see her ever again either. I hate her.'

7

She Said

How desperately one tries to make the unattached man fit the hole in one's life! All the stumbling blocks like the pigskin lounge suite, the black walls covered in swords, the pictures of himself in Cavalier costume and the drinks poured out in the kitchen, are stuffed to the back of one's mind while one hopes it's going to get better. I don't want to travel home in the car with him singing pom pom pom to that music and placing my hand on his bulging penis.

For the purposes of a piece he was preparing on the contemporary social scene, grieving over the advent of the "new" manners of the young (or lack of them), Conroy Sweeting was looking up his old school rules which were printed in a little black book.

Rule 1 read:

It is against the law of the land TO SMOKE before you have reached the age of sixteen. After that age you may ask the Rector on occasions when you think, and he knows, that you deserve a reward. Of course it is an expensive and sometimes deleterious luxury.

Smiling to himself, Sweetie turned the page.

Be well on your guard AT TABLE, lest the mere animal shows on the surface. If you saw animals in the farm yard with their trotters in the food trough, and all the rest of it, you would not be disgusted. They don't know better, having no code of table manners. You do and you have a code, the same as that at home or in the parlour. 'Pass the marmalade please' is better manners than rising and stretching for it. Helping oneself first is a token of ill breeding. It's not done in polite society . . .

Marigold Belper was waiting in the outer office to give Sweetie's secretary some of her personal correspondence to type. As her small sharp eyes scanned Karen's desk for evidence of anything her husband was concealing from her, she spotted a pair of gold pear-shaped earrings and popped them into her pocket.

When Karen returned to her desk she missed them immediately. 'Oh, what's happened to my precious little Dior earrings?' she demanded.

'What earrings, darling?' Marigold murmured vaguely as she pulled a chair up beside the secretary and riffled through her papers. 'Now, your first job is to ring the Electricity Board. You'll need their number, which is here. There's an exasperating muddle over the account for our cottage in the country and they've cut us off. Tell them . . .'

Sweetie got up and closed the door.

. . . Don't refuse a dish as not being good enough for you, though good enough for Tom, Dick and Harry: and don't leave helpings of food on your plates. We all know what that means. It's bad form and we could give it a worse name. It's also bad form, or rather bad manners, to have your elbows on the table. Table manners proclaim the man and the boy. In the Refectory 'facilis descensus averni!'

Sweetie made a translation in the margin: *'The descent to hell is quick!'*

He was still reading on, deep in the past, when his phone rang.

'Is that Conroy Sweeting?'

'Yes, it is.'

'My name is Joy Sadler. I was wondering if you'd be interested in an idea for an article in *Plain Speaking*. It's . . .'

'Did you particularly wish to speak to me? I'm very busy.'

'I thought you were the editor.'

'I am the editor,' he acknowledged testily.

'Well, my article is about drink.'

'The evils of?'

'It's really about women. When they drink and why.' She gave a smothered laugh. 'For instance, I had to have a quick snort to make this call.'

His impatient intake of breath was audible. 'Miss Sadler, could we . . . look, may I pass you over to my . . . ?'

'Just a minute. I'll put it in a nutshell for you quickly. It's only this. You see, I've just joined a little group rather like Weight Watchers and we try to monitor our drinking. As you know, the number of allotted weekly units for women is tiny. It seems to me, I want to say, that women don't drink so much at parties or in pubs. Their drinking is because of the shocks of life and fatigue, isn't it? They used to do it because their husband was always away working. Now they do it because the man is at home doing nothing. I mean, women these days have jobs, run a household, manage the children and cook while the New Man plays the guitar all day. He doesn't want to be responsible. So my point is that liver damage . . .'

'Miss Sadler . . .'

'All right, sorry, but liver trouble – just let me say – for women is increasing. Women drink, let's face it, because men upset them. Actually, I must not use my own name or everybody will assume I'm an alcoholic. I'd like to be called Utley, please, my unmarried . . .'

'Mrs. Utley, forgive me; I'm rather busy. Could you send in your article marked for my attention? Keep it to about seven hundred words, will you, then we can have a look at it.'

'Yes, do we arrange . . . I mean, how much . . . oh well, all right, thank you. I hope you like it. When d'you think you would be able to put it in?'

'It's always a question of space, I'm afraid. I can't make any promises. Thank you for thinking of us. Good day to you.'

In her sports shop Joy put her telephone down feeling nervous and dissatisfied with the conversation. Conroy Sweeting didn't sound very keen. She felt much inclined to ring Ruth Bly to discuss it, but didn't like to. The situation vis à vis Len might be awkward.

As she sat drinking coffee and pondering, a gang of youths arrived on the pavement outside the window. Her first weeks of shop-keeping had taught her that this was bad sign. It usually meant they were all about to surge in, swarm about and steal trainer boots and T-shirts. Her predecessor had been hit on the head with the cash box and knocked to the ground. It had taken her several shop-lifting shocks to grasp how they operated. And, as it was, the shop seemed to have the skids under it. It wasn't doing well. She didn't wish to be the cause of its ruin gathering momentum. Now, she simply went to the door and greeted the assembled boys pleasantly.

'Hallo. If anybody wants to come in, come one at a time, please. I'm afraid the shop is too small for all of you at once.' She let the first boy in then snapped the catch on the door. 'What are you looking for? Can I help with anything?'

Nonplussed, the youth stood there. 'Shorts,' he answered, in a disinterested tone.

'Football shorts? Squash shorts? Running shorts?' She stepped to the trays and held them up, knowing he wasn't going to buy a thing. 'Would you like to try some on?'

Cornered, he gazed at her with dull hatred. 'I'll think about it.'

'Do.' She led the way to the door, unlocked it for him then popped her head out. 'Anybody else want anything?'

Nobody did. Silently, they dispersed.

What amazed her was that these boys seemed to expect to be treated like criminals. They didn't take offence. Probably because they were criminals. She gathered up her writing things and made ready to go home. She locked the shop door in three places and struggled with the steel shutters.

Getting home in the evening traffic was a slow process. She tried to use her time sitting in the car to work out her writing programme for the next day. She planned to finish her *Plain Speaking* article by the end of the week if the shop was quiet enough and without too many nerve-racking visits from thieves or bailiffs. She never knew exactly what debts remained outstanding. A mounting number of goods were still on order. They never arrrived because the bills were unpaid, but the shop owner dealt with the courts. He taught at the London Business School.

Waiting her turn at traffic lights, in the clogged queue of crawling cars, her eye focused idly on a young man coming along the pavement with a dog at his heels. So many of the homeless sat begging here by the tube station with their dogs. She always looked anxiously to see the state of the animals, guessing that many of them would be in for a bad time. She never passed without giving a coin to help with a meal.

This dog was brown, woolly, young, thin and panting, with a wolfhound's head, and collarless. Its master was a thickly-built swaggering skinhead with a bullying stupid face. What a fate for that poor beast, Joy was thinking, before it gets lost or run over.

The queue moved, then stopped again. The lights turned back to red. The skinhead had stopped outside a hamburger bar and was ordering his dog to sit and wait at the edge of the pavement.

Panting, it was spinning in nervous circles. The man kicked it, but the dog went on moving, its thin body hooped. It was kicked and kicked until the buckled body flopped into shaking stillness. Nobody stopped and intervened. The man went in for his hamburger.

With some difficulty, Joy manoeuvred into the side of the road. Leaving the car parked on double yellow lines with the lights flashing, she followed him inside.

He was sitting on the far wall of the restaurant at a table on his own. She walked three quarters of the way across the room then called out to him, 'I saw what you did, you know!'

He stared. The small brutish eyes registered nothing.

Her voice rang out much louder. 'I saw you kick that dog!' Her chest was hammering.

He got up and sauntered over to her while other people kept their heads down and went on eating. He put his malevolent face right into hers, one finger jerking upwards under her nose. 'I don't care what you saw. You *dope*.' With that, he returned to his seat and she was left standing there.

'You shouldn't have a dog. I'm going to report you.' Defeated, Joy walked outside and passed the craven dog. She opened her car door. Then suddenly she turned back.

She bent over him, letting him smell her hands while she started to murmur nonsense in a low soothing voice. 'Good boy! You are a good boy, aren't you? Why don't you come with me, baby dog? Trust me. You've got to trust me and I can rescue you. I promise you it'll be all right.' He let her touch his head. 'There. Beauty face, come! Come quickly, please! We've got to hurry. It's all right, I promise. You good beauty!'

She walked a few steps and crouched, holding out her hands. The dog gave a little growl but his tail wagged feebly between his legs and he moved towards her so that now he was almost beside the car door.

'I can't beat about the bush. In you go!' As she put her hand under his light bony paunches, his head whipped round. 'Please don't bite me, baby chap.' She glanced back into the hamburger bar and thought she saw his bruiser owner standing up. She half-lifted, half-tossed the young collapsible body into the car, then she jumped in herself and started the engine. Amid a noise of brakes and angry horns, she drove straight through the red lights, panic rather than daring spurring her spectacular getaway.

'Well, good, good, good. We did that all right anyway,' she said shakily, only daring several streets later to look in the driving mirror. 'Dog stealing, there's nothing to it, is there, little chap? He asked for it and now he's got it!' To her relief, there appeared to be no pursuit of any sort. Slowly, she turned to the dog who was standing on the front seat beside her in his usual hooped position. 'Settle down, lambface, for God's sake. It's going to be all right, you know. I know it is, but how I'm not too sure. I'm going to find a lovely home for you. We'll just have to think what to do for the best.' He wasn't responding but she could see that he was listening.

'Well, I don't know about you but I am shattered.' She went on talking nonsense to him until they turned into Burbage Road. 'Here we are. Homey, homey. What about some chicken and brown bread for supper then we can think what to do next?' She knotted her scarf round his neck but he followed her quite happily into the house. He had a long drink of water then at last he lay down beside her, still panting slightly. She had a glass of whisky but her legs went on shaking as she started to prepare their supper.

'You *stole*?' Clive repeated incredulously, later in the evening, over the telephone. 'Are you saying you have stolen that dog?'

'Yes.'

'But couldn't you have got hold of a policeman?'

'Clive,' she said wearily, 'the police can't cope with dog problems any more. Anyway, what could they do about it? They didn't see the kicking. That man might get a paltry fine, that's all. He'd still have the dog. I'm so sick of all these awful thugs who are ruling our society. There's a dog across the road who isn't being treated properly. I can hear it barking now because they've shut it out in the rain. I'm going to take some action over that too, when I can think what to do. I shall just start taking the law into my own hands. Well, actually, of course . . . I've started.'

'You could ring the RSPCA.'

'I don't even know where the nearest one is.'

'There's a branch near my old office. We can hand your stolen dog in tomorrow on the way to my parents.'

'Good Lord, no. Nobody would want him. He'd be put to sleep. He's very p . . l . . a . . i . . n,' she said, spelling it out while she watched the brown woolly dog watching her, lying with his head on his paws. 'Will your parents mind if he comes with us?'

'Oh, Joy, must he? My papa loathes animals. No, of course he doesn't *loathe* them but he doesn't particularly want them around with guests staying. That dog will have fleas, you know.'

'I can't leave him shut up alone for hours on end, especially when I've just taken him in. Look, let me go to your parents another day. That's the best thing.'

He groaned. 'How can I alter it now? They're all geared to meet you. Look, this is most difficult. I thought we always kept Wednesdays and Saturdays for seeing each other. Okay, never mind then, leave it as it is. My mother won't object. She had dogs before she met my father.'

Clive's parents owned a guest house called Stapleton Byng, close to the Sussex Downs. He described it to Joy as they drove down there in his new white Vauxhall Cavalier, the car awash with Vivaldi. 'Yes, I shall probably take the house over myself one day, when my CSS commitments have tapered off a bit. My two half-brothers, from my mother's first marriage, have never shown any interest in it.' As his parents were well into their seventies, he explained, they now had a charming couple helping them to run it. They had recently met the Teftys in Spain.

'It sounds most agreeable,' Joy said.

He turned towards her with his little flirting power smile. 'It is *most* agreeable,' he agreed, mimicking her. As they whizzed along in the fast lane, he sang to the music 'Pom, pom, pom.' He wrinkled his noise at her and made baby noises of twosome cosiness. 'Happy?' The tops of his arms were pink and freckled and plump in the short-sleeved shirt. His legs were strong and stout in their camper's sandals.

'Mm . . .' She put her arm through to the back of the car to cosset the dog. 'Are you happy?'

He nodded, closing his eyes, smiling. He was radiating cleanliness and bounce. 'I feel fit for anything.'

She had an uncomfortable feeling that he was play-acting to jolly things along, but going on jaunts with him gave her a pleasant sense of reassurance that she was part of the normal world of couples again. She quite enjoyed that.

'I must warn you,' he said, as they pulled up outside an attractive old stone house like a vicarage set back among trees, 'my mother will go on about having her leg off. Take no notice of it. Nobody does. It's become frightfully boring.'

'Oh, my goodness, poor . . .'

'No, don't take any notice,' Clive insisted, getting out of the car. 'Do we have to walk the doggie a bit before we go in?'

But I shall have to take notice, Joy was thinking. She was aghast. What an appalling situation. She must make it her business to comfort Mrs. Pownall if everyone else was being so callous. She could talk about leg amputation if she had to, even if they couldn't. What a shocking thing! Surely Mr. Pownall and the charming couple were being sympathetic to her even if Clive had no normal filial feeling for his mother. There were people who found handicaps and lack of perfection repugnant. How vile. And how he could call the charming couple *charming* when the despicable . . .

'Oh, there's Garth Tefty,' Clive said, as a bearded man came out of the house to see some people off.

Garth and Dorothea Tefty were charming but they were

busy looking after the reception desk and dining room. Clive's parents received Joy in a private sitting room furnished in a chintzy and cluttered manner with many dolls and ornaments from foreign places. In the bathroom, fluffy animal covers hid the toilet rolls. She warmed to his mother at once and tried not to let her eyes go anywhere near her legs. Dinky Pownall made her think of the colonies, the Indian Army, certainly of expatriate Spain. She was a knowing, tough old bird, a good-hearted battered battler. She looked like an ex-Gaietey Girl. Mr. Pownall seemed a bit fierce. He was wearing a blazer, with a cravat in the neck of his shirt, and had the same bouncing military bearing as his son. He obviously didn't like the dog and fixed it with a hostile eye.

'It hasn't been near my rockery, has it?'

Responding to his hysterical tone, Joy wheeled in alarm. 'Is there poison down?'

'There's no poison down but there's a filthy mess of some sort on the lawn.'

'Well, let's hope its not human,' Dinky said humorously. 'I'm sure this lovely boy hasn't done any harm, Denis. I'm like Joy. I know dogs. I prefer them to humans.' She fondled the dog's ears while he did some nervous circling. 'Clive only knows cats . . . doesn't want to know 'em unfortunately. He takes after Denis.' She closed one eye to release a barrage of smoke from her cigar. 'Who's a big soft sweetheart then?' She put her face down to the dog. 'He's a real Heinz boy, isn't he? What a miracle you rescued him, dear. Clive told me.'

Still uncomfortable at Clive's father's lack of enthusiasm for the animal, Joy smiled gratefully. 'My legs still shake when I think about it. I'm sure that sort of man probably carries a knife. I'll have to steer clear of my usual haunts now in case I bump into him again.' She patted the dog as he settled uneasily beside her. 'You know he kicked him several times but people just walked on.'

'I'd have kicked *him*,' Dinky said vehemently. 'Or I would have done in the past. I'm a mess now. I couldn't kick anything. Has Clive told you I've got to have my leg off?'

'Ohhh . . .' Joy strove to get shock, reassurance and sympathy into one long vague muted sound. She thought she heard Clive groan. 'Well, Clive was telling me . . .'

'What's your poison, Joyce?' Denis Pownall demanded. 'Martini?'

'Thank you.' A distinct chill was coming from the two men. It made her even more determined to give comfort.

Clive said: 'Joy likes white wine or scotch, daddy.'

His mother chipped in. 'Nothing for me, Denis. I'll have my usual little glass of Aqua Libra.' Her face pleaded mutely. She wanted to talk. She was consumed, Joy guessed, with unimaginable horrors.

She leant forward, feeling her way. 'Clive was telling me you haven't been feeling very well, Mrs. Pownall. Are you in great pain?'

The face crumpled. 'Great pain, dear. Awful, awful pain. I've been going up for test after test. I haven't slept a wink, you know, for two months.'

Clive stared ahead.

'On the rocks, Joyce?' As Mr. Pownall placed a glass of whisky on a small table beside her, his stomach rumbled – a deep longish growl like an alsation. Her dog growled back.

'I want to scream my bloody head off,' said Dinky. 'Pardon my French.'

'*Oh . . . dear,*' Joy managed, from the bottom of her heart.

'And how's life in Motspur Park?' Denis Pownall enquired with a loud deliberate casualness, turning to his son. 'Are you getting your new place in order?' He stood with his back to the unnecessary fire, lifting his blazer to warm himself, as they started a determined discussion on the merits of double glazing.

Was there a streak of sadistic derangement in these two men? Joy was astonished. She raised her glass to Dinky. 'Good luck!' she said, with meaning. 'Does anything help the pain?'

'They can't help me, dear. They say there's nothing they can do for me. It hurts to walk now. My bladder feels as if it's on fire. You know, it's costing a bomb, seeing all these doctors, and I'm in hell day and night.'

'Do you think the bladder trouble could be due to nervousness over the leg?' Joy mused gently. 'Losing a leg, I've heard, is not as bad as it sounds. I mean, it's not the end of the world, by any means, although I'm sure that's what you're thinking at this minute.'

She heard Clive gasp and faltered, 'I know . . . er . . . we . . . I know one, no no, one or two people who have li . . . lived p . . p . . perfectly happily after a leg operation. Women apparently adapt much better than men do.' She gave Mrs. Pownall an uplifting smile of pronounced spiritual strength. 'Do the doctors say that?'

The poor woman looked too bashed to respond. Her head had sunk into her neck. She looked stiff, as if her limbs had stuck. Her cigar was forgotten. 'Mr. Trustam Ellis says the only thing he can do to take the pain away is to take my leg off. He's the top surgeon and he can't find out what's wrong with me.' As tears filled her eyes, the possibility dawned on Joy for the first time that there was nothing wrong with Mrs. Pownall at all.

She tried to change the subject but Dinky Pownall wasn't having it. She was too well away to stop now. She embarked on an intimate catalogue of her medical experiences while Joy sat nodding with her head sympathetically on one side, her eyes glued intently to her hostess but her mind moving onto other matters.

'I should have been getting on with my *Plain Speaking* article instead of coming here. What am I doing? Bugger it, what a fool I am! How pathetic to be clutching at straws like the Pownalls. It's all alien. It makes me feel lonely as if I've somehow slipped beyond the pale in middle age. At least Dinky Pownall has her husband beside her even though he appears to have made her suicidal. Clive and I have nothing whatever in common except the dancing. That's given us a spurious closeness for the time being. I wish though that I'd been able to give more, to nurture him a bit, but there's no vulnerable chink for me amidst all the nose wrinkling and giggling and puns. If I could be myself with him it would probably all be over. How desperately one tries to make the unattached man fit the hole in one's life! All the stumbling blocks, like the pigskin lounge suite, the black walls covered in swords, the pictures of himself in Cavalier costume, all the shallow bouncing and the drinks poured out in the kitchen, are stuffed to the back of one's mind while one hopes it's going to get better. I don't want to travel home in the car with him singing *pom pom pom* to that music and placing my hand on his bulging penis. The annoying thing is, Clive doesn't really want me either. He wants a fun doll. Why should I feel undermined by that? Strike me pink, who does he think he is? Presumably he is of average intelligence? Is he? I don't know. Anyway, he's perfectly pleased with himself. He thinks he knows everything worth knowing. If I raised George Eliot in conversation he'd know nothing, and be bored stiff, despite his English degree. George Eliot bores me but I'd prefer to be talking to the person who isn't bored by her. I can't ask Clive why Mr. Cross jumped out of the bedroom window on their wedding night. I don't want to talk to people like Mr. Pownall in blazers with cravats at their necks. And what is a fun doll? Is it a jangly blonde with the neck to wear a fur coat in public? Would she want to marry Clive? She'd want a rich dentist with a fast car who'd buy her a town house on an estate of like-minded upwardly-mobile funsters . . .' Joy gave another lugubrious nod at Mrs. Pownall, who was still in full flow, 'Mm . . . oh, dear.' The heat in the room was stifling.

'Clive is much like his father with his high forehead and ginger winged eyebrows, but more benign as yet, thank heaven. There's an odd hint of Mephistopheles in both cases. They've got the same blazers too. Blazers to go with

What's your posion? and the blob shoes. That's it, of course. Clive's dated. Certain people seem to stop at a certain period in their lives and cling to that style and those attitudes for ever. Clive goes dancing on, twinkling and twirling, rubbing noses and . . .'

'C'est la vie,' Dinky said disgustedly, 'I'd call it daylight robbery, wouldn't you?'

'Yes,' Joy replied, coming to attention. 'I definitely would. Yes . . . um, dear me.'

'I guessed why Mr. Chalker gave us such a whacking bill after my last examination – we only get a tiny percentage back from BUPA, you see – I said to Denis at the time – didn't I, Denis? "His Nibs is paying us back for damage to his premises!" ' Here, Dinky, who had perked up considerably after airing her troubles, gave a wheeze of embattled laughter.

Denis said: 'Charlie Chalker wants his annual holiday in the West Indies. We're paying for that.'

Relieved at the relaxed turn the conversation had taken, Joy smiled round at the two men. 'But why was Mr. Chalker paying you back?' she asked Clive's mother.

'Ooh, no, Joy, I can't . . . don't ask me to tell you that embarrassing story. You'd think I was terrible!'

'Tell me,' Joy urged, hoping to build on the improving atmosphere. 'You've got to tell me now.'

'Honestly, I laughed all the way home from Harley Street that day. It was a Monday morn . . .'

'It was a Tuesday,' said her husband.

'Tuesday, that's right. I went for my examination and it was torture. Excrutiating pain. I really don't think I could have faced it if I'd known what was coming. Well, Charlie Boy, that's what I call His Nibs, put his little pipe inside me and pumped me full of liquid. I can't describe the horror of it. I thought I was going to burst. There were two nurses standing by because I expect some people pass out.

'I warned Mr. Chalker that I wouldn't be able to control myself. I was jabbering at him . . . Denis and Clive think

73

I'm exaggerating but I was really screaming at him: "Stop, stop! *Please*!' and that sort of thing, and he was giving me stern looks down his spectacles. He can be a bit frosty at the best of times. They're like God, aren't they, these top Harley Street chaps? He said "Mrs. Pownall, you have nothing to fear. We have patients here every day and we haven't had an accident yet. Now, would you be kind enough to sit on the commode over there, please, and pass water for me. I need to listen to the flow".'

'Heavens,' Joy said.

'My dear,' Dinky Pownall buckled forward with laughter and rested her hand on Joy's knee. 'I seated myself on this throne with a wooden surround and when I looked down through my legs I could see the linoleum floor. I thought "Oops! Qu'est-ce-que c'est?" I couldn't see any receptacle because they'd forgotten it, you see, but I didn't say anything. I was in such a state. I was so dazed I assumed it was another of the mysteries of modern medicine, so I went. An avalanche poured straight through the chair and onto the lino. Mr. Chalker's face. Oh, Joy, I could have died!'

'Only Harley water, Ma,' Clive said promptly, with a hearty roar of laughter. 'God shouldn't object to that!'

They were all still laughing as Dorothea Tefty put her head round the door. 'Gong in five minutes,' she said. 'Dinner's ready!'

Meanwhile, at the Cavalry and Guards Club in Piccadilly, Conroy Sweeting and Ruth Bly were having a reconciliation dinner. Sweetie was a rare visitor to the Cavalry Club. He was usually to be found at the Beefsteak but, having just had the unpleasant experience of being blackballed by the Garrick for the second time, he didn't relish the prospect of bumping into journalistic cronies who might be rejoicing at his humiliation. He was talking to Ruth about cricket and the problems for the committee of the still fairly exclusive Wordsmith team. She was giving him her undivided attention because she was rather relieved to be holding on to her *Plain Speaking* column.

'We're not encouraging George Holgate to play cricket with us this year,' he declared. 'The Wordsmiths have a certain style, and that is what our members like. We've had some jolly good fixtures and we want to renew them. George is too exuberant for us. When we played Hurlingham last time he bowled bouncers, and every time he took a wicket he did a cartwheel. Our bowlers shouldn't be doing cartwheels.' Sweetie paused to pass her the bread basket. As he glanced up, his gaze settled on two new arrivals seating themselves at a table on the other side of the dining room. 'Oh, hurray! Look who's just walked in – one of my oldest friends, Marcia Galway-Lamb. She's done something peculiar to her hair. We'll have coffee with her later.'

Ruth looked. She recognised the Chinese girl from the singles club in the Melstar Hotel. The person sitting opposite her, in a po-faced little dress of peacock blue with knife pleats and Peter Pan collar, was Tania Galway-Lamb.

'Marcia?'

'Yes.'

'Tania you mean.'

'Over there. The two females. Marcia must be entertaining someone from the British Council.'

'But Sweetie, that is Tania Galway-Lamb. His real name is Tony. He's a captain in the Life Guards.'

'Yes, Marcia's his mother. He's my godson,' said Conroy Sweeting, in a flat, wondering voice. 'Trussed up like a tart. You know him too, do you?'

Ruth nodded, most reluctant to admit to the singles evening in the Cromwell Road and hoping Galway-Lamb would be equally reticent. 'Yes, I met him somewhere.' At that moment he turned and saw them. After a long wooden stare, he waved.

Sweetie stared back, then he helped himself to more cheese and changed the subject.

The meal went on. Into a silence, when the gentle buzz of diners' conversation had momentarily dropped, Ruth heard Tania's loud warm voice addressing her companion. 'Oh, you are naughty! I'm going to smack your widgy little wrist!'

Later, as they stood up to leave the dining room, Sweetie glanced across again. 'Well, I suppose something has to be said,' he observed bleakly and led the way to the other table.

'Hullo, Uncle Conroy,' his godson declared pleasantly, remaining seated and neglecting to introduce the Chinese girl. It was clear something awful had happened to his face. It seemed stiff and flattened. The jaw had taken on a Desperate Dan aspect and only the lower lip moved when he spoke, like a ventriloquist's doll. Working slowly, the wooden stare gave way to a simpering smile of apparently gross insincerity and lasciviousness with a bunching of the lips and crinkling of the eyes.

His godfather stepped backwards. 'What's happened to your face?' he demanded. 'Were you on manoeuvres?'

'I was assaulted by a friend of hers,' Galway-Lamb nodded at Ruth. 'I've run up a monumental medical bill and I intend to sue. Have you got his address? I'm going to take him to the cleaners.'

'No,' she replied in an emphatic rush, aghast, and hoping he didn't mean it. 'And he told me he was going bankrupt. He hasn't got any money at all now.'

Unable to disguise his disgust, Sweetie spoke again. 'I should think you've broken your poor mother's heart,' he said brusquely, 'dressed up like some damned swine. You look like a shitbag.'

'His mother was one of the finest horsewomen in the country,' he added, in a dazed voice, as they went down the stairs.

In the hall the porter was talking to the club secretary, Major Fox. 'Captain Galway-Lamb is here, Sir, with his daughter. He's booked a double room for to-night in the name of Mrs. Galway-Lamb.'

'Oh. Good. Thank you, Joe.'

'He appears to be in lady's attire, sir. A frock and tights and lipstick and that.'

'I see,' Foxy replied. 'Well, I hope he hasn't used the coffee room, has he? I must speak to him. The ladies' subscription is less.'

8

She Said

Leo . . . !

Ruth was almost beginning to get used to the fact that she was probably never going to see Leo again. Although he remained at the back of her mind, she wasn't thinking about him for once as she leafed open a copy of *Harper's & Queen* in the hairdressers. A headline and a row of photographs caught her eye. LONDON'S MOST ELIGIBLE BACHELORS.

Amid a selection of matrimonial plums – a PR man in a beautiful Armani suit who snatched short rests in the Seychelles, a pop star promoter with a topiary haircut who went clubbing and businessmen with keen eyes and Peter Jay mouths who owned shoots or played polo – was a picture of Leo. She felt a shattering surge of sick excited shock.

She couldn't take her eyes off the article. She shut the magazine and opened it again as it all came back. The hope. The waiting. The disappointment. Such a longing for him had suddenly come over her.

She had really believed they were going to be together, that she was going to help him through his bad patch, but he had literally evaporated, after taking her to some jazz films, like the Cheshire Cat. She'd rung once or twice but there was no reply. Seeing him being offered like this, as a perfect prize for a perfect partner, churned her up all over again. It made her feel even more rejected and shut out of his existence. She brooded on the picture, envious of the person who'd been with Leo to take it, envious of the journalist who'd interviewed him. Had he found her more interesting? Had he lectured her on visual images and Mickey Mouse? Had he made her eat jelly for breakfast? Surreptitiously, she removed the page.

Len Derbyshire, 47. Visionary animation genius who picks up all the prizes. This reclusive rough diamond is a sleepy charmer who has been everywhere and done everything. Led a union mutiny in the Merchant Navy. Jumped ship in Australia. Ran a diving school in Tunisia. Writes books. Is he cuddly teddy or wicked subversive? Nobody knows because nobody really knows him. He doesn't drink. He doesn't smoke. He says he's never killed a fly but his work is full of black thoughts and anarchic humour. He'll do anything for anyone except commit himself.

Life was so bloody *hard*. *Why* hadn't he rung? She went home with the article tucked in her pocket. Waves of depression kept flooding over her as she tried to resist the temptation to ring him. She had to forget it. She poured one small drink. Then a bigger one. Then she wrote a note. She carried it about with her, and posted it two days later.

He telephoned at once. 'It's Lee . . . o,' he said, sounding most amiable. He invited her to dinner.

This time she saw his flat. Ruth was dumbfounded. What she'd imagined for him was something Gothic, witty, airy – bare, perhaps, but artistic. Something essentially masculine but stylish. What she saw was a cesspit. The mess was indescribable.

'Leo!' she said, standing in the hall.

'Yes, I've got to do it up,' he replied.

On two floors, his maisonette looked as if there'd been a protracted fight down the stairs involving a trail of old shoes, clothes, car seats, discarded suitcases, bicycle pumps and pieces of odd electrical equipment. Leo had been living with the chaos mounting since he moved in. He didn't notice the sink filled with unsavoury unwashed pots, and the stove was encrusted with grease. There were two grubby junk shop fridges festooned with magnetic numbers. He didn't think about dust, far less see any. On the kitchen surfaces there were heaps of old newspapers, letters, computer magazines, parts of plugs, string and other miscellaneous rubbish.

'Leo!' Ruth said again.

In the sitting room there were computers on trestle tables round the walls, which needed painting, and more papers everywhere. In the middle of a stained and motheaten blue carpet, sitting beside a guitar and a clarinet, was a giant tabby cat curled up in a round red Cosipet bed.

'That's Jacob,' Leo said.

'Hallo, Jacob,' Ruth went on staring silently, still clutching the costly box of handmade chocolates she'd brought with her. 'I thought you'd written a book on how to organise your life.'

'I know. I am trying to organise it, but the place isn't structurally sound. There's a lot to do before I start to tidy up.'

She laughed. 'But has the woman from *Harper's & Queen* been here?'

He laughed too as he led the way back to the kitchen. 'She's used to it. Avril Aitken should have mentioned the mess in her description of me in case any of the readers get too excited. I've known her for years, you see. I think she even got her *Harper's* job through me.' He was milling about, bringing frozen packets out of the fridge. 'She only put me in because she needed an extra bachelor to fill up a corner. We cobbled something suitable together and, anyway, why not? I've had scores of articles written about me. I'm a lot more talented than those other guys.'

Ruth nodded, a trifle doubtfully, definitely put off. 'I know you are.' She felt let down. Her problem was that Len Derbyshire was the real thing. A dedicated, struggling, self-absorbed, shambling childlike genius living in an outlandishly eccentric world of his own. Although it had not dawned on her yet, she didn't actually want the genuine article. What she wanted was a smart fake who earned a massive salary and was seen to be living his life in distinctly dashing circumstances.

Nervously, she dusted a chair with her hand before sitting down at the kitchen table in her new pastel pink leggings. She pushed the gorgeous chocolates across to Leo who looked extremely pleased.

'Can I have one now?'

'Certainly not. You'll never stop. Are we going to have a little drink?' she ventured.

His face fell. 'I've forgotten your wine. I'll have to go out in a minute. D'you want some juice or a cup of tea in the meantime?'

'No, thanks,' she replied in a tired voice. 'I'll go and get wine. Where's the offey?'

'Coffee?'

'The off-licence.'

'Out the door and round to the right. About twenty yards along. Here, take some cash with you.' He pulled out a five pound note. 'Get yourself something reasonable. You can go and have a drink in the other room while I'm getting our food ready.'

'I've got some calls to make for my column.'

'The phone's in the sitting room, by the door.'

She tapped her briefcase. 'Thanks. I've got one of my own.'

Their supper was individual chicken kievs half-cooked in the microwave, with a large packet of mixed vegetables. These were followed by trifle in little cartons. A meal Ruth found uninviting but endearing. At that point she was beginning to feel he might easily turn out to be resistible.

Perhaps for this reason, this time, their conversation flowed. There were no tense pauses when they were out of communication. Leo was relaxed and attentive and doing his best to make her evening pleasant. He questioned her about *Plain Speaking* and about her family. He said he remembered her mother's name and seemed rather impressed.

'You're the right shape. Why didn't you dance?'

'It didn't occur to me. After my mother died I was even more set on being part of an ordinary family who all sat round the table together at regular times. I wanted a normal life of every day things. Because I hadn't got it, and other children had, that was all I dreamt about. I was very much a lost soul. I longed for my father to want me more than he ever did.'

'My father was a bum. I only have one really vivid memory of him. When I caught diphtheria, he flushed my white mice down the toilet. I didn't go to see him when he was dying in hospital. He wasn't a bit like my mother who was hard-working and generous and always laughing. Everybody took their problems to her and she used to sit there knitting while she listened. She wasn't from a gipsy background herself, so after my father died we left that life and went back to Enfield where she came from.'

'Can you remember living with travellers?' she asked eagerly. 'We could do an article about your childhood in *Plain Speaking*.'

'You romanticise them,' he said disapprovingly. 'Well, I don't. I detest them. I never talk about it because they're dreadful people. They steal. They're lazy. They've stopped travelling now to live on housing estates and cause trouble. They don't pay their rent. They send their kids out – nine years old, mark you – to start thieving. My mother was an honest woman. I don't know how she stood it.'

'And you loved her?'

'She was an uneducated simple soul but a marvellous character and I was the apple of her eye. When I went off to sea she warned me not to go with bad women and not to get dirt in my belly button.'

'And did you go with bad women?'

'Of course. I went to the West Indies at sixteen. I was totally innocent. I didn't know what a bad woman was.'

She laughed. 'What were the bad women like?'

'I can remember the first time I went with a girl. I was in a bar and I was asked if I wanted to. I only had the faintest idea what it meant. Anyway, I was led upstairs to a room with a queue waiting outside the door. Guys were going in and coming out within about two minutes. When my turn came, I went in and there was this girl lying on the bed wearing high-heeled shoes and nothing else. She greeted me impatiently, saying: "Come in! Hurry up. Get on top." It was all over in seconds. Whilst I was still pulling on my trousers, she poked her head out and the next man came in.'

'Your mother would have had a fit. She's dead now?'

'She died nine months ago. That's added to my general gloom. The trouble with my company started about the same time she got ill.'

'Oh, Leo.'

'Yes, it was a bad patch. My mother had given me her savings, you know, at some period when I was really down and out. It wasn't much, a few hundred quid or something, but it was all she had in the world. Now I keep wondering whether I could have done more for her. Not that she wanted for anything. I used to take her my washing sometimes just to make her feel needed. At least she saw me make a name for myself, even if there wasn't much to show for it. She always kept her faith in me without any proper understanding of what I was trying to do.'

'Does anybody understand what you're doing?'

'Hardly anybody,' he told her, smiling gleefully. 'I'm always ahead of my time. You use a computer, don't you? Come and see my latest one.'

They went into the other room where Jacob was playing by himself with a yellow ball. Leo kicked it for him then he sat down and tinkered happily with his computer. 'Now we'll make up a little story for you about a beautiful girl called Miss Bly who is going out for a walk. Miss Bly's Outing,' he typed as a long-legged blonde bombshell in a picture hat appeared on the screen. 'There she is!'

Ruth laughed. 'If only I had legs like the other Miss Bly. I'm flattered.'

'We'll give her a briefcase because she's a busy journalist, and here comes the sun shining for her but it starts to rain very suddenly. Look! She'd better take shelter under a tree.' Leo pressed another key and produced an oak tree in the rain. 'What would you like to see next on Miss Bly's Outing?'

'How about a rainbow?' Ruth suggested helpfully, suddenly feeling rather exhausted.

'Okey dokey . . . a rainbow,' he said triumphantly.

'What miracles! I can't do that on mine. Could she dance for joy?' She was wistfully eyeing one of the sunken armchairs. 'Talking of dancing,' she added cautiously, 'have you heard any more from Tania Galway-Lamb?'

He spun round in his seat giving her an excuse to go and sit down.

'Joy keeps telling me to get in touch.'

'Oh, don't do that,' she warned hastily. 'He might sue you. He could say he's got medical bills for you to pay, or got to have plastic surgery. Leo, don't let him get your address, whatever you do.'

'Don't worry, I've no intention of it,' he replied, turning back to his computer.

Ruth seized on the clarinet and guitar which were lying beside her. 'Do you play these? Will you play for me? Why not send Miss Bly home to bed?'

'I don't want Miss Bly to go home just yet.' He picked up his guitar and perched on the arm of a chair. 'Tell me what to play for you,' he said. And he played whatever she requested.

'Hold on,' he muttered each time as he picked out the chords of the new tune. While he played *Sweet Georgia Brown* for her, holding her eyes with a quiet tricky little bed smile, she knew she was lost again. Later on, when there were such terrible troubles between them, that scene always came back to her because she was so overwhelmed with tenderness and excitement and respect too, then, for all he'd accomplished on his own from his hopeless gipsy start. Her problem was that she fell in love anew every time she saw him. He was such a potent touching mixture of shyness and swank.

Unflatteringly early, he started to yawn and, once he'd started, the yawns gathered momentum. 'I'll have to go to bed, Ruth,' he told her apologetically. He stood up then bent down to kiss the top of her head, 'Coming?'

So it wasn't a ploy. This time she didn't feel offended. She realised he couldn't help it. He couldn't stay awake.

His bedroom was no surprise because she'd prepared herself for a monstrous shock. The ill-made kingsize bed was propped up at one corner on books, and the bare boards on the floor were only partially covered by a thin drably-faded rug. A dirty old net curtain was draped across to cover half the window. There was a scruffy table hidden beneath piles of newspapers and old letters.

'I've got a bit to do in here,' Leo said.

'Please say no more,' Ruth replied. 'I'm taking it in my stride.'

As if he had no time to waste before sleep took a fatal hold, he started to make love to her immediately. As she stood, absorbing the dishevelled bleakness of the room, he pushed her gently onto the rumpled bed. He undressed her slowly, kissing her solemnly on each new uncovered part. He got up to remove his own clothes, tossing them towards a chair. He lay beside her then, his finger inside her. Gradually the shock of his solid heavy hairiness subsided. His alien smell, so different from Sweetie's long bony hairless body, grew familiar and became a thrill.

'I expect you want me to use one of these?' he said, producing a condom from under the pillow, 'But it's been so long since I slept with a woman – good or bad – I doubt if I'm any danger to you.'

She laughed. 'The rubber will have rotted.'

That first time was the delight she had imagined it was

going to be. She forgot about Sweetie. She forgot about the awfulness of the bedroom. Leo was talking, gabbling little half-whispered words to her. He wasn't sleepy any longer. He came to life, drawing her with him to a fever of excitement. She lay afterwards in the darkness listening to his breathing and smiling to herself at the memory of his noisy anguished shouts. She reached out to touch him, entwining her fingers in the hair at the back of his neck.

Leo sighed sleepily, grunted, then coughed like a dog with a bone stuck. In a flurry of bedclothes, he bounced himself into the air to turn over and face her. The bed slid off its books and tilted. As they rolled into each other, there was a terrible prolonged splintering as the end of the bed smashed slowly through the floor. It stopped, leaving them suspended.

'Leo!' Ruth gasped, terrified.

He managed to shift gingerly and turn a light on. A piece of plaster fell off the wall, showering their heads and shoulders.

'Keep still,' he commanded.

Cautiously he climbed off the bed and tested the boards where he was standing, then he helped her get off and took her out of the room.

'Oh, God,' she said in an awed voice, trying to see the size of the hole in the floor, and how much of the bed was through it. 'What a disaster! I can't believe it. I didn't take you literally when you told me this place wasn't structurally sound.' She pressed her hand flat across her mouth in a gesture of shock to stop herself laughing. She shook with a sudden loud hysterical gust. 'I'm s . . . sorry,' it started muted but then the words came in almost a shout. '*I d . . don't mean to la . . laugh!*'

'This is more than I can stand,' he said coldly. 'Jesus Christ. I want to leave the country.'

'You can come and stay with me,' she replied, trying to control herself.

'No thanks.' Grimly, he collected her clothes and passed

them to her. 'Look, you go downstairs. Keep out of the sitting room.'

She dressed and made a cup of tea for them. Leo joined her in the kitchen in his dressing gown. They sat drinking with plaster in their hair. Jacob reappeared and climbed serenely onto Leo's knee.

Ruth was half-expecting to hear the bed drop through the ceiling. 'You could come to me for a bit,' she repeated, trying to be serious. 'Wouldn't that help? I'd love to have you.'

He felt a black wave of rage and self pity. Why laugh? If that catastrophe was a stroke of luck for her, it was pretty well curtains for him. He was at the end of his tether and he DID NOT WANT TO GO AND STAY IN HORNSEY. He wanted to shout it at her. Get off! Get off my back, woman. Give up, will you? I have nothing to offer you. Get it? No company, no money, no home. No hope.

'Why don't you come?' she insisted gently. 'You can work in the sitting room.'

'No, I couldn't do that to you. Thanks, Ruth. I have my computers.'

'Bring it. Bring them.'

'I can work downstairs here.'

'With all that noise? Workmen banging and trampling?'

'There's Jacob too, you see.'

'Well, he can come.'

'He's better here. The old lady next door always takes him in when I'm away. Anyway, I don't need to be away. I can sleep in another room.'

'You could easily be killed. Leo, really, it's not safe.'

In the end, when they'd had another look at the damaged bedroom, he was persuaded. With the choice of being maimed for life or a week or two in Hornsey, he reluctantly chose the latter. 'You are being most kind,' he declared, ungraciously, too appalled to look at her properly. 'I hope it won't be a lot of trouble. I'll just come to you at bedtime, shall I?'

'Leo, don't be silly. I'll be cooking for us. You can have jelly for breakfast. Bring all your stuff. You can come and go when you like.'

9

She Said

*At fifty you can't take any more shit from people.
I don't want to marry anyone now. I want to
marry my dog.*

'I'm going to have to steal another dog,' Joy said to Jill.
They were out in their dog-walking clothes, strolling in Hyde
Park close to where Jill lived in Queen's Gate Gardens.
'Dog stealing is incredibly exciting and rewarding. I can't
recommend it highly enough.'

Jill laughed. 'Well, it's been a great success with Brown.
I like that name for him. He is a Mister Brown. What are
you going to steal now?'

'I'm going to remove that poor dog who's left out all the
time across the road. I can't stand it any longer.'

'But you are going to keep Brown?'

'Oh, of course! There was never any doubt about it really.
I may have kidded myself at first, but once I'd got him I
couldn't part with him. I adore him.'

Poppy, Jill's little dog, was pattering obediently along
beside them while the woolly brown dog romped wildly with
a red setter and a beagle. Whenever Joy watched him, Jill had
noticed with amusement, there was a small smile of maternal
pride playing round her mouth. It was there now.

'Look at him!' Joy said. 'He's getting so confident. At first
he wouldn't let me out of his sight. He's very well behaved
in the shop, you know, and I feel much safer with him beside
me. It's much more relaxing coming to Hyde Park. I don't
keep imagining we're about to bump into his owner.'

They walked slowly back towards Jill's car and stood chatting, watching Brown hopelessly chasing the ducks.

'Let me run you back,' Jill offered.

'No need. It was kind of you to pick us up. Brown can do with some more walk and we can always get a bus for the last bit. It's such a nuisance Matt borrowing my car at weekends, but I feel I must help him out with all his stuff for the stall. I'm so relieved he's found something to do. At least it takes the heat off the Rastafarianism.'

'What does his father think?'

'I don't know what Roly thinks,' Joy said. 'I don't know that I ever did. He's quite capable himself of suddenly announcing he's become a Rasta. That's where Matt gets it, except that Roly probably would have gone a stage further and gone to live in Ethiopia, or wherever it is. Roly's mad tangents were what brought our marriage down. He's irresponsible. Roly's interest in children evaporated as soon as he pulled his trousers up.'

'It's interesting, isn't it,' Jill observed, opening the car door for Poppy, 'how you've gone from one extreme to the other? Clive's so dependable.'

'It's a lower gear,' Joy mused thoughtfully. 'It doesn't lead to so much angst. But Roly made me laugh. And that's what everybody wants, I suppose. I'd put that first, wouldn't you? Clive doesn't make me laugh.'

'The amusing ones are usually trouble. They can be very lacerating to live with. The problem is never getting all one wants in one cocktail. If you're out of a marriage you want to get into one, and if you're in one you want to get out. D'you think you'll marry Clive?'

'At fifty you can't take any more shit from people. I don't want to marry anyone now. I want to marry my dog. I think Clive is jealous of him.'

'Is Clive coming to-night?'

'No, he's fighting in Basingstoke. He never comes after battles.'

'Well, do let me take you home,' Jill insisted.

'Come and have tea, then. That's a good idea.'

Gossiping contentedly, they drove back to Joy's house. They found a parking space at the other end of the road and got out of the car to walk back. A furry yellow mongrel, hovering in the gutter, looked up as they approached and streaked joyfully across the road to greet Joy. All the dogs swirled round each other in friendly fashion.

'Hullo, Lucky!' Joy said, patting him then patting the other two. 'Hullo . . . hullo, you good boy. Come on then! Are you coming in as well?

'This is the one I'm going to steal who is left out all the time,' she explained to Jill. 'I'm getting beside myself. You know, those men went away for a week and left him to fend for himself. I fed him and he came for walks with us. I can't wait to do them down.'

'He's gorgeous, isn't he? Can't you report it?' Jill suggested.

'He'd only be put in a cell somewhere. He might not get a home. There are so many unwanted dogs. Those men are off somewhere now. There's been no sign of them since yesterday.'

She opened the doors into the garden. 'Let's have tea out here, then there's less chance of a fight. I'll give Lucky something to eat while the other two aren't looking.'

She put the kettle on and brought out a tray with pieces of buttered malt bread on it. 'D'you remember we always had this at those special school teas when we had to invite Miss Benstead and make conversation?'

Jill gave a little shriek. 'You were marvellous with her! She was such a bat, wasn't she? She'd sit there with that grim mouth and gimlet eye. Everybody was paralysed with fright. We relied on you to race through *The Times* and open up with an erudite piping about some new archaeological find in Mesopotamia. D'you remember when you told her you were going to be a vet?'

'She said, "Veterinary surgeon, Joy", and pointed out that I was fourteenth in biology, and sitting with my legs apart.'

Giggling together, as they'd been doing for nearly forty years, they went on drinking their watery Lapsang until the sun went in.

'What about a nippington?' Joy suggested. 'I'll go and get the bottle, then I can show you my article on drink which I'm sending to *Plain Speaking*.'

'You know Poppy has a crush on Lucky,' Jill remarked when she reappeared. 'She won't leave him alone.'

In the middle of their third whisky, Joy suddenly had an idea. 'Jill, why don't you take Lucky?'

'What?'

'I mean take him. You steal him.'

'Joy, dear one, don't be silly. How could I? I know he's gorgeous but he looks a bit like an alsatian. How can I?'

'You could. You work a lot at home. You've got one dog. Two is nothing. He's so eager to please. I can't have him because I live opposite. But you can. Oh, Jill, do.'

'But what about my father? I spend so much time going to Tewkesbury to the nursing home.'

'How is your father, by the way?'

Jill laughed. 'Actually, Pa could not be better. He's eighty-six and he's on top form now. I must tell you, because it's so funny, but he was bored stiff with himself. He got depressed because he had nothing to do. He kept writing letters to newspapers which were never printed until he penned a fierce attack on the IRA and that went in.

'He immediately got a letter from them saying they would be coming to get him. He was thrilled! Then he winged one off about Islamic fundamentalists and got a letter from them saying he was as good as dead. His life is transformed. I don't know who he's going to castigate next. I'm absolutely terrified.'

'I can remember the uproar when he sent a Valentine card to Miss Benstead. She was absolutely livid. But he had four dogs himself, Jill. Surely you can take Lucky with you?' It took Joy two more drinks before Jill was persuaded. 'Listen, as I said, we are fifty. We can't stand by with all this bad behaviour going on. Come on, are we going to put a stop to the rise of the super yob in this country or are we not? Look at the cruelties, look at the crimes, look at our collapsing culture. There isn't a film for us to see because each new release is more revolting than the last. I see the cretins browsing in the video shop searching for videos called *Serial Axeman* and *How I Screwdrivered My Granny's Brains Out & Ate Them On Toast*. Those men have asked for it and now they going to get it. We've got to take Lucky, haven't we?' she implored earnestly.

Jill fell back in her chair, overcome with drink, fanning herself with her napkin. 'Yes,' she said.

Over Ocean Pie and broccoli for supper, they worked out their plan of campaign. At midnight there were still no lights on across the road. They took the dogs out by the garden gate. Jill went straight to her car with Poppy. Joy waved and sauntered away in the opposite direction with Brown on his leash and Lucky following.

Several streets away, in a quiet crescent of stately houses, Jill was waiting. Joy popped Lucky into her car.

'Dog stealing is heaven, isn't it?' She whispered triumphantly. 'Most satisfying. We mustn't tell Matthew or Clive because they're so disapproving. Oh, hell! I meant to show you my *Plain Speaking* article on drink. I'm using a nom de plume, of course,' her voice went up the scale to a high squeak, 'lest anybody realises I'm the alcoholic dog thief!'

Mission accomplished, they parted, smiling to themselves like Mona Lisas.

In the office on Monday morning, Sweetie rang Ruth early. He normally didn't arrive until mid-day on a Monday. 'Got a minute, Roo? I'd like a word with you.'

He was on the telephone when she went in. Sweetie's

room always had the same pleasant smell of soap and freshly-laundered shirts. He was leaning back in his chair, swivelling from side to side, his white hair attractively tumbled, and one long leg in a green sock thrust out. He looked genial but sheepish, she thought. Marigold had been at home so they hadn't been able to meet, and consequently she hadn't had to mention Leo.

'No, Charles, no. Very, very sorry,' he was saying firmly. 'No can do. Not this year. Marigold's feeling a bit cheap lately and one thing and another, and I've got too much on my plate.

'That was our village vicar in Oxford,' he explained to Ruth.

She bent down to retrieve a piece of paper, with scribblings on it, which had fluttered to the floor. *Jerusalem*, she read, *Jesus Christ Is Risen Today!*

'Does he want you to read the lesson?'

'No, no, no.'

'What's this, then?' she asked, holding up the sheet, assuming he was attempting to conceal his movements from her as usual.

'Oh, that . . . nothing!' He dismissed it airily, screwed up the page and tossed it towards the waste paper basket. 'Only my list for er . . . Desert Island . . .'

'They've asked you? Sweetie! How absolutely . . .'

'No, no.' His nose twitched with something between a smile and a sniff. 'They haven't, no. They might think of it someday. Just amusing myself. Jotting down a few thoughts in an idle moment.'

'Now come and help me plan our next *Plain Speaking* lunch.' He flung an arm out sideways to embrace her and held onto her firmly round the hips while he kissed her. 'I'd like you to be there yourself, of course. At least I shall have a chance to see you then. I was wondering if you had any suggestions as to whom we might invite this time? I want to try and get one or two younger people for a change.'

Ruth was pleased to be involved because mostly she wasn't. She knew the monthly lunch was rather difficuult to organise now the *Plain Speaking* offices had been moved out to Kingsbury. Nobody seemed able to grasp where that was and they could never be bothered to find out unless they were elderly codgers with nothing better to do. Not that the food was going to entice them either. Last time she'd gone she'd had a piece of goat's cheese followed by a lump of venison which looked and tasted like a big job. It was always served by the catering girls, Charlotte and Arabella, who bobbed up and down at two spy-holes in the dining room door, observing the guests and the progress of the courses.

Ruth couldn't really think of anyone who would particulaly wish to come. 'What about the advertisers? Wouldn't they be pleased to . . . ?'

'Oh, we don't want them,' Sweetie exclaimed impatiently. 'Travel agents and that sort of thing. Arriving here in leisure wear, drinking like fish and talking about time shares. I'm so fed up with the deadliness of the working classes.' He looked up, smiling enquiringly, as his secretary came into the room. 'Coffee time, Karen, is it?'

Karen smiled politely. 'I'll go and get it. There's a message for you from Bexleyheath Literary Society. They're sending someone to meet you at the station at seven thirty.'

'Why?'

'You're giving a talk to them this evening.'

'I know nothing about it. You should have reminded me.'

'I did.'

'Bexleyheath? I can't possibly go. I've never heard of them.'

'It's in your diary. You arranged it six months ago.'

'Get me out of it.'

'Mr. Sweeting . . . um, oh heavens. Please not. What on earth would I say to them?'

'Many regrets. Mr. Sweeting is most distressed . . . called

away on urgent business. Too much on his plate. You can think of something. Bring some coffee for Ruth too, will you please, Karen?'

Ruth said, 'That's a bit naughty. Very hard on her to have to tell these whoppers. They'll be terribly upset, you know.'

'Roo, how am I to edit *Plain Speaking*,' Sweetie queried plaintively, 'if people from Bexleyheath keep bothering me?'

Minutes later his secretary reappeared with coffee. 'I told them you had flu. They were devastated.'

The editor looked pained.

'Thanks, Karen. Here's my ten p,' Ruth said. 'I expect you went to the machine, didn't you?'

'Yes, how much do I owe you?' Sweetie asked expansively, reaching into his pocket with a masculine flourish and paying for the first time in weeks. His awesome demeanour normally crushed his secretary into paralysed embarrassment so she dared not attempt to claim back these paltry sums each day. His debt to her for coffee, Snow Shimmer hair rinses and cigars, plus his wife's personal shopping, currently stood at two hundred and four pounds fifteen pence. On top of Marigold's occasional thefts, it often seemed to Karen too high a price to pay for working in an interesting atmosphere.

'I've been thinking,' Sweetie said, swivelling in his chair. 'Marigold wants me to invite Arnold Pope. He lives in Buscot, the next village to ours. And I might ask my godson. He hasn't seen the new offices.

'Tania?'

'Tony Galway-Lamb.'

'Will he come in drag?'

Sweetie tilted back his head with a disgusted "Ohhh!", looked down his long thin nose and closed his eyes at the memory. 'He knows perfectly well how much I disapprove of him getting himself dressed up like a bloody tart, and we don't want Arnold molesting him either. His mother's terribly worried, Roo. She's asked me to keep an eye on him. I must admit I haven't been an attentive godparent. I shall try and make up for that. Marcia thinks it's happening because he never had a father. He vanished when Tony was two. Bit of a Lord Lucan affair, I gather.'

'D'you suppose he had a gay life at Charterhouse?'

'Oh, that doesn't mean anything. Didn't we all? Buggery's the norm. What else is there to do at school?'

'I expect he wants to keep in touch with the feminine side of his nature. But why do transvestites always ape the most trivial aspects of women?'

'Yes, it's misogynistic,' Sweetie agreed briskly. 'I'm appalled.'

'Well, don't you think it's a bit risky to ask him to come to the lunch?'

'Darling, he may offend your feminist principles, but he wants to see you again. He wants to talk to you about someone.'

She stiffened. 'Who?'

'Some dancer he met through you. You know, the chap who damaged his face. I think he's going to sue him.' Sweetie picked up a letter from an enraged reader and idly glanced at it (*"I am a left-side paralytic, Sir, but not a dolt . . . "*). 'Do we know the dancer's name? Les, is it? Len something or other? Buggers jumping, my father always used to say, when he saw ballet. Can we get in touch with Les?'

'He hasn't got any money,' Ruth said emphatically, anxious to preserve Leo from a writ, 'so it really wouldn't be any good suing him. And in any case, it wasn't his fault.' She made a mental note to take ill on the day of the lunch. 'I mean where would it end if everybody started suing everybody else for falling over them at dances or in church or making love?'

'Mm . . . true. Yah.' He nodded agreement. 'But that fall damaged Tony's facial muscles. If he gets a smile on his face, he can't get it off. It causes a great deal of confusion and unpleasantness, and it doesn't make his career in the Guards any easier.'

Ruth remembered Tania's lewd simpering. 'Ghastly,' she said.

'Yes, well, Roo, think about the guest list, will you? I'm a bit pressed today. We might try to slip off somewhere together next week or I could probably come round to you. Marigold's hoping to persuade somebody to send her to the Middle East, but nothing's come up yet.'

As she went out of the room, he'd already gone back to the verse he was turning and decorating for the next issue of *Plain Speaking*.

> *Though the way be steep and weary,*
> *The sparrow falls, its voice unheard,*
> *Yon distant light keeps me cheery*
> *I know that You will keep your word.*

10

He Said

I can't have this cloud of disapproval hanging over me all the time. You know that I'm fond of you but I can't add your needs to the rest of my problems. I don't want any more demands to meet.

Almost as soon as Leo went to Hornsey to stay with Ruth, irritations arose between them which caused tension. Maybe for him she was the right person at the wrong time. Maybe for her he was the wrong person at the right time. She had a mental picture of the man she wanted and she pushed Leo into the frame. What he was like, and what she thought he was like, were two entirely different things. She couldn't help starting off with the highest expectations and the highest standards. There were fresh flowers everywhere, jelly for breakfast, three perfect courses for the lovingly-prepared little dinners on her beautifully laid table. She always lit the candles. She didn't like to ask to be paid, and when he offered rent she refused. She behaved as if she was in love because she was.

Leo lolled on the sofa while she was cooking, went on lolling while she washed up, got out his bedclothes halfway through the evening and passed out on the sofa in the middle of *News at Ten*. The sitting room looked as if several laundry bags had been emptied all over it.

Ruth didn't say anything but one evening, a couple of weeks later, his bedclothes simply disappeared.

'Sorry,' she called from the kitchen, where she was wiping

the fridge. 'I haven't had time to do any washing. You'll have to come into my bed for to-night.'

Of course his sofa bedclothes were never offered again so he couldn't go back to sleeping in the sitting room. He guessed the next move would not be long in coming.

It was a matter of days.

'I know you're not in the mood, and it's such a depressing time for you, and all that,' she began carefully, as she joined him in bed where he was reading a computer magazine, 'but I think I'll go out of my box if we don't do something. Couldn't we go out to eat somewhere or go to a movie?'

'I'm not in the mood really. Perhaps I shouldn't come to you so early so that you can go out. Let me give you some money.'

'You know, I do find it a bit hurtful that you are still so preoccupied,' she went on. 'It makes me feel I'm totally irrelevant. You don't notice me, do you?' she added, half-jokingly.

He put down the magazine and took off his spectacles which had one side missing. 'I do,' he declared amiably. 'I notice what you say. I notice what you're wearing. I notice your splendid dinners, don't I?'

'You eat them, yes. But I don't think we talk enough,' she said, trying to be encouraging. 'I ask you what you've been doing, but you don't ask me.'

'I know you're going to tell me. Well, I talk about my work. Or lack of it. We're talking now.' He yawned. 'Come to bed. This critical note is bringing on my narcolepsy.'

'Narcolepsy! You use that when it suits you! It's a very convenient way of switching off.'

'It's a medical condition. Now can I switch the light off, please? Then we'll talk.' He put his arm out for her and she lay with her head against him. 'We have to get to know each other, Ruth. It takes time to adjust. Tell me what you'd choose to be if you were in a circus?' he asked in an indulgent voice.

'I don't want to hear any of your old well-tried brothel party tricks.'

'You can find out a lot about someone from the way they answer my circus question. What would you be?'

'I'd be a clown,' she answered crossly, saying the first thing that came into her head.

'Because you're shy.'

'But I'm not shy.'

'You must want to hide yourself behind the make-up . . . smiling while the heart breaks.'

'Don't be silly,' she replied crossly. 'If you'd made any attempt to get to know me, you would realise a clown was the last thing I would choose to be. Who wants to be a hearty tumbling fool? If my heart were breaking, I should say so. You are a sod. If I were a clown, I'd torture you. I'd throw water at you. I'd burst balloons in your ear.' She folded her arms and lay stiffly silent.

'What's the matter?'

'Nothing.'

He left it like that.

Disappointed, she turned her back on him and lay awake in the dark mulling over his shortcomings.

He came and went without explanation. He made mysterious telephone calls. She knew he sloped off to the cinema on his own. He watched the most extraordinary television programmes and he despised chat shows, so she couldn't watch any.

He took telephone messages from her friends as if they were voices from outer space. He never remembered who they were and never produced any friends of his own.

The first dinner party they gave was for her friends. Leo assumed it had gone off successfully enough. In his opinion, oysters and champagne was going a bit over the top and he'd had to tease her out of dinner jackets because he hadn't got one. He hadn't wanted it to happen at all, but he'd tried to join in and be helpful. The main thing was that he was there as requested to talk to her friends.

He and Ruth cleared up together afterwards in what he imagined was a companionable silence and by the time she woke in the morning, he was already up and gone. When she arrived home from *Plain Speaking* that evening, he was lying in bed with his shoes on.

As she bent to kiss him, she tried not to see the bits of muck on her new grey duvet cover. Why was he lying on the bed at this hour? She didn't want to nag. 'What have you been doing today?' she asked, sounding tense.

'Thinking.'

'What d'you mean?'

'I mean . . . thinking.'

'Thinking what?'

'Thinking of ideas. Next century I'll probably be revered as a genius.'

'Did you get any ideas?'

'"Have it on while you have it off." Shall I send it to the Prime Minister for the Aids campaign?'

'Where did you go this morning?' She took off her skirt and jacket to change into trousers. 'Did you have an appointment?'

'No,' he said, closing his eyes. 'I normally go and see Jacob in the morning and inspect progress on the ceiling. I try to do bits of my own work while I'm there.'

She planted herself in front of him in her slip. 'But why don't you bring Jacob here?'

'He wouldn't like it. He likes clawing my furniture. He's happy with old Mrs. Rudge next door. She loves him. I buy his food for her.'

Unnecessarily, despising herself, she removed her bra while she rummaged in her drawers for a T-shirt. She was so constantly reminded of the frailty of her own position in his life that she felt forced to descend to these last-resort tactics for gaining attention. 'You didn't say whether you enjoyed last night. Did you enjoy it?'

'Sure. It was fine.' His eyes opened, rested momentarily on her breasts and closed again. 'I got on all right with your friends.'

'Did you mean to be rude to them?'

'I don't understand.'

'When I suggested moving to more comfortable chairs to have our coffee, you shouted, "Oh, don't move them now! They'll be going home soon".'

'Well, they were, weren't they?'

'They were when they heard that. Their jaws dropped. You were sitting there beside Anita just staring ahead and yawning.'

'I think Anita and I had said all we'd got to say by that time.'

'I hope you passed things to her at the table. You never noticed when anybody's glass was empty. Did you ask her about herself?'

'We had some conversation. I tried out my circus question on her. She said she'd stopped being a mortgage broker and was training to be a trapeze artist. I suggested it might be a bit late to start training for that at thirty-one but she told me it was never too late. I analysed her personality for her. I made jokes and listened . . .'

'You didn't listen to anyone. You crammed food into your face and held forth like Dr. Johnson.'

He beamed. 'Your friends were like teenagers round a rock star.'

'Because they're polite. They let you dominate. It was ridiculous. They didn't want to hear that simplistic, idiotic stuff about circuses, particularly not Anita who's got a professional job in a show at Kilburn. We'll have to go and see her.'

'No thanks.'

'Why not?'

'Why should I want to see that girl fall to her death?'

'Yes, you've made it clear you're not interested in my friends.'

'No, well, I'm . . .'

'You've made it clear you're not interested in me either.'

Spot on, he thought silently. 'Ruth, you fret too much about everything being perfect. Just relax. I try to please you, you know. I bring you things.'

'You bring me things from junk shops. If you bring flowers, you always present them to me as if you're making up for something.'

'You want me to be something I'm not.'

'Yes. Well, it isn't any good as it is, is it? I can't . . .'

'I'd better go back. This isn't working.'

'You'd better go back when the ceiling is ready,' she replied in a flat final motherly tone which disguised her shock. 'I'll start the supper.'

'I'll lay the table for you.'

He looked cast down after that and she felt contrite. She kissed his head as she brought dishes to the table.

'We will be all right, won't we?'

'Yes, we will.'

He caught her hand next time she passed. 'If you want,' he said, 'we could go to the British Film Awards in a fortnight's time? I was one of the judges in the animation section. I never bother to go usually, but I . . . well, would you like to?'

'Oh, yes please,' she said, delighted, kissing him again, 'I'd adore it.'

Ruth took an afternoon off to go and choose a dress for the awards ceremony, relieved to have an excuse to go shopping. She'd always enjoyed it but, since she'd met Leo, she'd turned into a shopaholic. She couldn't stop looking at clothes. It had become a drug. It comforted her.

It had to do with her current moods, feelings of rejection he caused or moments of elation. When the clothes lust was upon her she couldn't rest. A particular garment she'd seen, a Jean Muir, a Frank Usher, an Escada, could become an obsession. The instant answer to her problems, the key suddenly to perfect happiness. She knew it was nonsense, that it was neurosis. She'd stand in the shop, bewitched, imagining Leo's reaction, imagining herself more interesting to him, more confident, but as soon as she arrived home with her purchase she lost enthusiam for it.

She sneaked all these buys into the flat without showing them to him. She didn't like to admit she'd been spending again when he was in such a worrying financial state himself. To someone who loved grubbing about for bargains in secondhand shops, who'd known real poverty and had even led a union mutiny, hundreds of pounds for a piece of clothing might seem incomprehensibly decadent. Although the first to perk up at the sight of her red boots and black stockings, he definitely had a puritanical streak where vanity or possessions were concerned and she was getting worse because she was getting nowhere. He didn't find her attractive enough.

She chose a red mistress's dress because his fantasies were so babyish. It was long and straight with bootlace shoulder straps and a floppy bow on the hip.

'I've got a dress I think will do for the film awards,' she remarked casually at supper, planning to dress up and stun him afterwards.

'Good, yes, wear anything. Don't dress up or get anything specially. They go in jeans to these things.'

'What will you be wearing?'

'I've got an old black velvet jacket. I always wear that if I go anywhere, which I never do.'

'It's all right for you. I don't want to go in the wrong clothes with all those glamorous actresses.'

'Oh, you don't have to be glamorous to go to the film awards. Anybody can go.'

After that remark she couldn't bring herself to show him

the new red dress. On the night she wore a black suit with a cream blouse.

'You look very nice,' Leo said.

He had a white polo neck under his velvet jacket. 'So do you,' she responded.

They both set off to the theatre in a buoyant mood. He was pleased because she was. He was glad he'd agreed to be one of the judges and had an impressive event to take her to. She was pleased because they were going out together. This was what she'd been waiting for.

As they put the car in the carpark and made their way to the theatre, she could hear a band playing tunes from *My Fair Lady*. The moment stayed vivid in her mind because the romantic gaiety of the music matched her mood. They rounded a corner and suddenly they were walking down a red VIP carpet towards an array of photographers with all the musicians sitting alongside their route. Smiling girls in long bare evening dresses stood waiting to present them with programmes. In the foyer there was a gathering cocktail crush as the guests arrived and greeted each other. It took her only one dismayed moment to realise that every other woman there was in full evening dress, jewels, the lot. The men were all wearing dinner jackets. She recognised actors and one or two television personalities. It was obviously a most glittering occasion.

'Look at the women.'

'What?'

'All the women, Leo. Look at the women's clothes.'

'What about them?'

'They're in sodding long dresses,' she said between her teeth. 'I am the only person not dressed up. You said they'd be in jeans.'

'I thought they would be.'

'Have you got the invite?'

Unabashed, he pulled it out of his pocket and read it, grinning. 'Men black ties . . . ladies long dresses.'

She stared at him, incredulous. What the hell was he smiling at? The red dress would have been perfect. 'Why didn't you tell me?'

'I guess I didn't bother to read it properly. I wasn't going to go.'

'You've made me look a complete fool.'

'It's all right. It doesn't matter.'

'Leo, for heaven sake, it matters if I go to the supper party dressed like an office clerk. I'll have to go home and change. Did you do this on purpose?'

'You look fine to me.'

'It's embarrassing. You're one of the judges.'

'I'm not embarrassed by you.' He regarded her with kindly amusement as if he were big enough to take it.

'Well, you've ruined the evening for us.'

'Ruth, don't be silly.'

She felt silly herself but she couldn't stop. 'I'm going . . .'

'No.'

'We look as if we don't belong. We look as if we've gatecrashed.'

'I don't belong. I don't belong to anything.'

'I know,' she said bitterly. 'That's why I'm going home.'

'If you leave this theatre now, I'm never going to speak to you again.' He half-turned away as if detaching himself and gazed about over the heads until he saw somebody he knew and greeted them. 'Excuse me, Ruth. I'll be back in a minute.'

She was left there, upset and furious with him, and furious with herself for blowing up such a small thing out of all proportion. Suddenly feeling an object of pitiful curiosity in the chattering crush, with her odd clothes and gnarled expression, she opened her programme and pretended to study it.

Leo hadn't bothered to look at the invitation because he hadn't wanted to go. That arsehole hadn't taken her over to meet his friends because he didn't really wish to be associated with her. She'd tried to persuade herself their relationship was going to grow into something and she'd kidded herself it was happening gradually, but it wasn't. They had had some good moments then there were always rows, like now, when the communication went awry and it was hopeless. The trouble was he hadn't chosen her. She'd chosen him and he didn't intend to pull his emotional weight. He didn't make love much because he was always falling asleep. He fell asleep because he couldn't face life and he used her flat like a hotel as she'd invited him to. She loved him but he did not love her. It was ridiculous. The only thing to do was to tell him, reasonably, to get out. His flat wouldn't be ready for weeks and weeks. She couldn't wait for that. He was destroying her with his indifference.

She was leafing sightlessly through the programme, taking nothing in. She stopped suddenly at a picture of Leo in a judge's tableau, with youngish men and sprightly, smiling women grouped about him. In her undermined state she had an instant spasm of irrational jealousy. What the hell were those women looking so smug about? One of them was gazing at him in doe-eyed smiling wonderment. What were the smiles for? Sex, probably. No wonder he didn't bother to do it with her. Right!

She started forcing her way through the crowded foyer to the doors. Suddenly she stopped short. There, in front of her, three feet away, nodding intently at Germaine Greer, was Marigold Belper. The old snatcher was wearing Sweetie's secretary's missing earrings. Horrified, Ruth melted back into the crush.

'Sorry, sorry,' Leo said, reappearing and seizing her hand. 'I haven't seen that guy for years. We once travelled together to an animation festival in Zagreb. Ah, great, are we moving at last? I'm afraid our seats are not too grand. Row P. I hope I don't nod off.'

He nodded off almost immediately the awards started and the procession of stars stepped onto the stage. On they came to music and applause. Judi Dench, Maggie Smith, Sean Connery, Michael Caine. Leo slept through a succession of snippets from nominated films. Ruth nudged him awake for his own animation winner. Still the names were called. Jeanne Moreau, François Truffaut's widow, Billy Connolly talking from the States. First-timers who talked too long. Others who could scarcely talk at all. Was Sweetie sitting in the audience? Ruth peered at the backs of heads but she couldn't see him. Please God, don't let him see us, she prayed silently, wistfully thinking of the delicious gossip he and she could have had about it all.

When the roll call was finally finished, the audience formed into a slow-moving queue to the supper room. Inside the entrance a few tables had been specially laid for sitting down, and beyond these there was a buffet. Most people were making for that.

Leo moved no further than the nearest big round table, set for twelve. 'We'll sit here,' he said, pulling out a chair.

'Can we?'

When Leo was being noisy and eccentric, he seemed enormously conspicious. He created a disturbance now with his Dr. Johnson act. Talking bombastically about his own film triumphs, he pushed the cutlery aside in a clashing bundle and picked up the menu. He set down his one-sided spectacles, bumped the table with his knee so that the glasses shook, crumpled a napkin and scattered crumbs from two rolls he ate so fast they made him choke.

Ruth was staring at him, assuming he'd got nervous. 'Did you have sex with any of those judges?'

His jaw dropped. 'What?' He couldn't believe she'd changed the subject.

'Those animation judges. Did you sleep with them? Why was that woman smirking possessively at you in the programme picture?'

'Are you crazy? I've known those women for years. They're fans of mine. I know their husbands.'

'Oh,' she said, wishing she'd kept quiet. Tears filled her eyes at her mismanagement of everything and she reached for the *Reserved* card in the centre of the table. 'This is Richard Attenborough's table. We're sitting with the nobs.'

'Blast,' Leo sighed, starting to get up again. 'We'll have to move.'

Ruth caught sight of the guests of honour, approaching in a stately party led by Lord Attenborough. 'Leo, quick!' she hissed, pulling his arm. 'They're coming!'

He swung clumsily from his seat with a corner of the tablecloth caught between his legs. He drew it askew as he departed causing knives and forks to clatter to the floor.

She gave him a push to keep him moving, hoping they would merge unidentified into the buffet queue. She glanced back to catch Sweetie's eye. He was standing watching, from the fringes of Lord Attenborough's party, looking down his long thin nose, his face an enigmatic study of sardonic amusement.

'Yours, I believe?' An amused voice spoke behind them.

They turned.

A friend of Leo's was holding out the specs he'd left behind on the table. 'We made the same mistake,' he remarked, laughing. 'The hoi polloi are meant to queue for the buffet, methinks! How are you, Len?'

'Jack Crombie . . . Christine . . . meet Ruth,' he said.

Ruth recognised the wife as the beaming judge from the programme photograph. Christine Crombie put her arms round Leo.

Apart from Joy Sadler, these were the first old friends of his that Ruth had met. She liked them straight away. Although all their conversation was about animation, they managed to make her feel included because they were so friendly.

Partly to satisfy herself, and partly to make a good impression, she asked so many interested questions about the process of judging that Christine was agreeably flattered and suggested they both came to dinner in Sidcup at the first opportunity.

Leo was obviously popular. He kept disappearing for more helpings of rum baba and bringing back other people to join them. If this was his world, Ruth was thinking happily, she felt quite at home in it. She talked to animators and producers, carefully positioning herself out of sight of Sweetie who was sitting with the nobs, and half-listening all the time to what Leo was saying, noticing again that he seemed to have no small talk. He either talked shop or he made sweepingly provocative pronouncements which produced loud hilarious arguments. If he thought courtly sociability was called for with a woman, he fell back on the Middle Eastern brothel routine. She heard more than one cautiously astonished voice claiming she'd like to be a bareback rider or a lion tamer.

He didn't start yawning until they were in the car.

'You see, you didn't yawn,' she said.

'I had a nap before we set out.' When they reached home he immediately slumped on the sofa, threw his head back and closed his eyes.

She perched on the arm. 'What a lovely evening! Shall I make tea for us?'

'I don't want any.'

'Juice?'

He yawned, shifted, patted her hand and announced he was off to bed.

'Oh, Leo!'

'It's two o'clock.'

'I know, but let's talk a bit.'

'I'll talk to you in bed.'

'But you never do. You'll be asleep before I get there.' She pleaded. 'Look, I am a woman, you know.'

'I know you are. And you looked very attractive to-night.' He was searching through his pile of computer magazines. He glanced up vaguely, stifling a yawn by contorting his mouth like a dog eating a spider.

The drink, the strain and the sight of him pulling that idiotic face made her suddenly lose her temper.

'Well, what are you going to do about it?'

He leafed through his magazine and said nothing.

'I said,' her voice grew ridiculously loud and menacing, 'what the hell are you going to do about it?'

'Do about what?'

'I AM A WOMAN.'

'Ruth, don't start . . .'

'I want to know.' She folded her arms as if preparing to sit up all night.

'Please let me go to bed.'

'Why should I? I'll only be up all night with annoyance. No, I won't let you go to bed. I want to talk about this.'

'Not now. All this bellicose accusation brings on my narcolepsy and then I can't work.'

'What work?'

'Things I'm involved in at the moment . . . jazz, computer animation, philosophy. My ideas for . . .'

'But why fantasise? Why don't you get a job?'

'I don't work like that.'

'You worked in advertising. You told me you won the Silver Bowl. Well, be a docker again then, be a sailor, run a driving school. But why not be a copywriter?'

'I don't like advertising. They don't like me.'

'But if you need the money, let them snap you up.'

'I don't fit. I see through it. So you gain the power to manipulate people. It's meaningless.'

As she saw it, he didn't want a job in advertising because he didn't want her. 'D'you know what I think? I think you're a shit. You're using this place entirely for your own convenience and you treat me like a whore. Not physically. Mentally.'

He nodded ruefully. 'I'm no good at getting on with women,' he admitted in a distant voice. 'I don't know what they want. I thought ladies enjoyed being treated like whores.

My first girlfriend was a whore. I had to treat her like a lady or she got offended.'

She sighed. 'Don't be stupid, Leo. I only want to know where we are meant to be going?'

Looking tense and switched-off, he shrugged and suddenly bustled out of her way into the bathroom.

She followed, kicking the door open like a gunman entering a Western saloon bar. She stood there, arms akimbo, while he urinated. 'You said you liked being here. You eat here, sleep here, but you're not making any emotional effort. You shut me out. I'm asking you – do you want us to be together or not?'

He sat down on the edge of the bath and smoothed his fingers into his forehead, as if trying to erase the pressures from his life, while he found the right words. 'I don't know what to say to you. It's such a bad time for me, you see. You know that I'm fond of you but I can't add your needs to the rest of my problems. I don't want any more demands to meet.'

It was what she'd feared to hear. 'What demands am I making?'

'I think you want a commitment from me to some sort of regulated life together, a flourishing social life with all your friends . . .'

'Listen,' she said, cutting in with earnest urgency to salvage the situation. 'You said you liked being with me. I mean, if you do . . . well, our relationship has to to grow, hasn't it? You said we had to get to know each other. If the basic liking is there, we can make it work. Your mood will change when things get better. It isn't as if one keeps meeting people one likes. What I'm saying is that you don't seem able to make much emotional effort. You shut yourself up in your own private little dream world, having narcoleptic attacks whenever . . .'

'But I can't have this cloud of disapproval hanging over me all the time.'

'It isn't a cloud of disapproval. I'm only asking you to contribute a bit more. Not financially. I've got all I need. I've got the flat and a job and my car. Anyway, you do enough. I'm not asking for anything from you except a more positive approach. Give us a chance. I know it can be lovely because it is, when it is, isn't it? D'you see what I'm trying to say to you?'

He reached out for her with an awkward, sympathetic, reluctant movement.

They both saw what she meant. Other men found her extremely attractive. She wasn't used to being sexually turned down and she couldn't stop asking why.

He left her that night because in the end she drove him to it. When they got into bed she still felt too aggrieved to calm down. He didn't make the loving moves that would have soothed her, and she couldn't stop fretting about their limbo state. She went on yammering at him until he stopped answering. With a martyred sigh he turned over and went to sleep. The frustration of his humped back and even breathing sent her beside herself.

She thumped up and down on her back. 'I don't understand why I have to lie here with you taking no notice of me.'

He didn't answer.

'D'you hear me, you narcoleptic prick?'

'Ruth, please stop forcing your emotions on me.'

The hurt stunned her. She rolled over on her tummy because momentarily she found it hard to breathe.

'You're an emotional cripple. I'm not surprised you've never managed a sustained relationship with anyone. All my friends think you're mad, you know.'

She waited a few minutes, afraid she'd gone too far, but she still couldn't stop talking. 'Look, I'm sorry to go on but I can't help it. I do love you. D'you love me?' She listened to herself appalled, knowing she would regret it. 'Do you love me?' She gave him a sharp dig with her foot.

He half-turned. 'Don't corner me, Ruth.'

'If you can't answer, why are you here?'

'Don't make me say things to you I don't want to say.'

'I want you to say them.'

'I don't want to hurt you.'

'If that's the situation, I honestly don't know why you're here.' She gave him another kick. 'I hope your cock rots!'

'I'd better go back.'

'Yes, go.'

He pulled the duvet round himself. 'I'll go in the morning.'

'You'll go now,' she said, shoving him. 'I don't want you in this bed another minute.'

He went and she was heartbroken.

She waited each day hoping he would ring to suggest a meeting but he didn't. After twelve days of panic, she rang him and persuaded him to come back. When she heard they had found more cracks in his flat, with signs of dry rot, she was extremely relieved.

The weeks passed and she tried harder than ever to be careful to nurture him. She made his existence with her immensely comfortable and she began to feel instinctively that being with her was gradually becoming a habit to him. 'The healthily-eating man does not have jelly for breakfast,' she could joke now. 'He has bran flakes.'

But there were bad times. Sometimes she was so wound up she couldn't speak to him for hours. Speechlessly, she vacuumed the bedroom twice in one day to get him moving. When she gave him a shopping list with "Carrots 1' on it, meaning one pound, he came back with one carrot and she tipped a jug of milk over his head.

There were nights when she had to leave their bed and sleep alone in the sitting-room sofa because his heedlessness overwhelmed her. Every so often she threw him out.

He went home and camped as best he could with the builders there, both of them knowing that before long she would call him back and that he would come.

The last time she did it his flat was completely uninhabitable. The fact that it happened in the middle of the night, when he had nowhere to go, added a delicious zest to her vengeful satisfaction. She changed the locks.

But when her anger had evaporated, she was terrified. She woke each morning with a searing sense of loss spreading over her because he'd gone. This time it was over, she knew.

Leo borrowed a friend's house in Mitcham. He asked her to pass on his new telephone number to anybody who rang for him.

'Come back here,' she begged. 'Don't stay in Mitcham.'

'I don't want to come back,' he replied. 'We've proved it doesn't work.'

Instead of passing his number on, she took messages for him, using these as an excuse to telephone and talk. Stuck in Mitcham, he seemed pleased to chat. His mood was just as low, she was gratified to discover. He might not love her but there was definitely something between them. He never bothered to find anybody else.

One day he told her he'd been tinkering with a children's story he had written ten years earlier. As nobody was interested in it then, he'd put it in a drawer. It was about a dog called *Chelsea Charlie*,, a sort of football-playing cross between himself and Winnie the Pooh.

'Oh,' she said, half-heartedly. 'But couldn't you do another award-winning cartoon?'

'They don't make money. I sold the last script for five hundred quid.'

'You're never going to make a penny, are you?'

'I've got ideas. One of them might make it.'

'Leo, you live in a dream world. You're like a bum.'

'I've always survived. I don't need much.'

'I've told you, I can support you. You can get on with what you like. I know how talented you are but the things you're interested in just aren't going to make you a millionaire.'

'If I thought that,' he replied, 'I'd slit my throat.'

'I'll have to go now,' she told him suddenly, 'I have to see the doctor.'

'What about?'

'He thinks I've got an ulcer. It's your behaviour.'

It wasn't an ulcer, as it turned out. It was a baby.

11

She Said

I could lie on the bed and weep for a thousand years.

'I was disappointed to read your review of my book on metropolitan orchestras,' Arnold Pope complained over the telephone to Conroy Sweeting. 'I think you missed the point.'

'Can you tell me what the point is?'

'Why not read the book properly, my dear chap?' Pope admonished him with a somewhat grim laugh. 'Then you'll see the point.'

Sweeting was extremely irritated. Reviewing this ass's book had been Marigold's idea and now he had to put up with this nonsense. He allowed him to babble on because he had to be careful not to alienate Arnold Pope. Apart from his wife's connivings to get herself on to his guest list, Sweetie was in the middle of building a swimming pool at his Oxfordshire cottage without planning permission which he'd decided was unlikely to be granted. As he'd successfully campaigned to put paid to several of the villagers' applications for extensions and other bits of new building in the past, he was anxious to keep this illegal enterprise of his a complete secret. If old Arnold got wind of it, he didn't want him blathering about it to any of the locals who would undoubtedly take their revenge.

'Will you be at home on Sunday?' Pope demanded. 'I thought I might pop over from Buscot with a few ideas for a biggish country piece we might chew over together?'

'Sunday, no,' Sweetie said at once. 'No, I'm sorry, Arnold. We won't be coming down.'

'When can we expect you?'

'I don't know. Marigold's got commitments in town and one thing and another.'

'But you'll be having the church fête in your garden as usual, I suppose? I can see you then.'

'Not this year. Too much on our plate unfortunately,' Sweetie replied, smoothly. 'I've already told the Vicar. Pity about that but it's a lot of work.'

'Oh,' Arnold Pope said, disappointed. 'That won't go down well. Everybody here regards your fête as an institution.'

As their conversation finished, the phone went again.

'Mr. Sweeting?'

'Yes.'

'You've made a terrible blunder.'

'I'm sorry?' he said crossly.

'I am completely stunned,' Joy Sadler said. 'In fact, I could drop dead with embarrassment. You've printed my article on women drinking at home with my own name on it. I thought we'd agreed that I was to use the name Utley?'

'Did you wish to speak to me, Mrs. Utley?' He frowned at his secretary who had allowed this call to come straight through to him and picked up the latest issuue of *Plain Speaking* to find her piece. The headline was *In Our Cups!* by Joy Sadler.

'Of course I want to speak to you. You're the editor, and thanks to you I am now known to thousands of people in Britain as an alcoholic.'

'I shouldn't let that worry you.'

'It does worry me and I hope it worries you. As I am not an alcoholic, how do you think I feel?'

'Madam, if I may say so, you appear to be getting needlessly worked up over a small slip on our part and, frankly, I don't understand why. There's no stigma these . . .'

'I want to know what you're going to do about it?'

'It's too late to do anything, I'm afraid.' He shook his fist in the air. 'I'm sorry to be unhelpful. It was a good piece. I liked it.'

'You'd better print something to say that the name Joy Sadler was mentioned by mistake.'

'Let me look into this, Miss Ut . . . Sadler. I can only apologise, but I'm very busy. I have somebody waiting to see me. Leave it with me, will you?' Conroy Sweeting brought the conversation to this unsatisfactory conclusion and put the phone down.

'Karen, another time – I've told you before – don't automatically put everybody through to me. How am I to edit this magazine if every nutcase is put straight on to me?'

'She's Ruth's friend.'

Sweetie wandered off to the lavatory. On the way back he looked into Ruth's little room.

'I've just been duffed up by your alcoholic friend.'

'What?'

'A Mrs. Ut something. She didn't want her name attached to her article on drink. Women always want to do everything men do but not admit to it. Why are you wearing cigar cutters in your ears?'

She laughed. 'They're rockets. What are you talking about?'

'Ut Sadler.'

'Oh, Joy! I thought that was quite a funny piece of hers. She's Leo's friend.'

'My dear girl, that doesn't exactly endear her to me,' Sweetie said. He hadn't found an excuse to sack her yet, as she'd expected, but he had taken Ruth's defection to Leo rather badly despite the fact that he'd refused to leave Marigold Belper and marry her himself.

'Marigold remembers him. She says he used to be extremely aggressive, had a big chip on his shoulder. He'd taught himself practically everything he knew and was always trying to prove he was better than anybody else.'

'A characteristic unknown in the offices of *Plain Speaking*, I suppose?'

Sweetie smiled. 'How is Leo?'

'He's living in Mitcham.'

'Is it over?'

'Except that I'm pregnant.'

'My poor darling Roo! He has wronged you,' Sweetie positively cooed at her in a forcefully fulsome voice. 'Have you got his address?'

'Sweetie, he hasn't a penny.'

'Does he know?'

'Yes.'

'What's his reaction?'

'Dunno, really . . . speechless. *Wondering* is the word I would use, but he won't hear of an abortion.'

'The working classes are so totally irresponsible, aren't they?' He sat on the edge of her desk and doodled on her copy of *The Independent*, becoming more dulcet by the minute. 'What did you see in him?'

'Perception, originality. Vulnerability, I suppose . . . swank . . . it's a potent sexual mixture, isn't it?' she went on, remembering Leo's tricky little bed smile as he played *Sweet Georgia Brown* and turned her legs to water. She wished she hadn't started talking about him because it brought on such a surge of desolation. 'I liked him, you know. He's mad, he's impossible, but I think he's a genius, probably. I thought he needed me but, as you can see,' she shrugged, 'he doesn't.'

Minding the sports shop with Brown beside her, Joy Sadler was in a state of shock about the publication of her article. The conversation with Conroy Sweeting had made that state much worse. She kept trying to read it but could get no further than the headline – IN OUR CUPS! by Joy Sadler. *A humorous look at the reasons why women do their drinking at home and the increasingly serious consequences for their pockets, their livers and their marriages . . .*

Embarrassingly flippant phrases caught her eye ... *clink of bottles in the wardrobe ... a drink to go out, a drink to recover when I come in ... a snort or two to write this article. Cheers!* She kept going hot with shame. She never said "Cheers!" What would the children say? Who would have seen it?

As if in answer to her question, the telephone rang.

'It's only moi,' said Dinky Pownall. 'Snap.'

'I'm afraid I can't ...'

'We share a problem, ma pauvre petite. I read your article in *Plain Speaking*.'

'Dinky, I'm sorry, I can't speak now,' she said, too appalled to talk. 'There's somebody in the shop.'

'What?'

'I said I can't have a conversation now. Sorry. It's too difficult but I'll try and ring later.'

'What?'

'I'll be back soon. Bye.'

Recently Clive's mother had taken to ringing her at the shop. Quite often she seemed to be a bit tight. She rambled on, blocking the line, and she kept saying "What?" all the time then never listening. Her sprinkling of French phrases grew more profuse under the influence of drink. Clive said they'd started when Hove was twinned with a town in France. The French party had stayed at Stapleton Byng. The Mayor kissed Dinky's hand on the landing and, afterwards, carried away with the excitement of it, she fell fully clothed into the bath. A second visit to the guest house was cancelled because Denis announced he was not having any more French wogs all over his garden.

Joy made a cup of coffee and tried to calm herself. What did it matter what Mrs. Pownall thought? The good thing was that *Plain Speaking* had liked her article and published it. The unfortunate aspect was that her association with that magazine was now over.

The phone rang again.

'Forgive me if I have hysterics,' Jill said. 'I've just read *Plain Speaking*.'

'I am having hysterics. I could lie on the bed and weep for a thousand years.'

'Don't be silly, I didn't mean it. But I thought you said you were using a nom de plume? Anyway, it's marvellous. A hoot.'

'I could drop dead with embarrassment. It's so exaggerated.

'Yes, but who reads *Plain Speaking*? Nobody we know.'

'Clive's mother does. She's rung to say she's an alcoholic too.'

Jill couldn't control herself.

Her call was rapidly followed by one from Joy's mother who lived at Cromer in Norfolk. 'Well, you've made a fine fool of yourself with your article about drinking.' She spoke, with a reproachful dying fall to her voice. 'Everybody here is astounded by it. They'll think you've sunk very low in London. Why ever did you do it?'

'I don't know what you mean. It's a serious observation on the problems of our times, although it was meant to be quite humorous.'

'There's nothing humorous, dear, about a drinking woman. A man may get away with having too much to drink but a woman, never. She's always disgraced. Men can't stand a woman who drinks.'

'Yes, well, I have no thought of pleasing men. That's the least of my worries. I'm not a drinker anyway. The whole point of my article is that women are told they are constitutionally not safe to drink practically anything. What bad luck for us, is what I'm saying.'

'Anybody who takes more than two drinks is usually not asked again.'

'Well, fiddlededee is all I have to say to that. Drinking doors still remain open to me. I thought you never read *Plain Speaking*.'

'A lot of people take it here. They've been asking me if it could be you. Mrs. Dobell cut it out and put it through my letter box. Grace is quite the lady, you know. She'll be terribly shocked by it.'

'If that's Grace Dobell, the one whose moustache cream nipped her, I'd like her to have a flea in her ear.'

'I think people feel a bit sorry for me. One or two of them have crossed the road when they've seen me coming. I think they don't know what to say to me. Haven't I always warned you to keep your own counsel?'

'Ma, I'll have to go, I'm afraid.' Joy put the phone down as two men in motor-bike gear came in to the shop. Brown growled faintly beside her and she held his collar. 'Yes? Can I help?'

They glanced about in silence. They were older than the usual boys who only came in to make trouble.

'How much are them shirts?' the bigger one demanded, pointing to a make of coveted sweatshirts.

'Twenty-nine ninety-nine. Do try one on if you'd like to.'

He handed his helmet to his companion and disappeared behind the curtain with a red one. Seconds later he came out with it pulled over his own T-shirt.

'That looks rather good,' Joy said. Brown growled again so she hauled him onto her knee. Rough male voices still upset him because he hadn't yet forgotten the bad treatment he'd received in the past.

'What d'you reckon?' the big one studied himself in the glass and turned to his friend for approval.

'It's great,' the other said, already moving towards the door. 'Make up your mind.'

The first man picked up sweatshirts in each colour and fanned out the five cellophane packets in one hand to choose. Red, blue, gold, black, green. 'What d'you think then?'

'I think the red one suits you very well with your dark colouring,' Joy remarked helpfully.

The door was open and the waiting friend stepped outside

with the two helmets. Suddenly, with incredible speed, the other man whirled round and sprinted after him. One minute he was beside her and the next he wasn't. Joy made a small sound of surprise like the wind sighing in the trees. He had stolen six sweatshirts.

She went outside but there was no sign of them. They must have jumped on their waiting motorbike for the get-away. She felt completely bewildered. That man had seemed amiable. Why trick her when she was being trusting and helpful? As she put her hand on the telephone to ring the police, it rang again.

'Joy, can you get to an AA meeting right away?' Dinky Pownall said urgently. 'Go now. Don't touch another drink.'

Joy twitched with nervous irritation. 'I haven't touched a drop,' she said tersely, her chest knotting. 'And I am not going to touch one.'

'What?'

'I'm not an alcoholic, you know.'

'We have to admit we've got a problem, cherie,' Dinky said in a thick wise voice, 'before we can be helped.'

'I don't want help. I don't want a drink.' Joy was studying her strained white face in the mirror beside her desk. In her shocked state she suddenly decided her eyebrows looked very peculiar. They were sparse. 'How are you feeling?' she asked Dinky automatically.

'I'm at the end of my tether.'

'Is it the pain?' She poked her left eyebrow to see if it was going to come away in her hand.

'I don't want my leg off, Joy.'

'No, and I'm sure that is not going to happen.'

She hiccupped. 'What?'

'Dinky, if I am sure of one thing, it is that you are not going to have your leg off.' She listened while there was a suspicious clinking and heavy breathing, guessing that Mrs. Pownall was helping herself to another drink.

'Joy? Good . . . you're still there? Didn't I ever tell you

what my specialist said to me? He can't do any more for me, you know. He said to me last time I saw him "Mrs. Pownall," he said, "I . . ."'

'Yes, but wasn't that a sort of semi-joke about your leg?'

'Wot?'

The silence was thunderous. Jesus Christ, how could she listen to this repetitive balderdash when her left eyebrow was visibly dwindling before her eyes? 'Wasn't that a joke the specialist made about your leg because it wasn't true he needed to take it off but he didn't know what . . .'

'Balls.'

'He must have been saying he could only take the pain away if he took your leg . . .'

'Balls.'

'All right, well, I'm sorry if you . . .'

'I am sorry, Joy. I happen to have a highly developed sense of humour and a semi-joke to me is not about having my bloody leg amputated. That doesn't make me laugh. D'you know? It does not tickle my funny bone one little bit.'

'No.'

'I am scared stiff. That's why I drink. I don't know why you drink. You mustn't let it spoil your friendship with Clive. Is that what damaged your marriage?'

'No.'

'It's unfair, isn't it. Men have no patience with women who drink. It's the women who stay with the men. Men always leave. Is that the reason your husband went?'

'No,' Joy said, riled. 'I sprayed him with insecticide.'

There was a thoughtful pause at the other end before Dinky Pownall gave quite a respectful chuckle. She said, 'I don't think Clive will stay with you for long, dear, if you do that to him.'

'No.'

'Don't spray him, Joy. You seem to be getting on so well together. Why don't you both come down here on Saturday? I'll have our little bottles of Aqua Libra ready.'

'That sounds lovely, but please could we come on Sunday, Dinky? Clive's got the Battle of Marston Moor on Saturday.'

His mother laughed. 'All this fighting! He must get it from Denis. Sunday then. Come and meet my two sons from my first marriage. Talbot and Nick are extremely worried about me. They're going to have a tête à tête with my specialist about my leg. Clive doesn't get on with them but they're nice boys.'

'Lovely. We'll look forward to it. I'll ask Clive to ring and confirm. I'd better go now. There's somebody lurking outside the shop. I've just had one awful theft. I don't want another.'

'Cheerio for now,' Dinky said cheerfully. 'Take care.'

To Joy's relief, the man didn't appear to be a bailiff or up to anything sinister. He gazed through the window, at the goods, at her, then he moved off and disappeared. She got up to switch the sign on the door to CLOSED then she put Brown's leash on and departed.

They walked the long way home to go across the park. She left the car behind these days so the dog got enough exercise, and she had to make sure she kept well away from the area where she'd picked him up. She stopped now at an off-licence to buy a bottle of whisky for Clive, suddenly self-conscious, as if the man was likely to recognise her as the drunken author of the article in *Plain Speaking*, a magazine he would not be reading in a million years. Clive, she knew, would be even more embarrassed about her own name being on it than she was.

By the time she reached home she was exhausted. She glanced at her winking answer machine, listened to a message from Claire, shrieking with laughter about her debut in *Plain Speaking*, then she simply wiped the other messages off without hearing them in case there was anybody else talking about alcoholism. She poured herself a glass of whisky then lay on the bed, which needed clean sheets for Clive coming. She had an hour and a half to change them, iron his pyjamas, clean the bathroom, find some flowers to pick, stand on a stool in various parts of the house to replace three light bulbs and get the supper ready. She hadn't the strength for any of it. She lay marvelling at the sensation of over-whelming tenderness produced by the sight of the back of Brown's head on the pillow.

At least when she got to bed to-night she would be able to rest undisturbed like a beached whale, which was a relief. On the nights before his battles, Clive didn't make any attempt to get it up. He was saving himself to meet Cromwell's army.

Now the warmer weather had come and Clive's battles were raging so regularly, their dancing had stopped too. Really, Joy reflected, it was quite satisfying the way they had created such a stable situation between them. Their meetings had developed a definite momentum. It was illogical of her to mind that Clive only wanted to spend Wednesday nights with her and Saturdays, providing there were no battles, because the arrangement suited her very well too. Perhaps he'd decided that that was all their relationship could stand, that it was liable to break down under the weight of more meetings and he'd made a sensible commitment to the amount he could cope with. She couldn't help feeling aggrieved because she didn't enjoy being controlled by Clive. The only reason he was coming on a Friday this week was because he was taking her with him the next day to see her first battle in a Hertfordshire village called Crawston.

He arrived, spruce as ever in his blazer. 'No barking!' he said jovially as she opened the front door. 'And that means you!' he added to the dog.

'How's you?' he said to Joy, bunching his lips for their greeting.

He bounced into the kitchen in a proprietorial manner with a bottle of wine and presents of coffee, which he popped into a tin, and peanuts which he tipped into a dish. Then he looked round helpfully to see if there was any slicing or stirring to be done. Was she the highspot of his week? Joy wondered. And did he assume he was the highspot of hers?

Their supper went a bit too fast, leaving a lot of time to be filled up with sitting. When they'd had coffee, she had to open the corner cupboard, pretending to be looking for something, while she yawned and yawned into it. Twice she got up and went out to the kitchen in order to look at her watch, dismayed to see how the time was dragging.

'I shall need nine hours' sleep or I'll be fit for nothing tomorrow,' Clive declared, but at nine-thirty he started watching the fourth episode in a television series called *Sweet and Sour*, a saga about badly-behaved married couples changing partners.

Clive watched it intently, his back very straight, commenting approvingly on the hairstyles. 'This is English literature at its best!' he called after her as she went out to the kitchen again.

'Oh, poof!' She made a rude exasperated gesture with her fingers. 'It's crap!' She stepped back into the room again, on a wave of annoyance, determined that he should hear the truth and grasp it. 'It's shallow, it's so coarse-grained. The stuff is designed to appeal to the most brutal numbskull. Can't you see that nastiness and violence are taking the place of any kind of wit or profundity?'

'I like it,' Clive said. 'Perhaps I am one of the brutal numbskulls.'

Appeased, Joy laughed happily with him. 'You may become one if you watch much more of this.' With that, she slumped beside him on the sofa and grew absorbed in the story herself.

When it finished, they went up to bed. 'I'll be fit for nothing tomorrow,' Clive said. He shut himself in the bathroom and spent a long time washing.

There was definitely something deeply unarousing about a lot of washing, Joy decided, lying on the bed with Brown while she waited to clean her teeth. She swung one leg into the air and studied it, surprised and depressed at its heftiness. And her fourth toe was looking buckled and misshapen. That's what you get when you're fifty, she told herself. Buckled toes.

She rolled Brown onto his back and rubbed his tummy. 'Who's mummy's lambie mothball, then?'

The dog made little moans and wriggled with delight, waving his head from side to side in the depths of the pillow.

'You're the tops!' Joy sang to him, kissing his head. 'You're a gay Te Deum. You're the tops . . . you're the Coliseum!'

'Water's dripping down the side of the house.' Clive reappeared from the bathroom, radiating cleanliness and vigour, and tweaked his freshly ironed pyjamas from beneath the pillow.

'I know. I can't deal with everything,' she answered, too tired to move.

'I can deal with it. It's probably from your loo. I like to do things for you.' He sprang into bed. 'All these unhealthy blankets! You need a duvet.'

'I don't like 'em.'

'I'm going to drag Mrs. Sadler screaming and kicking into the twentieth century if it's the last thing I do.' Smiling cosily, he leant over to kiss her. Baby rosebud closed-mouth kisses . . . phut phut phut . . . like the ones she gave to Brown. 'Hurry up,' he urged. 'Come to bed. I hope we're not having the doggie in here, are we?'

'Of course.'

'Joy, no. Oh. Must we?'

'I can't shut him out.'

'Is he liable to bite me in the night?'

She laughed. 'Don't be silly!'

'You know this dog is a substitute for something, don't you?'

'Substitute for what? He fills me with utter pleasure. People fill me with utter annoyance.'

He sighed. 'You won't meet the challenge, will you?'

'Only too readily. I find myself barking at people all day long.'

She left the dog lying across the bottom of the bed while she went to clean her teeth. When she came back, Clive was lying with his eyes closed and his nose poking over the edge of the sheet.

'Put the pooch downstairs, sweetie.' He spoke in the thin long-suffering whine of the interrupted sleeper. 'He's dribbling on the blankets.'

'My mite never dribbles.'

'Be a good girl. He's going to trample over here and dribble on me.'

'Clivey!' she said, trying to humour him with a helpless squawk. 'I can't put him outside. He's used to being with me.'

'Can't you get him unused to it?'

'Come on, be kind. He's not an ordinary dog, you know. He's been ill-treated. He'd think he was being rejected. You go to another room if you like but I promise he'll stay at the bottom of the bed on my side. He won't disturb you.' She turned out the light.

'You know I have to sleep with my legs in the Y position.'

'Is it a superstition?'

'If my legs are not in the Y position, I can't relax,' he said petulantly, thrusting them out wildly to dislodge the dog. 'If I don't relax, I'll be fit for nothing tomorrow.'

'You'll mash 'em.'

For a few minutes there was silence then he snored lightly. Brown shifted himself.

Joy reached out her hand to cosset him. 'Sly boot,' she murmured.

'What was that?'

'It's all right.'

'He's not chewing my shoes, I hope?'

'No. I was only saying "Sly Boot".'

'That's your new name for me, is it?' He took her hand under the clothes. 'Go to sleep, poppet.'

'Clivey?'

'Yes?'

She had to pinch herself with her free hand in case she shouted with laughter. 'Will any people be killed tomorrow by mistake?'

'Oahh!' He shot up in the air, flinging off the blankets and uncovering her. The dog jumped off the bed and barked.

'God love us.'

Clive was waving his arms. 'Ewff! Ewff!'

'What is it?'

The dog was moving in a sort of enquiring half-moon round the bed, still barking a bit, his head on one side.

'This bed is full of fleas.'

'Clive, do pipe down. Please.'

'Oahh! Oahh!' He leapt from the bed, dancing about and scratching himself.

The dog danced too, rushing at him and backing away.

'Get off, fleabag!' he shouted, smacking at the sheets. 'Joy, get me a piece of soap, will you.'

'Stop it. There aren't any fleas.'

He pointed dramatically at a small red mark on his leg. 'What's that, then? I've been bitten.'

'I'll get the antihistamine.'

'No, no. Don't get it. I'd never use that.'

Wearily, she shook out the sheets and remade the bed. 'I'm sure we won't find any fleas. I haven't seen any on Brown. Now, d'you think you could recapture the Y position?'

'How can I relax when I'm itching?' he asked plaintively, getting back into bed for yet another examination of his leg. 'There are three bites. Three flea bites.'

'That's it,' she murmured soothingly, covering him up. 'I think you'll get off to sleep now, won't you? Are you in the Y position?'

'Naughty of you to make fun of me. I shan't sleep a wink.' He kissed her and turned over with a little sniff, making grumbling noises to himself.

She put the light off. 'Sleep well,' she said. 'Old bean.'

Just as she'd expected, his light snores started up almost immediately. Brown snored too, and dreamed, with happy hunting cries and little shakes. She lay listening to them.

12

He Said

*Of course I'll be fit for ~~nothing~~ today. I didn't
sleep a wink.*

'Of course I'll be fit for nothing today,' Clive declared as
he bounded into the kitchen for a hearty breakfast. 'I didn't
sleep a wink.'

While he ate orange juice, bran flakes, a boiled egg and
toast, Joy finished off the picnic she was preparing and put
the packages in a carrier bag. 'If you're feeling so tired, why
can't you pretend to be wounded early on in the battle and
have a rest under a bush?'

He gave her a pained look. 'Our performances are choreo-
graphed with enormous care. This is history, you know. It's
pointless if it isn't authentic.'

'I must say I am looking forward to it. I feel most
excited!'

Clive drank the last of his coffee and stood up. 'D'you want
me to put my things in the dishwasher?'

'Yes, will you? I'm just going to throw the sandwich crusts
out for the birds, then I'm ready.'

'Oh, don't bring all those dreadful pigeons into the garden.'

'Why not?'

'They're all diseased. Don't feed them. Don't encourage
them.'

'Yes, but they exist and they probably don't get enough to
eat. Some of them always look very motheaten and decrepit
to me.'

'Jolly good.'

'*Clive!* Do they suffer or do they not? That's all one needs to ask oneself, surely?'

He shook his head as if marvelling at the depths of her nuttiness. She stared at him as if waiting for the sign that he wasn't being serious. When none came she stalked out into the garden.

They took about an hour to drive to Crawston where the Battle of Marston Moor was to take place on some playing fields. They arrived at the same time as the trucks bringing cannons and costumes. Even the spectators' car parks were already starting to fill up.

Clive left Joy to join the rest of the cast which was to be swelled by several hundred local people who were going to act as extras. They were receiving their last minute instructions from the producer. As she strolled round the edges of the ground with Brown, she caught snatches of conversation as the armies prepared for battle.

'What ho, Mistress Mundy!'

'Darling, I've put a little patch on that hole in your tunic. Promise me you won't wave your arms about too much, will you, or it's not going to hold.'

'How can I wave, my precious? I can't move. I've got a trapped nerve, my doctor says. At least I can groan realistically. If Sir Toby lays a finger on me today, I shall kill him!'

'Where, oh where has my lunch box gone?' sang another despairing voice. 'Has anybody seen a brown sandwich with a bite out of it? An ac . . . *tor's* life is not a happy one!'

As Clive and Joy found a quiet place to sit down with Brown and have a picnic lunch, people with the same idea began to pour into the ground. What seemed to Joy like literally thousands of school children tumbled from coaches with Birmingham on the side and Oxford and Watford and Milton Keynes and Lichfield. There were stands, rows and rows of benches and plenty of standing room for spectators.

Tents had been erected for Information, Refreshments, First Aid and Toilets.

Joy had just started undoing their picnic packages of egg and lettuce sandwiches, chicken legs and tomatoes, when a woman's voice greeted Clive. 'Oh, hi! *Clive!*'

'Den!' he responded delightedly. 'Where've you been?'

'Florida, darling! Visiting my mother who's gone to live there. It was *wond* . . er . . ful!' She hugged Clive, her arm right round his neck. She was small and blonde and pretty with a bright tough little face and a slender figure in lime slacks and a lime and white shirt with a glass of champagne on the chest. A drunken smiling cat was curled up in it. "Happiness is a tight pussy!" was printed underneath.

Clive said, 'Joy, this is Denise.'

She held out her hand. 'Hallo, Joy.'

'Are you going to have some lunch with us?' Joy asked, hoping she wasn't because there wasn't enough.

'We'll come and join you,' Denise replied. 'I'll go and get Barry, my husband.'

She reappeared with her husband and a picnic that put Joy's and Clive's to shame because they had quail's eggs and hot pheasant soup and champagne. To Joy's chagrin, Clive ate most heartily from their lunch, smacking his lips and paying Denise lavish compliments. Barry did accept one of Joy's egg sandwiches.

'Clive and I used to work together,' he told her. 'So did Den until she started her own business. Bubbly, Joy?' He offered her a glass of champagne.

'Oh, Barry, well, thank you . . . how lovely,' she replied awkwardly. 'We've only got mineral water. How debonair of you to be drinking before battle! I must say I don't care for the look of that First Aid tent. Do a lot of people get injured?'

'Accidents happen, inevitably. Arms are broken, ribs crushed that sort of thing. The pain threshold goes up as our armies get carried away. About once a year somebody gets killed.'

'Heavens! Oh dear, I didn't realise that. I think Clive is meant to be fatally wounded in today's battle. Are you?'

'Yes, I'm done for. Clive is too, is he? Who are you today, Clive?'

Engrossed with Denise, Clive didn't hear. They were laughing loudly together. 'He's William Welford,' Joy said.

'He gets it too.' Barry's pleasant face dissolved with amusement. 'It's curtains for the worthy William.'

They both glanced at Clive who was looking anything but worthy, Joy thought, annoyed. He was flirting with Denise.

'I was called a foxy lady at a dinner party in Florida.' Denise squared her shoulders and stared at Clive rather challengingly, waiting for him to endorse the compliment.

'I think you're a very foxy lady,' Clive said.

'Foxy?' Joy repeated, her voice deliberately bewildered. 'Does that mean that you're crafty?'

Denise bridled. 'It means witty and sophisticated and street-wise,' she explained, her shoulders moving in time to her words. 'Everybody knows what it means over there.'

Joy could feel her neck reddening. 'I'm most surprised,' she said, 'because they don't have foxes in that part of America.'

Deinise shrugged but she was unwilling not to have the last word. 'It's a phrase that's part of our current pop culture. There's a shop in Wimbledon called *Foxy Lady*. You work in a shop, I believe, Joy?'

'Only while I'm trying to write.'

'What are you trying to write, Joy?'

Suddenly Joy had had enough of her. 'I'm writing a biography of George Herbert,' she said.

'Are you now?' Barry rejoined enthusiastically. 'You mean the composer?'

'Actually, no. I mean the poet.'

'That's right,' Denise assisted. 'He's a minor Victorian poet, Barry.' She had the last word.

'Well, Clive and I had better get a move on.' Barry stood

up and started packing the picnic things away. Joy began to do the same. Brown stretched and started nosing about in the grass assuming this was a prelude to more walks.

'D'you notice how things suddenly go very quiet before a battle?' Barry remarked, 'Everybody starts going to the toilet. It's nerves. You can almost feel the expectant tension in the air.'

'My hero!' Denise flung her arms round his neck and hung there, kissing him. 'I hate these battles, Joy. I know they're a superb spectacle but I've really grown to dread them. Men! They are so babyish, aren't they! I never see Barry or Clive once the fighting starts. It's just bedlam. If you've got any ear plugs, just stick 'em in!'

'Den always gives us a telling-off beforehand,' Barry said, patting her behind. 'I hope you're going to enjoy it, Joy.'

'Barry, I'm sure I will,' she said. 'Clive, shall I take the car off now and find a place to park where Brown won't be terrified by the noise?'

'Make it as safe as possible, will you? There are so many lunatics around.'

The moment had come. They stood awkwardly together then kissed with poignant smiles as if the war was real. 'Good luck,' she said, 'Please, be very careful.'

The trouble was she drove further and further away from the battle ground. This position was too exposed to dog thieves, that position had too much sun. It took ages. By the time she'd decided upon a cool secluded place for the car, the drums had started. A shiver went down her spine. The Battle of Marston Moor was under way!

Hurriedly, she adjusted the windows to leave Brown air. 'You be a good chap. Shan't be long.' As she was locking the car door, Clive's telephone rang. She walked off, then she went back. She nearly didn't answer it.

'Is Clive Pownall there?' asked a man's voice.

She smiled. 'He's taking part in a battle.'

'Can you get hold of him? It's desperately urgent. Tell him

it's Talbot. Our mother has been taken ill. We're waiting for the doctor now.'

Muffled cannons went off. 'You think he ought to come at once?'

'If he doesn't come, he may not see her again.'

For a few seconds Joy stood where she was, transfixed. What should she do? Take the car for speed? What about the fright for Brown? No, no, she decided frantically, she must run herself.

She started running. A hundred yards and she was out of breath, her heart bursting and sweat trickling down her face. Omigod. Poor Clive. Quick! Quick! Poor Dinky. She slowed for a stitch then started up again. The precious minutes were passing.

As she drew nearer the battle field, the booms and shouts and screams grew more deafening. The air was filled with thick black smoke and the smell of gunpowder.

The spectacle put her in despair. Her legs were shaking. She nearly wept. It was a melée beyond her wildest dreams. How could she find Clive? There were hundreds of men fighting. Soldiers setting off cannons, soldiers pitching from horses, soldiers fighting hand to hand, soldiers injured, soldiers dead. Omigod. 'Excuse me . . . excuse me, please.' She pushed her way through rows of standing spectators to a corner where there seemed to be a large knot of Cavaliers. She put on her glasses and peered steadily at each whirling, cursing Royalist figure bashing his enemy with the wrong end of his musket or finishing him off with a bayonet. Was that Clive's back? No, no . . . not straight enough . . . was that . . . with a moustache? No, it wasn't. Oh, please God . . . Please let me see him. Let me get him to his mother in time. William Welton . . . William Weatherby? William whatwasit?

Beside her a hoarse-voiced teacher was instructing a school group. Pointing and commenting and adding bits of useful information from the history books.

'Come on, Cromwell!' shrieked a bald girl in pink wellingtons with a ring in her nose.

'Belt up!' responded a male voice rudely. 'Cromwell's an agitator. Who needs it? Good old Charlie!'

'Go on the Round'eads!' The bald girl put two fingers in her mouth and whistled. 'The King's a big pooftah!'

'The Royalist army was not inspired by the King's leadership,' the schoolmaster explained, 'but Charles I was not a gay. And anybody who says pooftah will be punished.'

Another cannon went off beside them. 'Kill! Kill!' shrieked the girl in pink wellies.

Suddenly Joy saw Clive in a little armour hat like a harebell. He was aiming his musket at an advancing cluster of Roundheads when she positively screeched 'CLI . . . VE!'

He seemed to look directly at her and she waved. A wild beckoning. Come in Boat Nine!

He stood still with a puzzled stare and was felled from behind by a giant wielding a stave. He sank like a stone, rocked a bit in a stiff boomerang shape then lay still.

'He'll be fit for nothing,' Joy thought, as she nipped under the ropes like a streaker and ran out onto the battlefield.

She was vaguely aware of a communal gasp from the audience. Half-expecting to be hit by a bullet, she dived among the grunting, flailing actors, receiving a kick on the shin and mud in her face. She kept up a high genteel cry: 'I have a message for Clive Pownall!', dodging and weaving as best she could while she waited for the armies to divide before her like the Red Sea. But the men were fighting as if possessed. She felt a sickening blow on the back of the head.

'Gid out of it!' swore a Roundhead, hurling her back towards the ropes.

She staggered, walloped him and, cheered by the spectators, thrust her way through the scrum like a wild woman till she got to Clive. She reached him before the police reached her.

He was lying on his back groaning 'Mind my legs!' with

tomato ketchup oozing from beneath his breastplate. One thought crossed her mind. That harebell hat made his nose more common.

'Clive, it's your mother!'

His face contorted in slow speechless annoyance.

'Quick! Quick! Get up. We've got to go. Talbot says she's dying.' As she reached down to pull him up, a policeman seized her.

'All right, madam. *Out!*'

'See you at the main entrance!' she shouted over her shoulder as she was led away.

Waiting in his Cavalier costume, Clive's face was still dark with anger when she reappeared with the car.

'Was all that really necessary?' he asked, 'You know what my mother is. It's not another "wolf wolf" about her leg, is it?'

'It absolutely isn't. We've got to hurry. Ring your family now.'

He made the call as they pulled away from the battle-ground. 'We're on our way, Tol. How bad is she?' His face grew grave as he listened.

'It's serious,' he told Joy. 'The doctor hasn't come yet and she's refusing to go to hospital in an ambulance. I don't know if we'll be there in time.'

Joy never forgot that sad, reckless drive to Stapleton Byng, their feelings of impotence and the long helpless silences between them. She didn't know what Clive's thoughts were, brooding on the death of his mother. She sat beside him with her head thumping and her bruises hurting, remembering the nice things about Dinky and already feeling a genuine sense of loss.

From time to time she tried to take Clive's mind off his mother.

'What is Denise's business?'

'She sells dental equipment.'

'She's full of herself, isn't she?'

141

'Yes, she's a fun doll.'

She was a fun doll, Joy reflected in silence. That's exactly what she was.

By the time they reached Stapleton Byng, Dinky was dead. The doctor had arrived, got her to hospital but it was too late. Denis Pownall had gone with her and her two sons, Talbot and Nick, had stayed at home waiting for news. Garth and Dorothea Tefty, ever helpful, were sitting with them.

'We opened a bottle,' Talbot said awkwardly, 'to drink the old girl's health, really. Will you join us?'

It was clear from the scene of disarray that several wine bottles must have been opened. There were three empty on the table and a distinctly smoky atmosphere with overflowing ashtrays. Talbot and Nick were in their shirtsleeves. Pale and stunned, Clive listened as they described what had happened to his mother. He sat slumped with shock. Joy felt very sorry for him.

Nobody could think of much to say or do after that, so they all poured more drinks. Dinky had complained about her poor state of health for so long they'd all grown immune to it. Now that it turned out to be true, and she was gone, none of them could believe it.

Clive looked at Joy. 'Did I put my own clothes in the car?'

'Yes,' she said. 'I'll get them for you when I take Brown for a walk.

'Still fighting, Clive, eh?' Talbot boxed into the air. He could hardly conceal his amusement at the blood be-spattered Cavalier costume and winked at the others. 'He was always fighting Nick and me when he was little but Dinky wanted a girl by the time he came along so she was forever dressing him up in fancy clothes.'

'I've got three sons myself,' Joy responded quickly. 'And I was just as pleased when the third arrived. I never wanted daughters.'

'How old are your boys, Mrs. Sadler?' Dorothea Tefty enquired politely, to keep the conversation going.

'They're grown up. The eldest teaches in America, with a child of his own. Guy market-gardens in Worcester and Matthew works on a weekend stall in the market.'

Dorothea smiled cosily. 'What does Matthew want to do?'

'Nothing,' Joy replied. 'He's very religious. He reads the Bible.'

Joy had no wish to talk about her own family when they had just lost a member of theirs. She felt she ought to say a word or two in praise of Dinky so she remarked, somewhat hypocritically, how much she was going to miss her frequent calls to the sports shop.

They all laughed at that, familiar with her addiction to the telephone and that set off the reminiscences. Another two wine bottles were fetched from the cellar, Dorothea produced some meat paste sandwiches and they each told their favourite anecdote about Dinky.

Talbot talked the most. He was a salesman, it appeared, so he was used to talking. He acted out his stories, in which everybody he ever met seemed to call him "Tolly", with his arms waving and his long legs working like a dangling man. He had a rather bogus honking laugh and a little head which seemed a great way off because of his height. Joy pigeon-holed him as a ne'er do well.

His brother Nick looked as if he might be the type to make his own wine and go on cycling holidays. He had a beard like Garth Tefty but was slight in build. A borderline ne'er do well, she decided.

Leaving Clive where he was, she took Brown for a long walk to the shore. She walked along, throwing stones for him, pondering on the scene in the house and her own part in it. So intimate yet so alien. Life was a series of chance happenings, she reflected. What made one take up one option and not another? No choice was ever perfect. It was all a question of mood. She was still involved with Clive and the Pownalls only because there was no urgent reason not to be.

No sooner had she fed the dog and put him back in the car, than Denis Pownall arrived home. He was as straight-backed as ever but he looked gaunt, sunken-eyed. His bounce was gone. He stood, dazed, wafting the fuggy air with his hand as Clive got up to greet him. They hugged awkwardly in the new *This Is Your Life* manner. His father patted him and nodded at his costume with a slight smile. 'Straight from Marston Moor?'

'But not soon enough,' Clive said sadly.

'Well, who'd have thought it?' Mr. Pownall gazed blankly round at the others.

'Yes, we won't see her like again,' Garth Tefty said.

'Dinky Pownall was a one-off,' echoed Dorothea, screwing out her cigarette with respectful emphasis.

'I'm awfully sorry,' Joy murmured. 'I liked her so much.'

'I know you did, Joy,' Denis said. 'And she liked you. You did a lot for Dinky, one way and another.'

'Have a drink, Denis?' Talbot suggested.

'Yes.'

As he was handed a glass of wine, Denis Pownall glanced curiously at the label on the bottle. He reached forward and took hold of it to have a better look. 'Well, what's this then?' he demanded, interestedly.

Talbot honked. 'An impertinent little wine.'

His step-father was obviously impressed. 'Congratulations . . . good stuff. Where did you find it?'

'In the cellar.'

'Your cellar?'

'Your cellar.'

Denis Pownall glowered at him. 'You should have told me if you wanted to drink wine like this. D'you know what it costs?'

'I'm sorry?' Talbot said, managing to sound both insolent and superior to matters of money.

'Yes, well, it's a bit too late to be sorry now, isn't it?' Furiously, his step-father eyed the empty bottles on the table.

His demeanour upset Talbot.

'She was my mother, you know.'

'I beg your pardon?'

'She was my mother too, and don't you forget it. Nick and I are part of the family, meant to be.'

'But you don't just walk in here and help yourself to rare wines from the cellar which are meant for guests. How dare you?'

The distressed atmosphere produced by Dinky's death worsened rapidly.

'You'd better know that I'm entitled to a share of what's in that bloody cellar. We all are.'

'Yes, we are.' Nick nodded, and muttered something ruder under his breath.

'You've always tried to cut us out, haven't you?' Talbot accused bitterly. 'But my mother worked hard all her life for this house and this business. It's ours as well.'

Clive saw his house beginning to vanish into oblivion. 'What have you ever done towards it except borrow money?'

Talbot stepped over to Clive and loomed over him menacingly. Years of resentment had welled up in him. 'Yes, and you, you're always sitting pretty, aren't you, Clive? Still dressed up like a fucking dog's dinner.'

'If you think you're going to come here and grab anything you want,' he answered grimly. 'You've got another think coming.'

Talbot punched him.

Clive rocked backwards into a glass-fronted cabinet. China treasures slid along the shelves and smashed.

As he struggled to get up, Garth and Dorothea Tefty jumped bravely between the brothers to stop the fight. Talbot's fist caught Dorothea in the throat. She sank to the floor, chortling as if partially strangled.

'Ohhh . . .' Joy said. 'Crumbs!' And crouched to help her.

With an astonished grunt of rage, Denis Pownall went for Talbot. He danced on the spot to work up the necessary force then struck him on the side of the head. His step-son reeled, lost his balance and fell heavily across the table. Bottles and glasses smashed. A dark stain spread across the pink carpet.

'Get out!' Mr. Pownall shouted at him. 'Get out and don't come back. We don't want you or your brother at the funeral either. D'you hear me? You are not welcome in this house. Now or ever.'

Sullenly, in the silence, the two men picked up their jackets and left. The others sat listening as Talbot's Ford Sierra started up. A minute later Nick's clapped-out Renault followed it down the drive.

13

He Said

I'm a father. Mother and child are doing well.
She's a gem and he's a gem. We'll probably be
getting married now.

'I'm a father, fun doll!'

'Leo! Oh, my goodness! Congratulations! How marvellous.
What is it?'

'A boy. Thomas. Mother and child are doing well. He's
called after Ruth's father.'

'Tom. How lovely.'

'Yes, it's what she wants. I wasn't allowed to choose a
name. Anyway, this is just to let you know I've moved
back in with her. I'm keeping my own place on as an office
because I need to work there every day, and that keeps Jacob
happy.'

'Is it going to be all right with Ruth?'

'Well, we'll probably be getting married now.'

'Oh, good. That is good, is it?'

'I like our family life. I'll settle for that.'

'I'm so pleased. She's a gem.'

'She's a gem and he's a gem. You'll have to come and see
us soon.'

14

She Said

*We haven't any friends and it's your fault
because you behave so oddly to people. You boast
at them and then you fall asleep. When we went
to that housewarming party, I saw a man sitting
beside you reading a magazine because he had
no one to talk to.*

After the initial awed rapture at the birth of their baby son
had worn off, Leo was reasonably contented with Ruth but
he could tell she wasn't contented. She never relaxed. She
created tension. She worried about money, worried about
their way of life, worried about the future.

'I'll have to keep on working,' she said. 'I don't want
Thomas to have the messed-up childhood I had.'

'We're getting on well,' Leo said.

'Yes, but we haven't any friends and it's your fault because
you behave so oddly to people. You boast at them and then
you fall asleep. When we went to that housewarming party
I saw a man sitting beside you reading a magazine because
he hadn't got anybody to talk to.'

'I listened to him when I woke up.'

'When you do listen to people's views, it's only to shoot
them down and do some more boasting. Nobody can understand what you do and they don't know what you're talking
about.'

'That's why I don't talk to them.'

'Do you realise that each time we come away from a dinner
party – that's if we can come away and you haven't left the

car lights on all evening and made the battery flat – I know that we are probably leaving that house for the last time. It makes me really depressed. The chances are we won't be asked again.'

'My dearest wish.'

It wasn't his dearest wish. He was perpetually worried himself because he was trying so hard to please her. He wished she'd stop hounding him. He adored Thomas and he enjoyed family life with a baby. He was amazed to be a doting father. He hadn't expected to be because his own father never doted on him. And Leo had hated him. He hadn't even visited him in hospital when he was dying. If life with Ruth was in a low emotional key, he accepted that. It was just that with all the tensions she created he didn't know whether he was on his head or his heels. If he lay down to think, she snapped at him. If he kept out of the way, she demanded to know where he'd been. Sometimes she wouldn't speak to him for days. He knew she cried sometimes in the night but he didn't know whether it was fatigue from the baby or because he didn't love her enough. She wouldn't admit to anything. He tried to look after her and help. He didn't mind not loving her enough. She minded it.

The things she took as insults or selfishness were frequently his inadequacies. He didn't know what women wanted. If he didn't take her out to dinner, it was because he had never in his life taken women out to dinner. He didn't know how to do it properly. People didn't do that sort of thing in his family. So he'd been scared of being humiliated by getting it wrong.

What put him off was an incident years ago in the States when he'd invited a classy college girl to a jazz club. She'd ordered scotch while he had Coca Cola. On his first sip he spilled some coke and made a puddle on the table. Wanting to smoke, the girl produced her cigarettes and held out the matchbox to him. Too slowly, it dawned on him that he was meant to take the box and light her fag. He opened it upside down and all the matches fell out into the pool of Coca Cola. He'd never forgotten the expression on her face. Now he was seeing it on Ruth's.

It could appear in a twinkling, any time, but particularly at mealtimes.

'I've forgotten to bring the butter,' she might say, with a martyred sigh.

Naturally, he carried on eating, expecting to get the butter when they wanted it. But the atmosphere brought about by his failure to jump to his feet there and then could start a row which blew up over days.

The trouble was she wanted him to throw himself into bourgeois life with all her own fervour. She wanted everybody to see that they knew how to lay a table or where to place the milk jug on a tray. He supposed she clung to this pathetic display of order because of the turmoil inside herself. And he found this middle class life a tedious minefield. He got on splendidly with the celebrated and the successful because they were communicating on another level – mutual acknowledgement. He got on with people like himself from the working class. He could speak to a conference of five hundred. It was Ruth and her basically boring friends who weren't compatible.

But she'd pushed him into the role of Provider. Not necessarily provider of love or money or babies, but provider of colour and entertainment. He was meant to offer a Way of Life.

Her dream scenario, he guessed, would turn him into a frenetically busy jet-setting figure in dashing fashionable clothes who sold his way-out ideas for massive fees whilst remaining hopelessly undomesticated, which was where she could come in. His famous friends from the world of television and cinema would be invited home to find a tasteful house running like clockwork. Out would come the oysters and champagne, and much more that no ordinary person had ever heard of, and she would be able to bask in their admiration.

'My goodness me, what a little whizz Ruth is ... having babies, running such a gorgeous home, holding down a job.' She hadn't actually gone back to her job at *Plain Speaking* yet. She'd taken to folding her hands in her lap and saying 'But what about the future?'.

He had to pretend he hadn't heard. He was happy to do things with her and share Thomas, whom they both doted on, although much of the time he didn't even want to touch her because she forced her emotions on him and made such colossal demands in return.

'You should have had a house ready for us,' she said on one preposterous occasion, 'somebody of your age. In my book if a man of thirty is still using public transport, he's a failure.'

'I use the bus because there's nowhere to park.'

'You take a cab,' she answered witheringly, probably thinking wistfully of the sweetie and his chauffeur, 'unless you are a total wimp. It's a mentality.'

'It's mental,' he said and went to chat to Thomas.

'Don't wake the baby,' she called after him. 'If you're looking for something to do, why don't you clean the cars?'

As soon as he'd cleaned her car, she clicked her tongue and then went straight out and did it all over again herself.

'And I iron all your shirts for you.'

'Well, don't iron 'em.'

Not the right responses, he knew. If he'd demanded why his shirts weren't ironed, she would have been better pleased. She'd still have given him a long-suffering rant about the role of women.

His clothes caused another running battle. They embarrassed her, she said. He supposed she wanted him to dress up like the sweetie. He'd always dressed in an outrageously downbeat manner for the same reason as not taking women out to dinner. He didn't want to get it wrong. And of course she couldn't stand him poking about in charity shops and finding old sweaters and T-shirts for ten p.

Their conversations were another minefield. He sometimes dreaded the evenings, when Thomas was in bed and out of the way. He spun out his bath and bedtime play knowing what was coming. 'Proper clothes. Proper jobs. Aren't you going to . . . ?' He did his best to steer the talk away from these floating mines. 'I'm a woman, you know. If you don't find me attractive you can . . .' Oops! Blast. Hit one. 'But I like family life, Ruth.' 'Yes, but what about the future?' Oh, shit! I've set off another.

What she could not stand, he suspected, was this hopeless penniless slob somehow sailing through life, having narcoleptic attacks which she didn't believe in, with nothing more than a clutch of Academy Awards to his name. It undermined all her values.

If the man is not challenging enough, Leo realised, the woman goes on making more and more unbearable conditions. She pushes and pushes until there's a break. Their break came when Thomas was about nine months old. Ruth threw Leo out.

That separation shocked them profoundly, now that they were parents. They went back together pretty quickly that first time. Anyway, Leo missed Thomas so much.

He wanted it to work because it had to work. In his depleted state, he kept on trying to be unobtrusive so as not to annoy Ruth. He kept it a secret if he sloped off to the pictures during the day. She even objected to him going back home to work in his own flat, convinced he spent his time in bed with the cat on his stomach – which he often did.

One day he noticed there was a small leak in her radiator so, filled with zeal, he planned to surprise and please her with his plumbing powers. Congratulating himself on taking the initiative, he scraped rust away from around the tiny hole, thereby making it a large hole. Water gushed out everywhere. The hysteric in the flat below started banging on the ceiling. Leo felt he knew in that moment what it must be like to be a three year old child alone and lost in Piccadilly Circus. In his panic, he rang Ruth who came home from work.

'Go away,' she said at once as she took in the scene. 'Just go away and leave me alone.' She called a plumber, soothed the hysteric, looked up her insurance. And hid Leo's tools.

But he did keep his eyes open after that, anxious to prove his competence about the house, and he wanted to be able to speak up first about any little jobs that needed doing because she made such a fuss if she was the one to notice and do the speaking.

'That back window needs a proper lock on it,' he asserted, in a masculine manner. 'I'll fix something.'

'Oh, yes,' Ruth said pleased. 'That is a good idea.'

The very day after he'd secured the window for her, and received fulsome praise, he forgot his keys. He had to climb up a drainpipe and smash the glass. He taped a Sainsbury's bag across the hole with the handles flapping in the wind.

She was incredulous.

While she was away with Tom, spending the night with her half-sister Melanie, he forgot his keys again and damaged the front door getting in. In the row that followed, his responses to her criticisms seemed to make her hysterical, and she kicked him out.

'We can get married if you want to,' he suggested in a letter.

She ignored his proposal. In her reply, she said she was reluctantly agreeing to a meeting with him for two reasons:

(a) to reinforce reality
(b) to discuss access to Thomas.

Things were patched up between them because the child missed his father. He was two and a half now. He'd waited in the hall repeating, with dogged monotony, 'Daddy's coming home soon', and refused to go to bed.

Thomas was a most engaging little boy. He had his

mother's features and his father's dark eyes, and he drew wonderfully imaginative pictures of rather grown-up subjects. There were some extremely happy family times, of course. In the good periods Ruth loved to muse with Leo on the sort of house they were going to buy and where it would be. Sometimes they even went to look at places. Leo had been working on some Open University maths films for the BBC and an animation studio was currently showing an interest in his story of *Chelsea Charlie*. Problems still existed but they gradually seemed to be solving them. When Ruth started on another clothes-buying binge, Leo knew it was a bad sign. She sneaked into the flat with outfits costing hundreds of pounds which she often never wore.

He didn't know what to say to her. Sometimes he'd comment casually, 'Oh, is that new?'

'No' she'd reply in a vague voice, smoothing and fiddling with the material so as not to have to meet his eyes.

'I haven't seen it before.'

'You don't notice what I wear.'

So he steered away from these bobbing mines and left it at that. He pulled the covers over his head and went to sleep.

When the end came, it happened suddenly and inexplicably, sparked off by a tiny unexpected booby-trap.

Leo went to the fridge for juice and helped himself. He poured it into a cup, drank too fast, spilled on his T shirt and left the cup unwashed on the draining board. He stood choking with his mouth open like a dog with a bone stuck. Ruth went to the telephone and ordered a furniture van. He had two hours, she said, to pack up his belongings.

'But why?' he demanded plaintively. 'What is it now?' She did make one coherent statement amidst an embittered rant about his selfishness and self-absorption. 'And you've always found me unattractive as a woman.'

Spot on, he thought silently, not for the first time. He gave one long last look at the uncluttered modish sitting room where he had never really felt relaxed and nodded at it to annoy her. She stared back at him with an Aztec mouth, the epitome of the neat child who plays in the sandpit and never gets dirty. He knew this time he wasn't coming back.

When he eventually got home, he dumped all his stuff from Ruth's flat in the hall and surveyed the mess with distinct relief. Thank goodness he'd hung on to his own place. He rocked Jacob in his arms, a daily routine they both enjoyed. 'Play belly bellies . . .' he murmured to the cat, rubbing his tummy. He'd think about his problems when he'd had a sleep.

As he got into bed, the telephone rang. BBC Television were thinking of doing a series of *Chelsea Charlie* cartoons in a five-minute afternoon slot each week. Correspondingly, his agent told Leo, *Chelsea Charlie* was to be marketed as a children's annual, small supermarket books, jigsaw puzzles, T-shirts, pencil cases, balloons, money boxes and anything else they could think of from building society fan clubs to children's vouchers for hotel chains.

It looked as if one of his dreams might actually be coming true.

Suddenly Leo began to make a great deal of money. *Chelsea Charlie* didn't take off instantly, but the lovable new dog character was launched with a flourish and pushed hard all year by the sales and publicity people. Leo was amazed. Nobody had wanted his story originally. Now it fitted. The studio had needed a project. The marketing company needed something new to promote. *Chelsea Charlie* was the right thing at the right time. And away he went!

It seemed odd at times to have such a success when so little of his heart had been in it. But he enjoyed writing the scripts and stories and he found he enjoyed the children's reactions because it made him feel all the closer somehow to Thomas. Hurrying home one day to watch *Chelsea Charlie* on television, he heard a child on the pavement beside him say to her mother, 'D'you know why I like Tuesday best? It's because it's *Chelsea Charlie*.'

When *Chelsea Charlie* won a BAFTA award, the ceremony was televised and seen by millions. Unfortunately, one of the millions was his old friend Captain Galway-Lamb, who happened at that moment just to have come off duty, and was lounging about at home in a raucous red dress from the Empire Stores catalogue. When Leo went up onto the platform and made his short speech of thanks, he leaned forward in his chair, suddenly excited. 'Is it? *Is* it?'

Galway-Lamb sprang up and tapped the screen. 'Got you!' he shouted triumphantly. 'Well, you've asked for it, buddie, and now you're going to get it!'

Next day, he hastened to see his solicitor and an action was set in motion claiming damages from Leonard Derbyshire for negligence, trespass to the person, and assault.

Leo received the writ on his knees, through the cat flap in the front door, having mislaid his keys and inadvertently locked himself in.

'But why is Tony Galway-Lamb doing it?' Ruth asked Sweetie, perching elegantly on the edge of his desk to eat a handful of cherries. She had resumed her old relationship with the editor and felt a spasm of pure pleasure that at least somebody was going to make Leo jump out of his skin. 'How embarrassing. I do hope I'm not involved in any way.' She dangled a cherry temptingly beside Sweetie's mouth, which opened to receive it.

'Poor Tony looks so very peculiar now, that's the trouble. I've told you, darling – well, you've seen him yourself – if he gets a smile on his face he can't get it off.' Sweetie held out a long white hand and studied his perfectly manicured nails. 'It's a recipe for a lot of disagreeableness in the Guards. He's already been beaten up and his prospects are ruined. How's he to become a general if he's grinning the whole time like a lewd northern comedian?'

'Not to mention being in drag, half the time,' she added, giggling. 'That's a handicap too, I should have thought, unless the Army chooses to regard it as showing initiative. Actually, I believe there is a trend towards blokes dressing in a much more feminine style. Well, you do, and I'm all for it. But why is Tony bringing this law suit now? I mean, why *now*?'

'He says he saw his attacker on television. He thinks he's in the money.'

'Huh, does he? I've yet to see any great sign of it.'

'Darling, he pays you for Thomas, doesn't he?'

'I know, darling, but I didn't ask for much, you know. I don't think he's got it, honestly.'

'Tony seems to think he's just won an award.'

'Yes, he's got masses of awards but no money.' She stood up and twitched down her new Escada skirt, suddenly anxious that Leo's earnings might be syphoned off in another direction. 'Anyway, I don't mind. It means more power to me to decide how often he sees Thomas, etc. He only sees him on Sundays. I've had to put my foot down. I'm not allowing any child of mine to stay the night in that cesspit.'

'Put it down hard, Roo, that's my advice. The rogue element in society is taking over. That chap, let's face it, has done enough damage already, dancing and screwing his way all over London.'

'Mm, I don't know. I think he's a recluse really.'

'He should be made to make amends,' Sweetie responded righteously, stirring a cup of coffee which put him £354.10p into his secretary's debt.

When Ruth had gone he returned to something he was preparing for the next issue.

. . . *A century earlier F. D. Maurice commended Hooker's ideal of a Christian state as 'an order which never proved itself to be more divine than when it watched over the vulgarest interest of the poorest creatures'.*

> *At no time has there been greater need for this vital message than in our present society. So much time is wasted blaming particular groups or rival systems but the problem is a basic human one: the ills of our world stem from its fallen nature.*
>
> *Our first need is for redemption and the means of grace. Such a belief does not mean that we must do away with any attempt to make life better for all but that we recognise the size of the problem.*

Sitting in the sports shop, keeping an eye open for bailiffs, Joy was trying to write an article on jockeys' increasingly flagrant use of whips in racing, and quietly worrying about Leo's impending court case.

She guessed she was almost bound to be called as a witness. Anyway, she'd already promised to support him if need be, in any way he wanted. Clive could be called as well. But poor old Leo. Another calamity on top of his computer company going phut. She didn't see how Captain Galway-Lamb could win, but how could you tell with juries these days? They seemed to take no notice of the judge's directions about the verdict and dreamed up the most astonishing figures for damages. They might easily feel sympathy for Tania Galway-Lamb, being a transvestite guardsman with a squashed face. Would he be appearing as a Cavalry officer or as a woman? Either way, he could be dangerously charming and amusing. Well, so could Ruth Bly. Most plausible. Whose side would she be on? Her behaviour towards Leo was so vindictive. Look at her hysteria over the unwashed cup and sending for that furniture fan. She was a bit dotty.

Leo was of the same opinion. His great anxiety over Galway-Lamb suing him was the effect on Ruth and whether it was going to damage his access arrangements with her over Thomas. He prayed she wouldn't be brought into the case at all but realised it was a serious possibility because of the Sweetie connection. He absolutely dreaded what she might say in her unbalanced state. He lived on tenterhooks, wondering whether he was going to see Thomas as planned or whether the meeting would suddenly be cancelled.

Ruth was being extremely difficult. She'd recently taken to winging off impromptu bombshells. The latest note complained that he lived above a laundry. Its doors were left open, she pointed out, to release noxious fumes from chemicals on filthy garments. Thomas was not to be allowed to linger near this doorway and he was to be kept right away from the disgusting black bags bursting with rotting rubbish, which littered the area round Leo's flat.

Whenever she cancelled Leo's promised meetings with his son, which she increasingly frequently did, there was never an explanation other than it was no longer convenient. He was still against taking her to court to establish his rights as a father. He'd simply given her the money she asked for and was inclined to think it was better not to stir things up any further. He idolised his child and he was trying to make his dealings with Ruth as civilised as possible. His idea was that they should go on outings together as a family sometimes, but she wouldn't hear of it.

The night before the case, Captain Galway-Lamb stayed at his club. He arrived quite late from a reception in full dress uniform, to the amazement and consternation of the secretary, Major Fox. Last time he was in gray lamé, and here he was calling out, 'What ho, Foxy!'

Foxy didn't mind whether he was male or female as long as he was consistent. Otherwise it made it awkward for the staff and members if this embarrassing pervert popped up in all the wrong places, using inappropriate facilities and flouting club rules. He pursued him to have a quiet word about it only to hear him talking to someone on the telephone.

'Lambkin? Yes, here I am, hard adjacent!' he was saying in an excited voice.

Major Fox stopped dead. 'Ohh!' he muttered, appalled, then he stood still, listening, and staring at his shoes.

'I've got a little surprise for you or should I say a big one!' Carried away with his own amusingness, Captain Galway-Lamb was now laughing and talking at the top of his voice. 'How would you like to be locked to the bed by rampant thighs? What . . . what? Yes, I'm wearing my uniform for you. Naughty little sausage. You want to rape me, don't you? You want to drain all my strength from me. I know!

'What's that? No, no . . . mustn't be overtired for court tomorrow. Of course I shall be dressed entirely in black apart from my oxblood belt. Okay, yah. See you there. You might get dinner out of me afterwards if you play your cards right. No, no. I tend to sleep like a log. Nighty night. Lots of love.'

It was too much for Major Fox. He decided to sleep on the problem and went off home to Putney.

Before he undressed and hung up his Tania clothes for the morning, Captain Galway-Lamb took a framed photograph from his case. It was a picture of himself, nude in fluorescent wig, taken in the days before his face was paralysed. He sat on the edge of the bed and laughed to himself as he signed it. *For a naughty little waglet from her exhausted valentine.* Then he wrapped it up in scented paper.

As it turned out, he did not sleep like a log. He hardly slept at all. Another member, Lord Postlethwaite (pronounced Posset), came in at four o'clock after a night of adulterous hanky panky with a call girl. He collapsed against the door of Galway-Lamb's bedroom and died. A dreadful commotion went on all night.

15

He Said

*Look at The Sun! The headline says SMILING
BULLDYKE LOSES FACE TO DEPLORABLE
DANCER. Oh shit.*

In the morning, all involved in the case assembled outside
Court Number Fourteen at the Law Courts in the Strand. Leo
arrived first, followed shortly by Joy and Clive Pownall.

Joy was full of nervous fluttering smiles to disguise her
anxiety but Clive was spruce and genial as usual, as if he
took court procedure entirely in his stride which, indeed,
he probably did, providing the action was not directed
against him.

'Good morning, officer,' he said to an elderly usher, looking
at his watch. 'Lamb v Derbyshire. Have you any idea how
long this case is going to last?'

The man raised his eyebrows. 'None at all, Guv.'

'It won't last long,' Leo assured Clive. 'What is there to
say? It's ridiculous.'

He was most relieved to see there seemed to be no sign of
Ruth amid the crowd of litigants and witnesses waiting about
for various court rooms to open. He thought he recognised
Tania Galway-Lamb, dressed in black, standing at the other
end of the passage. He stared resentfully but was too far away
from her to be able to tell whether there was anything actually
wrong with her face or not. She wasn't smiling anyhow. So
that was heartening. His spirits lifted. A thin white-haired
guy, tall and aristocratic, who looked to be in his sixties,
was in muted conversation with her. He was tapping a copy

of *The Times* against his thigh. Leo guessed, with a dart of annoyance, that this must be the Sweetie, her godfather. He turned back to Joy and Clive as Galway-Lamb's barrister arrived, greeted them, and drew her with Sweeting into a huddle.

His own counsel, Mr. Laurence Love, arrived in a flying hurry at the last minute, after an early morning row with his wife. Before Leo's resentment had time to take root, they were moving in to take their places in Court Fourteen.

'Silence!' shouted an usher, nodding at the Clerk of the Court, and in swayed the stately figure of Mr. Justice Shakeshaft, known affectionately to members of the Bar as Shaky.

'I don't like the look of this,' Joy was thinking to herself. 'This old boy could turn out to find Tania very fragrant indeed. Poor Leo.'

Everybody stopped staring about and sat to attention as Mr. Simon Shyer, QC for the plaintiff, began to make his opening statement in which he described the social embarrassment, the ruin – emotional as well as physical – that became the lot of Miss Tania Galway-Lamb after the muscles of her face were severely damaged on the night in question at the Melstar Hotel.

'Seeking innocent companionship with members of the opposite sex, my client, accompanied by a woman friend, went that evening to a respectable Kensington hotel for a meeting of a singles club.' With his fingers spread high on his chest and plucking at the lapels of his gown, Mr. Shyer sought to convey the air of any reasonable person strolling along the Cromwell Road in search of innocent companionship.

'A singles club is, by definition, for the single.' He removed his glasses as he glanced down to turn a page of his notes. 'The atmosphere at the Melstar, I understand, is sociable, cultivated and decorous. Members are accepted only if they have attained university degree status, thus a certain level of social discourse is guaranteed. There was dancing that evening, a mixture, I am told, of ballroom and disco.'

'What is disco?' the judge enquired, playing to the gallery.

'Disco, m'lord,' replied the barrister, unable to resist a flash of wit, 'is spontaneous movement which takes place more or less on the spot while the dancers appear to be experiencing a series of uncontrollable nervous spasms.'

'Thank you, Mr. Shyer,' said Shaky, making a note.

Mr. Shyer continued, 'It was towards the end of that evening that Tania Galway-Lamb danced for the first time with Leonard Derbyshire. From the moment he took her in his arms for an old-fashioned waltz, which has such a strictly formal step sequence . . .'

'Just a minute, Mr. Shyer,' the judge interrupted. 'We know it was a waltz, do we?'

'We do, m'lord. The tune playing at the time, I gather, was *If You Will Come to The Ball*.'

'Oh, yes.' He nodded. 'Please proceed.'

'From the moment Leonard Derbyshire took my client in his arms for the waltz, Miss Galway-Lamb relates that she felt a distinct uneasiness due to his odd behaviour towards her. He boasted immediately that his powers revealed she was born under the astrological sign of Scorpio.'

'And was she?'

'She is a Scorpio, m'lord.'

'The sign of the Scorpion,' Shaky beamed in a homely manner. 'So am I.'

Mr. Shyer bowed. 'An excellent time of year from all accounts.

'But to return, m'lord, to the conversation on the dance floor . . . a polite query from Miss Galway-Lamb, as to Mr. Derbyshire's apparently inexplicable knowlege of her birthsign, served merely to antagonise him. He bared his teeth at her in a snarl, which she has described in her own words as being like that of a wild beast, and gave her what she took to be a warning. My client did not catch the actual warning itself above the noise in the ballroom but she recalls such alarming words as *nark* and *nick* and *maniac*. Then he kicked her.

'Miss Galway-Lamb might have dismissed the kick as a lack of dexterity on the dance floor but for what followed. She enquired if anything were the matter but he didn't answer. He gave her a push. As she stumbled, her ankle twisting, he threw her to the ground and jumped on her. Again, you might say, it's possible he could have trodden on her accidentally in the crush but he remained upon her. He remained upon her, making no attempt to get off, trampling savagely up and down on her defenceless body. His considerable weight on her face and throat caused her to lose consciousness.

'This was no accident,' Mr. Shyer concluded triumphantly. 'I am suggesting to you that Leonard Derbyshire had been drinking heavily that evening. He had come to the Melstar Hotel in search of an unsuspecting partner for his own mysterious purposes. When he saw he was not going to have his way with my client, he turned nasty, tossed her to the ground and angrily inflicted the damage upon her that now speaks for itself. A once-beautiful face is spoiled and scarred out of recognition, the muscles permanently paralysed. Her prospects are ruined. Her life as a woman is turned into a desperate fight against depression, humiliation and despair.'

'Omigod,' Joy whispered, as she and Leo exchanged a long horrified glance.

Tania Galway-Lamb gave her evidence next. She had had strict instructions from her counsel to confine herself to the feminine role during the legal proceedings and not to bamboozle or shock the court with any disclosures whatsoever about the other side of her life. It would go down extremely badly, he had advised her, if it came out that she was a cavalry officer who had gone dancing at a singles club in women's clothes. She must give away no more than that she expected to be invalided out of the armed services as a result of this catastrophic incident.

It was clear from the moment Galway-Lamb swished up into the witness box, lantern-jawed and smiling, that Mr. Justice Shakeshaft did not care for the cut of her jib. In her swirling black calf-length skirt, jaunty belted jacket and new thrusting breasts from *Transformations*, she seemed outrageously tall and blonde and outgoing. She went on smiling as she took the oath. But it was much more than a smile. Her eyes were crinkled into slits and her lips stretched swollenly into a carmine rectangle as though stung by a thousand bees. To the judge, it was a thoroughly indecent smirk, to which he took instant exception. Unfairly, he found it grotesque. He watched her performance unfold, wearing a puzzled frown.

'This is probably one of the most unpleasant moments of your life, is it not?' Mr. Shyer suggested.

'Yes it is,' she replied, in her eager, furry voice.

'You have nothing to smile about?'

'Nothing.'

'And yet because of what happened at the Melstar Hotel, you cannot cease to smile?'

'The muscles of my face are partially paralysed. I can change my expression but only slowly and with an effort. It is acutely . . .'

'Could you change it now?' the judge interjected encouragingly.

She laughed, tossing her head coyly so that her dangling crystal earrings caught the light. 'I'd rather not, Your Lordship, with all eyes upon me.'

Shaky glanced at Simon Shyer. 'As you wish, Miss Galway-Lamb.' He turned back to her. 'Take your time. The court is here to see the expressions you can conjure up for us.

'Mr. Shyer . . . mmm . . . I don't know whether you will be introducing any evidence which might suggest there was a draught at the Melstar Hotel?'

'M'lord?'

'Forgive me . . . only a little theory of mine that the plaintiff might be suffering from Bell's Palsy? Sitting out after dancing in a cold wind from an open window could be the cause of a most marked change for the worse in her facial features for some period of time to come.'

'I am grateful to you, M'lord. It is not Bell's Palsy, in fact. I will be calling a doctor later on who will testify to the permanent nature of my client's condition.'

'Thank you, Mr. Shyer. Please go on.'

When Tania Galway-Lamb finished giving her evidence, Mr. Love stood up to cross-examine her.

'Miss Galway-Lamb,' he said, in a pleasant leisurely manner. 'It would be true to say, would it not, that before you and Leonard Derbyshire danced together later on that evening at the Melstar Hotel, you had already watched him dancing with other partners?'

'I hadn't been watching him.'

'But you noticed him?'

She shrugged. 'We'd passed each other.'

'You exchanged some jokes about him with other members of his party, didn't you?'

'I may have done,' she pouted. 'I can't remember.'

Mr. Love smiled matily. 'In other words, you had your amorous eye upon him?'

Mr. Shyer jumped up. 'My Lord! Amorous eye! I must protest!' He threw his arms out helplessly and clapped his head. 'Why should my client's eye be described as amorous?'

'Yes, come come, Mr. Love. I don't think we can allow that,' the judge interposed quite genially. 'What sort of an eye was it, exactly? Did you mean that the plaintiff's eye became amorous at the sight of the defendant, or did you mean that her eye is amorous in all circumstances?' Glancing towards the witness box he met an extravagantly lascivious stare from Galway-Lamb and almost shuddered. He turned hastily to

Laurence Love, who agreed that he had only meant to suggest the eye became amorous at the sight of his client.

'Miss Galway-Lamb,' he continued. 'Each time you danced past the defendant, you exchanged badinage, did you not? Some jokes were initiated by you about his dancing?'

'I've told you, I don't remember exactly what was said.'

'No,' Mr. Love said, 'but you must have found his dancing rather memorable to make jokes about it. Did you think he was a good dancer?'

'Not particularly.'

'You wouldn't have given him ten out of ten, would you? In fact, you saw him being shown the steps by one of his previous partners. I understand you called out "Slow, slow, quick – quick, slow!" and that you were making fun of him having a lesson. Would it not be true to say he didn't seem to know any of the dance steps at all? In short, his ballroom dancing was atrocious?'

'Everybody seemed to want to dance with him.'

'Yes.' Mr. Love pounced. 'You wanted to dance with him yourself, didn't you? Why?'

'I thought it would be fun. We'd all been laughing together.'

'You liked the look of the defendant. You *fancied* him. Did you think he had been drinking?'

'I assumed so.'

'He is teetotal. What gave you the impression he had been drinking?'

She gave a rather affected sniff. 'His behaviour was so strange.'

'Strange, Miss Galway-Lamb? In what way? It wasn't that you had butted in and forced your attentions upon him, was it? Simpered at him and cajoled . . .'

'My Lord! *Please!*' protested Mr. Shyer, throwing up his hands again in despair, '*Simpered and cajoled* . . .'

'Yes, come along now, Mr. Love,' Shaky said, quite kindly.

'I apologise, M'lord,' replied the barrister, 'but if my client's behaviour seemed strange, I am suggesting to you that he was merely trying to be polite and make the best of an embarrassing situation because he did not want to dance with the plaintiff.'

'He did want to dance with me.'

'If he did want to dance with you, Miss Galway-Lamb, he didn't invite you to do so, did he? You asked him to dance, did you not?'

'Yes, what if I . . . ?'

'Thank you. No further questions.'

The Chinese girl was called next. She told the court she had assumed that Leonard Derbyshire was having some sort of fit and should not have been there at all if he wasn't responsible for his actions. Her evidence continued until lunchtime when the proceedings were adjourned until the afternoon.

In the Ladies, Joy overheard Tania Galway-Lamb, from inside one of the cubicles, talking cheerfully to the Chinese girl who was in the one next door.

'I think I'm doing all right, don't you? And you, my sweet girl, were phenomenal. I feel Judge Shakeshaft is sympathetic. I've been receiving some most disturbed looks from him. I get the feeling he's one of us. Uncle Conroy thinks the medical evidence is bound to settle it.' She pulled the chain, emerging to wash her hands and powder her nose.

Joy stayed in her cubicle and listened.

'Look at my bags! They've never been worse, have they? It's all this worry. I need a dash more lipstick, I think, to smile at the judge. Wait a minute, precious . . . just a teeny dab of deodorant on the wrists. There! I really think my hair has to be combed under to look its best for this ordeal. Now, let me give you a little squeeze.' Joy could hear exaggerated sounds of lip-smacking kisses. 'Oh, you little scamp. I do feel rampant,' said Tania, as they went out.

Joy rejoined Leo and they went to a pub to have some

lunch. Clive had already gone ahead to shop for food for supper for the three of them.

'It's going against me already, isn't it?' Leo said, with the utmost gloom. 'Her face is a mess, and I feel very sorry for her, but I could be paying off the damages for the rest of my life. All my *Chelsea Charlie* money will go. I wanted to keep it for Tom.'

Silently, Joy agreed with him. She was feeling very sorry for Leo. Out loud she spoke most positively to buoy him up. 'No, no, when you give your evidence, they'll soon see the proper picture. That judge is not a fool. Anyway, he must think Tania is a bit much. Just you be yourself. You don't drink. Tell that to Mr. Shyer. The whole thing is ridiculous, as you said. Is it likely he is going to make her a gigantic award when she pushed you into dancing in the first place? Come on, don't be silly. You've got to stress that. You were minding your own business but she'd got her eye on you all along. Look, she was sidling up and pestering you, grinning and joking, and all that, long before she butted in and got you to dance with her. Tell them. Tell that to Mr. Shyer in no uncertain terms. There was an accident because that gangling git couldn't leave you alone. Don't mince your words.'

'No,' said Leo.

They ordered their lunch and sat down with drinks while they waited. 'I wish I'd never gone near the Melstar Hotel,' he said bitterly, sucking in his treble pineapple juice in what Joy couldn't help feeling, despite the circumstances, was a needlessly neanderthal manner.

'Leo, what are those shoes?' she exclaimed suddenly, glimpsing some grossly battered relics he must have found in a secondhand shop. 'Good God.'

'Oxfam,' he replied proudly. 'I mended them myself.'

'Who the previous owner was doesn't bear thinking about. I hope you won't catch some dreadful disease.'

He smiled. 'They cost fifty p.'

'You were robbed.'

He sighed and yawned. 'My clothes became an issue with Ruth. One of the many. They embarrassed her, she said. She couldn't stand me going into charity shops and rummaging about for bargains.'

'When is Ruth coming?'

'She's not.'

'What d'you mean? She hasn't refused, has she?'

'I haven't asked her,' he said. 'Things are bad enough between us already. I don't want to make them more difficult because of Thomas. She'll only say I can't see him at all. You see, she won't want to take my side against her boss's godson, will she?'

'Well, wait till you tell the judge that Tania is really a man.'

'Joy, I can't get into that. How can I? It could even swing him against me . . . exposing that mutilated transsexual with her agonising dilemma. Ruth would say it was reprehensible. She's into all this politically correct business. I shouldn't be surprised if she had a hand in setting up this case against me. She does everything to do me down over my son.'

'Why let her get away with it? It's laughable.'

'I know. But at least I'm not in the bad financial situation I was. I shan't make less than a hundred and twenty thousand from *Chelsea Charlie* this year. If I start paying out a lot for Thomas, that gives me a lever with her.'

After lunch, the hearing resumed with a clash over the medical evidence. The issue was how much of Galway-Lamb's smiling had been produced by her Melstar Hotel injuries. Dr. Maurice Stone, for the plaintiff, made much of her pain and suffering and the permanent damage of her facial muscles caused by the defendant's display of demonic dancing. Only equal, he tried to assert, to being attacked by a fourteen stone animal or run over by the front wheel of a small trolley bus.

His opinion that such a condition was inoperable, Mr.

Love argued, was disputed in medical circles. Was it not true to say that tired muscles were known to respond in time to heat treatment and exercises? The smiling was no more, he suggested to Dr. Stone, than a minor exaggeration of an unusually forceful and exuberant personality with which she habitually got her way in the world. In short, she was taking the court for a ride.

Escorted by a solemn lady usher, an ex-waitress from the law courts canteen who took her duties very seriously, Leo was next into the witness box. He put on his one-sided spectacles to take the oath, then he coughed his dog cough three or four times with his mouth wide open.

'Are you Leonard Derbyshire of 42 Meecham Gardens, London West Two?' demanded Laurence Love.

'No,' said Leo.

Shaky smiled at him. 'I think you mean "yes", don't you, Mr. Derbyshire?'

'Yes.'

Mr. Love took him through his evidence without a further hitch.

Then Simon Shyer stood up.

'Mr. Derbyshire, you say you don't dance. You say you don't drink. Therefore, I am finding it rather hard to understand why you chose to go to a singles dance at the Melstar Hotel in Cromwell Road.'

'I didn't want to go. I was keeping a friend company.'

'As a bachelor, not in your first youth, if I may say so, you must surely have had a quite natural desire to make the acquaintance of some young lady?'

'None.'

'Curiouser and curiouser. We've heard how very popular you were that night with the ladies. Did you have many partners?'

'Two . . . oh well, three, counting Tania Galway-Lamb.'

'You invited them to dance even though you are asking us to believe you don't know how to dance?'

171

'I didn't ask them. They asked me. Miss Galway-Lamb got rid of the person I was dancing with and took over.'

'Yes, well, we only have your word for that, Mr. Derbyshire, don't we?'

'It's the truth.'

'Be that as it may . . .'

'No,' Leo said angrily. 'Several people saw what happened. Let's have the truth.'

The judge interrupted. 'Just a minute, please, Mr. Shyer.' He looked towards Leo. 'Mr. Derbyshire, do you remember the name of the lady with whom you were dancing when Miss Galway-Lamb . . . er, took you over, as you allege?'

'Yes,' Leo said, needled into recklessness. 'It was Ruth Bly.'

'In that case, Mr. Love,' Shaky raised his eyebrows companionably. 'I've no doubt we will be hearing from Mr. Derbyshire's previous dancing partner later on?'

Laurence Love half-stood, bowed respectfully and sat down. 'Get a subpoena on Bly,' he said to his solicitor out of the corner of his mouth.

From that moment on, from Leo's point of view, the case took on the aspect of a nightmare.

'Why did you snarl at the plaintiff, Mr. Derbyshire?'

'I didn't snarl at her.'

'Do you deny baring your teeth?'

'I was yawning.'

'But you were angry.'

'Bored.'

'You gave a warning, did you not?'

'I was merely telling her that I'm a narcoleptic.'

'Mr. Derbyshire,' the judge said. 'I think we will need to know your definition of a narcoleptic. Can you describe your condition to us?'

'I have short attacks of drowsiness. That's all there is to it.'

'Thank you. Please proceed.'

Mr. Shyer pressed on. 'Why did you feel it necessary to tell Miss Galway-Lamb that you were a narcoleptic?'

'I was apologising for the fact that I couldn't stop yawning.'

Mr. Shyer was unable to disguise his satisfaction. 'You were not afraid, perhaps,' he asked in a deadly voice, 'that you were about to doze off during the dance and slump senseless upon your partner?'

'Hardly. She's over six feet, I should think. In any case we kept bumping into each other.'

'Do you receive treatment for your narcolepsy, Mr. Derbyshire?'

'It's not necessary.'

'I see. So you don't consider it anti-social to wake up from a short attack on the dance floor to discover your partner unconscious and scarred for life. Thank you. No further questions.'

Leo left the witness box bemused with rage and knowing he had made a bad impression. He hadn't said what he meant to say and he'd missed the opportunity to express sympathy for Tania Galway-Lamb. He stood for a second, wondering where his seat was, the faces before him blurring into incomprehension and hostility. The lady usher waved him along, then stood back to let him pass.

As Leo moved, the sole of his fifty p. shoe came unstuck, and tripped him up. He appeared to dive at the usher. One hand tore the gown away from her ample bust. With the other he grasped her head. The court held its breath while they swayed together. Mercifully, they regained their balance.

'Well, done, Mrs. Turnbull,' Shaky congratulated the dishevelled woman. 'A narrow escape!'

'I was trying not to tread on her toe,' Leo explained apologetically.

A woman in the gallery started laughing like a hyena. Joy kept her head down and pressed a handkerchief against her mouth. She thought she'd never ever stop laughing herself.

*   *   *

The press turned up the next day. They must have had a tip-off that Len Derbyshire was well-known in the animation world or that it was a hilarious case, or both.

With the arrival of the press the atmosphere in the court changed. It became sharper, more stylish. Somehow the stakes grew higher.

Ignoring legal etiquette, Ruth Bly arrived with Sweetie and Marigold Belper, looking tense and upset. She refused to talk to Leo as everybody gathered together in the passage before the courtroom opened.

Tania Galway-Lamb, a bombshell in a silken blue trouser suit, made the most of the occasion. She whirled glamorously among the other waiting litigants and witnesses, calling greetings in a loud voice and laughing. 'A narcoleptic of all things, my darling!' she was gushing to someone. 'The swine's shot himself in the foot.'

Suddenly, to her embarrassment, Joy found herself face to face with Ruth. Babbling pleasantly, she said the first things that came into her head, anxious to smooth over the awkward situation and help Leo. Then Ruth introduced her to Conroy Sweeting who behaved as if he'd never heard her name before, so she was obliged to forget his cavalier treatment over the article in *Plain Speaking* and exchange small talk with him.

Clive got talking to Marigold Belper, being a fan of her early military despatches for the Daily Express. Misunderstanding his introductory words, she took him to be a new curator at the Imperial War Museum who was also called Pownall.

They sat next to each other in the public gallery swopping war anecdotes. 'Having fighting talk' was the way Clive put it, with one of his exuberant manly laughs.

'Bloody people making friends over my dead body' was the way Leo put it.

Ruth Bly gave her evidence dourly but honestly in reply to Mr. Love's questions. All she was called upon to do by the defence was admit that Tania Galway-Lamb had butted in during her dance with Leo and pushed her out of the way. This she did. Cross-examined by Mr. Shyer, it was a different matter. He made no attempt to conceal his glee.

'Miss Bly, I believe you also met Mr. Derbyshire for the first time on the night in question at the Melstar Hotel?'

'Yes.'

'It would be true to say, would it not, that neither you nor the plaintiff escaped the experience unmarked? One of the fruits of your friendship with him was a child, I understand, whom he has since abandoned?'

'M'lord!' Laurence Love pleaded. 'This is completely irrelevant.'

'It's not entirely true,' Ruth said.

Skilfully Simon Shyer manipulated the evidence against Leo, his voice rising and falling dramatically as he wheedled the damning responses out of Ruth.

'I think it has been crudely said, in the past, before the days of feminism, of course, that ladies could be categorised as madonnas or whores, present company excepted naturally. Correspondingly, we men in our relations with the fairer sex have been likened either to beggars or beasts. I'm asking you to tell us, Miss Bly, whether in your opinion Leonard Derbyshire is a beggar or whether, as I'm attempting to prove to the court, he is a *beast?*'

'My lord!' shouted Mr. Love. 'This is preposterous!'

'Yes, Mr. Shyer,' the judge agreed crossly. 'You are really quite out of order with this line of questioning. Please stick to the point.'

Ruth looked across the courtroom at Leo and her heart turned over. 'The point is,' she said bitterly, and her throat ached with sorrow, 'he is just not interested. He adores the child but he . . . he . . . d . . . doesn't . . .' Her voice faltered. She gulped and sniffed and wiped tears away with the back of her hand. 'Oh God, I'm sorry but I can't . . . c . . . ca . . . can't . . .'

'Take your time, Miss Bly,' Shaky said kindly. 'Would you like to sit down? You can have a rest, if you like.'

'Thank you,' she said. For reassurance she looked round and sought Sweetie's comforting face in the gallery but his head was down and he was writing busily.

A verse was coming.

> *She's not a madonna, that's certain*
> *She might be a whore, at the least*
> *I am hardly a beggar myself*
> *Is it true I'm a closet beast?*

It was Joy who saved Leo. When her turn came she took the oath and dropped her bombshell from a great height. She told the court that Tania Galway-lamb was a captain in the Life Guards.

It changed the course of the case.

In his summing up the judge, who was prejudiced, naturally, but anxious to disguise it, said that this made no difference to his view of the merits of the claim. 'But I am bound to say it does effect the credibility of the plaintiff to start the hearing as a female and end it as a male.

'I find as a fact that the defendant is a deplorable dancer, whether suffering from the effects of narcolepsy or not, and the plaintiff, taking reasonable care for his own safety, should have realised that dancing with Mr. Derbyshire was a far from straightfoward act. But, seduced and amused as he was, he carelessly intruded uninvited during a waltz at the Melstar Hotel and the fact that there was an accident does not immediately attract damages of any sort.

'If he sportively cavorts on the dance floor, he must take the consequences. He voluntarily takes the risk of injury as, say, a rugby player takes the risk of a broken nose or turning his ears to cauliflowers. This is known as the principle of *volenti non fit injuria* and in which case I must find judgment for the defendant,' Shaky said.

'Omigod,' Joy murmured as she and Leo exchanged stunned glances.

'Oh, Leo,' Ruth said in her heart, relieved that nothing worse had happened.

Next morning the newspaper headlines were as arresting as both parties feared.

SMILING BULLDYKE LOSES FACE TO "DEPLORABLE" DANCER

'Shit,' Leo said.

16

She Said

Statistics show that married men are happiest, single women are next, married women come third and bachelors are last. They don't live long apparently.

'Fun doll?'

'How are you?'

'Depressed. Ruth won't let me see Thomas.'

'What d'you mean?'

'I suppose it's her way of getting at me. Now he's at school, she doesn't need me any more as a babysitter. I used to have him with me every day when she went back to work.'

'But you have rights, surely? Haven't you got an arrangement about access?'

'She's always got an excuse why it's not convenient. He's going to a party. He isn't well. She's got to buy him new clothes. Well, I can buy clothes for him just as well as she can.'

'Ruth won't want that.'

'No, but everybody seems to get to see my son except me. It's never my turn. I really hate her. I wish she'd catch cancer so I could have him. I wish she'd get Aids.'

'You feel she's controlling everything?'

'She *is* controlling everything. Wanting control is natural for men, but women are meant to make the relationships. Why doesn't she do it? She's going out of her way not to make one with me.'

'Well, you know, she did try. You didn't want her.'

'I do want her. I've offered her marriage.'

'And what did she say?'

'She just brushes it aside as if it's some kind of wild fantasy of mine. The point is, once you start respecting a woman as a person, you can't get on with her as a woman. Anyway, she's a bitch. I'm writing a book now on why men hate women.'

'But married men are meant to be in the happiest state of anyone, I read the other day. Single women are the next most happy. Married women come third and bachelors come last. They're not meant to live long, apparently.'

'All I know is that bachelor fathers are treated abominably. There's no thought for him and no thought for the child. The mother vents her fury by manipulating the child and denying him access. Everybody suffers. I can't sleep. I've never been so churned-up in my life. I had to lie on the floor this morning to stop my heart pounding. I thought I was having a heart attack.'

17

He Said

*Men hate women who use the children against
them to gain their ends.*
*Men hate women who play provocative games
and then try to act as if they were not.*

*Chelsea Charlie was sitting in the middle of nowhere, sniffing the air
in case he could smell any steak and kidney pies . . .*

Leo stopped typing, stuck. He couldn't think of anything
else to say because he couldn't stop thinking about Ruth
and Thomas. He hadn't seen his son for three weeks because
she wouldn't let him. He'd written letters. He'd rung. She
wouldn't even let him speak to the child.

He got up and went to the kitchen. Jacob followed him and
sat waiting expectantly beside his bowl. Leo gave him a Tuna
Dinner. He had to drink a pint of milk and eat half a sponge
cake to steady himself down before he started to type again.
This time he went very fast.

*Men hate women who play provocative games and then try to act
as if they were not.*

*Men hate women who use the children against them to gain
their ends.*

Men hate women who blame them for their own unattractiveness.

*Men hate women who allow them to spend more money than they
can afford because they know they are being exploited. A woman who
shows concern about how much a man spends is actually thinking it
is her money he is spending.*

Men hate women who demand their time for trivial things.

Leo had been looking foward to the Summer Fair at

Thomas's school. He was counting on that event to put things right. Parents were asked to help so he had assumed that they would all be going together as a family.

'Oh, I can't get into all that, I'm afraid,' Ruth said at once, when he suggested it. 'I've got far too much to do here. In any case, I'm terribly behind with my column.'

He was immensely taken aback. 'That's a big disappointment. I'll take Thomas on my own, then. Shall I come and collect him in the morning?'

'Listen, Leo, I'm sorry. Tom can't go.'

'Why not?'

He heard Thomas shout. 'I can go!'

'Why can't he go?'

'He's got earache.'

As he put the phone down, he could hear Thomas crying in the distance, 'I haven't got earache . . . I haven't g . . . got earache. I wa . . . want to go with Daddy . . .'

He was glad he was alone. He'd never known such a feeling of frustration, helplessness and blind rage. If Ruth had been there at that moment, he would probably have killed her.

Instead, he sat down at his desk and wrote a letter to *The Guardian*.

Dear Sir,
Your article on divorced mothers who use their children as weapons against the father by refusing or disturbing access, exposes a growing problem in our society.

The children not only lose the security and experiences they might have with the father; they lose their heritage, and all that entails, from his side of the family. Boys have no role model to look to and emulate. Girls have little opportunity to become familiar with male attitudes, which in later life will be a severe handicap to them.

There is no shortage of evidence that children deliberately deprived of their father's company by the mother resent her in later life, quite often to the point of hate. It has been shown

*clearly in many studies that the mother in these cases is simply
using her custodial privilege as a form of power and control over
the father for personal reasons. This provokes unreasonable actions
by the father which are then used to show his unfitness to see his
children.*

*Perhaps the most disturbing aspect of the problem is that so
many of these mothers who abuse their position are professional
women who use their independence and knowledge of the system for
their own ends rather than putting their children's needs first.*
L. Derbyshire
42 Meecham Gardens
London W2A 4JT

When his letter was printed, and he'd posted a copy of it
off to Ruth, Leo felt better. In fact, much better. And with
another copy of it in his pocket, he turned up at the school
on the day of the fair because he felt he should give parental
support. He wanted to be seen helping so that they all knew
he was Thomas's father.

There were to be stalls, competitions and games. The
preparations were well under way by the time he arrived.
So many people seemed to be milling about in a disorganised
way, he didn't know whom to approach. He chose a youngish
man with fair curly hair and glasses who was carrying
chairs and calling out instructions to other people over his
shoulder.

'You're Thomas Bly's dad! You write *Chelsea Charlie*?
Thomas has told us all about you and we've got all your
books here.' He held out his hand. 'Nice to meet you. My
name's Jim Pierce. I teach the ten year olds mainly, but I
often see Thomas. He's a great favourite in the school.'

'You probably see more of him than I do.'

Jim Pierce smiled.

'Can I give you a hand with anything?'

'That's very kind of you. Well, let me think. You'd be just
the person to make us some big signs so that people know

what's going on where. I was about to do them myself, so that would be an enormous help.'

Leo and Jim Pierce chatted together while they worked on the signs, and at lunchtime they had a drink together in the pub across the road. The Summer Fair was opened in the afternoon and Leo helped Jim on the Aunt Sally stall by walking up and down behind a cricket net with a top hat on his head. The hat bobbed along just above the top of the net and competitors were given five hard little balls for ten pence to try and knock it off. Leo pulled faces and did funny walks and the children loved it. There was always a queue of them waiting to knock his hat off. As the afternoon wore on, and word went round that he was the author of *Chelsea Charlie*, he kept being asked to sign his autograph.

'Thomas not coming?' Jim asked. 'Is he here? I haven't seen him yet.'

Leo smiled wryly. 'I've got marital problems.'

Jim groaned sympathetically. 'Don't tell me. I'm into all that myself. Is that why we haven't seen you at the school? You have my sympathy. What's your situation?'

Leo told him, as the fair drew to a close, producing his letter to *The Guardian*.

'It must be even more difficult if you're not married,' Jim said. 'I'm having enough trouble myself as it is, and I really don't know how effective the Children Act will be. Seems to be making things worse in many cases. I haven't seen my two daughters for over a month because my wife's been staying in Basingstoke. She says she's going to get married again and take them to live in the States. We're in the middle of the most almighty legal brawl over the children through our solicitors. It costs a bomb and even more in emotional wear and tear. I tell you, Len, it keeps me awake at nights. I've joined a protest group called Families need Fathers.'

The two men's troubles drew them together. They were relieved to find each other because friends who had not experienced their situation soon got tired of listening to the long embittered tirades about the mothers of their children. They met again a few days later to have a drink and compare notes, and Jim invited Leo to come to the school and talk to the children about *Chelsea Charlie*.

His visit was a great success. He saw Thomas. He got on well with the children and Jim suggested he come again whenever he could manage it.

That gave Leo an idea. If he established a regular link with Thomas's school, it gave him a ready-made excuse to see his son as often as he wanted.

'I could teach the kids animation,' he offered.

Jim was immediately enthusiastic. 'Brilliant,' he said. 'They have so little, many of them, in their lives. But I don't think we could pay you anything, I'm afraid, Len. We can't keep within our budget as it is.'

'I don't want paying,' Leo assured him. 'I'd like to come. I enjoy it.'

So he started going regularly to Thomas's school. As soon as they heard what was going on, the other teachers invited Leo into their classrooms. He gave up half a day each week to teach the children, but it was worth it. He always saw Thomas for a few minutes on these occasions.

Leo was a natural teacher and he enjoyed being a part of the educational world. He felt quite proud of himself when he told people he was teaching. He had his own unorthodox methods to keep the children interested and he had already started to print a simple book on animation with instructions and illustrations. At first he had to deal with the children's attempts to get the measure of him.

'You don't have to be good at drawing,' he'd assured Jim's class of ten year olds. 'Anybody can animate. You only have to learn a few basic rules on how shapes can change and move. You make up your own exercises.

'Now, let's start with a caterpillar. I want you all to draw two long sausages. First do a sausage stretched out and then do a sausage behind it, hunched up. See, like this.'

A big girl called Giselle, with red-gold hair and insolent eyes, did her drawing rapidly and then ran up to him. 'Is this right?'

Leo was taken aback. She'd drawn a penis.

He dismissed it off-handedly. 'That's not a proper sausage.' He got up from his desk and started moving round the room to look at all the other sausage drawings. He could hear stifled giggles as Giselle's penis was passed round.

'D'you think Giselle's a virgin, sir?'

'Quiet, please,' he said.

'Mr. Derbyshire!'

'Mr. Dar . . . bee . . . sheere!'

Hands went up and papers were waved wildly in the air. 'Can you look at my sausages, please?' Others got tired of waiting and clustered round Leo, making a noise.

'Giselle's a slag!' shouted a boy with a high squeaky voice, seizing her drawing and making off round the room.

'Shut up, dog breath!' she shrieked, clouting him. 'I'm not a slag, am I, Mr. Derbyshire?'

'Well, you won't get on very well as an animator if you can't do what's wanted.' Helpless to silence them, he simply got on with the job. When he showed the children how to make their caterpillars move, he got them interested and they started to concentrate.

With the little ones he taught the alphabet in pictures rather than sounds.

A is a witch's hat
B is a butterfly's wing
C is the handle of a cup
D is an ear or a cup on its side

'I need to have them early,' he explained earnestly to Jim Pierce. 'Once they're past twelve, they're too old for me.'

The only teacher who hadn't approached him was Mrs. Prescott, a beefy dominant woman who taught Thomas's age group and took Brownies. He happened to meet her in the staff room, dressed as Brown Owl, and offered to do a regular animation stint in her class. She refused at once.

'I'm sorry, Mr. Derbyshire, no. His mother has informed me that she does not wish you to attempt to see Thomas during school hours.' He could tell from her determined, aggressive demeanor that Ruth had already managed to poison this awful woman against him. Whenever he bumped into Ruth at the school, she studiedly ignored him. She wouldn't speak.

'Couldn't you come home and marry Mummy again?' Thomas asked sadly, 'I wish you and Mummy would talk to each other.'

Leo wished it too. What he found embarrassing, and tremendously upsetting, was when she arranged for another mother to collect Thomas from school. Often the mother would see Leo and call out to him. 'Oh, hallo, I didn't know you'd be here today. Thomas will be going home with you then?' He had to say that no, he wouldn't be taking him. Then, beside himself with bitterness and frustration, he'd have to watch his own child go off with a stranger because he didn't dare to alienate Ruth any further.

She used him, he knew, only when she was desperate. If she had to be away, or had things to do, he might be given Thomas to look after for a night, sometimes a few rare precious days. Things usually went along quite amicably after that for a little while until suddenly she got annoyed because the child was late back, or missing some piece of clothing, or was sick.

'You realise, don't you, that a social worker would remove a child from the conditions in your flat?'

'Why? If he's well-fed and happy, what's wrong?'

'It's disgusting. It's unhygenic. And it means your life is out of control.'

He'd look at the strewn clothes and discarded papers, wondering how he could live in such a state and then he'd forget about it again until he received another of her curt contemptuous little notes barring him from seeing Thomas in the foreseeable future. He retaliated with more letters to newspapers about fathers' rights which he sent to her. These letters seemed to have an effect. He wasn't sure why. They frightened her.

Fathers have rights, too

Dear Sir,

Studies show that children of divorced or separated parents (often unmarried) suffer emotionally, financially, socially and educationally. The case for non-custodial fathers having more involvement with their children is accepted by everyone with the exception of a few: those mothers who see their children as a means of retribution towards the fathers. Such mothers refuse or deliberately disrupt access to the children: often refusing even to allow fathers to phone, write, or give gifts to their children.

The law has recognised this problem with the recent Children Act which enables more fathers to gain access and even custody of their children, but perhaps the better solution will be the system finding favour in the US of parents being given joint custody, and children dividing their time between both parents, where practical.

Such a system is not so dependent upon the law, but upon better trained welfare officers who can evaluate the situations more in terms of the children's needs rather than taking the easy option of giving one parent the custody and letting the other parent work it out as best they can.

Len Derbyshire,
Meecham Gardens,
London W.2.

Next time he called at her flat with something for Thomas Ruth handed him an envelope round the front door without a word.

Dear Leo,

Your letter about access seems to me to be most unfair. It is not that I deliberately deny you access to Thomas. I thought we had a satisfactory system worked out with you seeing him on a Sunday every other weekend. Spontaneous unplanned meetings do not seem to work.

As you are not near, it would be pointless for you to collect him from school during the week. If I can't get there myself, I can arrange for another mother (a neighbour) to take him home until I can collect him. Any other arrangement simply leads to unnecessary confusion and it is essential in the circumstances for him to have a sensible structure to his life. Your oppressive behaviour towards him, and hysterical behaviour towards me, always leave him in a disturbed state. He understands that we do not get on together and this naturally upsets him. We should do everything we can to keep his life as settled and tranquil as possible. If Thomas is invited to a party on one of your access days, that is not my fault and I cannot compensate for it. You surely don't expect me to refuse invitations, on your behalf, from his friends?
Best wishes,
Ruth.

But things were better after that. He did see more of Thomas and he felt much happier. Leo lived for the child. Having him, he admitted, had made him become completely responsible for another human being for the first time in his life.

'I think I'm getting on better terms with Ruth,' he said to Jim. 'What I'd really like now is for us to do things together sometimes as a family. It would be nice for Thomas if we went for walks, or something, or went out for a hamburger occasionally. Do you think I should send Ruth some flowers?'

'I don't know, Len,' Jim answered, a bit doubtfully. 'Wouldn't she see that as a ruse?'

'Yes, is the answer to that. She loathes everything I try to do for her. I was thinking . . . it's Valentine's Day in a fortnight. Should I send her a valentine?'

Jim nodded. 'All women love valentines.'

Leo rang Joy and put it to her. She was equally enthusiastic.

'Oh, yes, that is a good idea,' she said.

'Good. I'll go out and buy one and get it over there.'

'Leo, not yet. Good Lord. Wait till the right time, for heaven's sake, and post it for Valentine's Day.'

'Yes.'

'And I think you'd better be very careful about the card and the wording. What I mean is don't go and get her some huge red thing with ribbons and a bleeding heart and a soppy message, or you'll put her back up. The words will have to be slightly humorous and touching, then I don't think you can go wrong. She should be very pleased with that. A valentine can hardly fail.'

'No, it can't fail,' he agreed. 'I can look after cats and flowers and make them blossom. I ought to be able to do it with ladies.' He laughed happily. 'You've got to take care of them.'

After he'd posted off the valentine card, Thomas's visits were suddenly cancelled without any explanation whatsoever. Leo was terribly worried.

Jim was amazed. 'She must be a strange woman. Is she at all lesbotic, Len? It seems very common these days.'

'That was a very bad idea indeed,' he said accusingly to Joy. 'She's obviously taken it in the wrong way.'

'I can't credit it,' she replied.

'It's made my situation much worse.'

'What did the card say on it?'

'Oh, they all say the same, valentine cards. I didn't really examine it. On the outside it said something like "Let's get more familiar", and inside it said "May I call you Val?"'

There was a strangled sound at the other end of the phone. Joy couldn't speak for laughing. 'Leo, how could you?' she said at last. 'May I call you Val? No wonder she's not speaking!'

Leo was too shattered to be amused. 'I'll just have to think of new ways of doing her down,' he answered grimly.

Men hate women because women curtail men's lives rather than extend them. What is more, women expect men to extend their lives for them. This impossible task is dealt with by men avoiding women a large part of the time. It shows in going to the pub: late nights at the office; various hobbies and interests that exclude women. The luckier men have jobs that take them out of the house regularly for extended periods.

Men don't believe that women "fall in love". They belive that women want to be in love, and like the state of falling in love, and to that extent they prime themselves for the situation rather like a professional boxer keeps in training without knowing who his opponent is going to be. It doesn't really matter.

Most men don't fall in love. They have infatuations when young, and often obsessions about women. Whatever their fantasies, in most cases the bother of chasing girls, the cost of entertaining them, and the problem of getting rid of them, soon becomes too much. If they find a girl who can satisfy their sexual needs and is easy to get on with, then they will settle for that. It helps if she is already pregnant.

'Where do I go wrong with ladies?' Leo asked Joy. 'What do you think they want from men?'

Joy thought about it. 'What everybody wants is response, isn't it? I think you've got to chat them up a bit, be interested. You've got to have the man-woman love exchanges. They like teasing and all that stuff.'

'I'd like to find a young woman to have another baby with me. I've been wondering whether I ought to go back to the Melstar Hotel to meet somebody else?'

Joy laughed. 'The dancing could prove costly. You might meet Tania Galway-Lamb.'

'Yes, that's all I need. Actually, I've been in touch recently with a girl I used to know years ago. She married a barrister but she's divorced now and lives in Stevenage. She's got two children about Thomas's age.'

'Oh good.'

'We didn't really get on before because she always seemed to have so many problems. Anyway, I asked her to come to a dinner party with me a few weeks ago. She arrived about two hours late because her car had broken down and it cost me thirty quid to send her home in a taxi. I haven't rung her again. I can't cope with all her problems on top of my own with Ruth.'

Leo's next move to do Ruth down, and reach his son, was to start inviting groups of children from the school to come and play games on the computers in his sitting room.

Thomas's teacher, Mrs. Prescott, did her best to stop it because she had heard so much to Leo's detriment from his mother. She was already convinced of his raging eccentricity but the parents were only too pleased to give their permission. They all knew Leo from the school, from their children's enthusiastic descriptions of the animation classes, and from his *Chelsea Charlie* supermarket books and the cartoons on television. At first they brought the children themselves, and came to see exactly what was going on, then they happily left Leo to it. It kept the kids out of trouble. Thomas wasn't going to be left out. Ruth was forced to give way and let him join in.

However Thomas had mixed feelings about it. He wasn't used to anybody else sharing the silly games he played with his father and all their private jokes. He was jealous.

'They take you away from me,' he complained to Leo. 'I certainly wouldn't like any brothers and sisters being a nuisance to us, would you, dad?'

They had just been watching a sword fight together in an old television film. Leo rolled up two newspapers and handed one to Thomas. 'Here's your sword.'

They fought like mad things, shouting, jumping and thrusting. Paper shredded all over the room.

'Now we'll have a sword fight on one leg,' Leo announced.

Thomas started hopping. 'Ooh yes, on one leg!' he echoed breathlessly. 'Come on, on one leg, you said.'

'Here's your shield.' Leo handed him a little badge saying *Thank you for not smoking!* 'I'll get mine.' He reappeared with the lid of the wastebin. 'Let's measure shields.'

Thomas couldn't stop laughing. 'Yours is much bigger,' he protested. 'I can hardly see mine.'

'Ah, yes, but I've got more to cover up. Right. Are we ready? Oh, just a minute . . . have you seen my box of tickles?'

Thomas pretended to search. 'No, I can't see a box of tickles.'

'There's a tickle under your arm . . . quick!' Leo tickled him until he was yelping with delight. 'Look, I'm tickling the air. Don't move over here!'

Thomas immediately dived at the air with his arms out to catch the tickle. 'I've got it! Where's the tickle box?'

The telephone rang. It was Ruth. 'Where are you?' she demanded. 'You're late.'

Alarmed, Leo glanced at his watch. He should have had Thomas back to Ruth three quarters of an hour before.

'Sorry, Ruth. We were just watching the end of a film. Here's Thomas to have a word. We're coming right now.'

'She's very cross,' Thomas whispered, sobering up.

'Well, it's all right. No harm done. It might be an idea if we stopped to buy Mummy a box of chocolates. What d'you think?'

The little boy considered it. 'I know the best thing to do, Leo,' he said wisely. 'You buy the chocolates and I'll give them to her with a message saying you are very sorry.'

The wisdom of children never ceased to amaze Leo. There was his son, with the situation between his parents completely summed up, learning how to manage them. The children at the school, many of them academically backward, were often a horrifying mixture of pitiful worldliness and raw naivety.

CONSEQUENCES

One afternoon, the worldliness of one of them landed Leo in serious trouble.

He was late at the school, still packing up his equipment and tidying up. He thought all the children had gone home. Outside the window Mrs. Prescott, in her Brown Owl outfit, was leading the Brownies in a song. Her strong raucous voice almost drowned the piping voices of the children. She was miming to the words with her big vigorous arms.

> *She sailed away*
> *On a sunny summer's day*
> *On the back of a crocodile.*
> *'You see,' said she*
> *'He's tame as tame can be',*
> *As they floated down the Nile.*
> *The croc winked his eye*
> *While she waved her friends goodbye*
> *Wearing a sunny smile.*
> *At the end of the ride*
> *The lady was inside*
> *And the smile on the croco's dial!*

Engrossed in making some notes for his next week's class, Leo didn't hear Giselle coming into the room. He'd always kept a wary eye on her since his first day when she'd drawn the penis. He could see she had great potential as a trouble maker.

This time she had an inflated condom on her head. She placed a note marked PRIVET on Leo's desk and stood there waiting for him to see it. When he took no notice, she picked it up again and plonked it onto the page where he was writing. He looked up. Giselle's face was half-masked. The condom was stretched under her nose and the red-gold hair stuck out.

'I don't talk to terrorists,' he said pleasantly and went on working.

When she'd gone, he picked up her note.

Dear Mr. Derbysher,
  Please meet me in privet in yellow room in five minutes please.
All my love
*Giselle*XXX

What did she want? He smiled to himself. Five minutes with Giselle Eden in the Yellow Room could get a chap five years. When he'd finished, he gathered up his things and went along to check that she'd gone home. There was no one in the Yellow Room. He didn't notice the condom lying on the floor. With his arms full, he managed to pull the door to with his foot but he forgot to turn the light off. Giselle's note fluttered away as he strode off.

Shortly afterwards, while parents were arriving outside and collecting Brownies, Mrs. Prescott noticed the light in the Yellow Room and was on her way to switch it off when the telephone rang. It was Giselle's mother wondering where her daughter was. She hadn't arrived home at the usual time.

Mrs. Prescott and her mother compared notes. Mrs. Eden said she would ring round Giselle's friends. Her daughter was sure to have gone home with one of them and forgotten to let her know where she was. Mrs. Prescott waited until she rang back. Nobody knew where Giselle was.

Brown Owl, who knew Giselle's reputation in the school, felt more alarmed than her mother did. It was in a most anxious frame of mind that she finally went into the Yellow Room to switch off the light. There she found Giselle's note, and then the condom lying on the floor and naturally, putting together what she knew of the girl's behaviour and Len Derbyshire's madness, she feared the worst had happened. She called the police.

Leo was exhausted after his afternoon with the children, but he was trying to do a bit of work on a new *Chelsea Charlie* story in a desultory way.

Leaving five Chelsea footballers standing helplessly, the little black and white terrier raced round the pitch on an opening lap of aerial juggling and close nose control.

'There he goes . . . *Chelsea Charlie!'* said the commentator. 'Very much at home in celebrity soccer! Right winger Kevin Graves chases after him. This game may be won on penalties but my money's on the dog. This dog is magic. Come on Kevin . . . oh, bravo! Graves has got the ball now!

'Passes to Mike Stainton. Stainton to centre forward Geoff Anderson. Dazzling footwork from Geoff but Charlie's in there tackling. Oh Stainton's down . . . my goodness, Charlie's got him!'

Leo got up and stretched. He went into the kitchen. Jacob followed him in and sat beside his bowl waiting for his fifth meal. Leo put some catfood out for him, then he finished off the remains of a cheesecake with a carton of toffee icecream, before he sat down to work again. He couldn't concentrate on *Charlie*. Instead, he sat thinking. When his thoughts flickered onto Giselle and her note, he searched for it but it wasn't there.

Because women are attracted to powerful men, men have to present themselves as powerfully as possible. If a man has not got the ability to do this, and a woman takes a scornful attitude towards him, his response will be in some form of physical or mental hate. In some cases it works, and a woman will accept this form of power, a possible explanation why some women put up with such terrible men and even love them.

Men hate women because they use the excuse of morality to justify their anger with men.

The moral stand that women take undermines their own position. It is fine to say that men should not desire young girls (or boys), but the fact is, most normal men desire any attractive girl. If she happens to be fourteen instead of sixteen, his instinct doesn't change, only his sense of survival. It means that some men who cannot control their instincts get themselves into trouble with young girls. There is no way such men could ever get help because women would not allow a man to confess to such an instinct. Hence the widespread child abuse that has come to light. It shocks most women, but it is understood by most men (not the same as accepted by most men).

After a time he felt an overwhelming attack of narcolepsy coming on. He started locking up. He locked the front door in three places, locked a wire mesh barrier at the top of the stairs leading into his flat, locked his sitting room to protect the computers and left the all-night jazz playing on the wireless. Then he went up to bed. The last burglary, which happened while he slept, had cost him a microwave, a video and his two best computers, and there had been considerable damage. Since then he'd had a mania for locks. A light went on if anyone approached the rather dark and concealed entrance and outside the kitchen window there was a muted red glow like the sign of a brothel. He lay down on the bed and fell asleep.

When the door bell rang he didn't wake at first. The persistent ringing wove its way into his dream. Jacob woke him by scrambling off the bed and under it.

Leo's keys slipped out of his pocket into a mound of scattered clothes as he stumbled out of bed, still half-asleep. In case thieves were already inside, he put Thomas's tank helmet on his head and snatched up a steel rod from an old bicycle as he came into the hall. He felt in his pocket for his keys to open the mesh barrier but they weren't there. Above the beat of jazz in the sitting room, he could a man's voice outside shouting: 'Mr. Prescott! *Mr. Prescott!* Open the door please.' The bell went again.

On the doorstep were two police officers (male and female), who had been goaded into action by Mrs. Prescott. In the hysterical confusion surrounding Giselle Eden's disappearance, Constable Goodall now seized upon Prescott as the name of her abductor.

'Mr. Prescott! We know you're in there. Can we have a word with you, please?'

Leo had had a lot of aggravation from people trying to trace the previous owner of his flat, who had diddled the Social Security and left a number of debts. Greatly angered, and with no sense of what time it was, he assumed some creditors had chosen to call in the middle of the night.

'Go away!' he shouted.

Constable Goodall hammered on the door.

'Mr. Prescott's gone,' Leo roared. '*He is not here!* I don't know where he is, so bugger off!'

'We'd like to ask you a few questions.' The policeman rattled the letter box. 'We don't want to have to force an entry.'

Thinking it must be thugs, Leo bawled his reply and clanged the steel bar several times on the metal surrounding the wire barrier. 'I'm ready for you! I've called the police.'

'We are the police.'

Constable Goodall lay down on the cement outside Leo's front door and put his arm through the cat flap to show his identity card. Then his face appeared in the hole. He stared up the stairs to where he could see a dimly lit figure in a tin helmet, standing behind wire and brandishing an extremely offensive weapon. He could hear a sinister thud of drums.

'Here I am, Mr. Prescott,' he said pleasantly, hoping to humour him.

'I am not Mr. Prescott,' Leo replied. 'Because I am Mr. Derbyshire.'

'Can you open the door for me?'

'I'm locked in,' Leo said. 'I've lost my keys.'

The face withdrew. There were murmurings, then silence. A few minutes later, the police car drove away. Leo went back to his bedroom, found his keys and put them in his trouser pocket. This time he undressed before he lay down.

Soon afterwards he woke again to hear his front door splintering.

'Jesus God Almighty!' he shouted, seizing his trousers.

He stood at the top of the stairs, bare to the waist, as police rushed in. In their wake he glimpsed a po-faced Brown Owl, some strange blonde woman and Ruth.

God damn and blast her to hell!

'I don't know what you want,' Leo greeted them, his dark eyes glittering with rage, 'but you'd better all explain yourselves mighty quickly. I'm going to sue you for illegal entry.'

Two policemen remained at the front door. 'Where is Giselle Eden?' Constable Goodall demanded, speaking above the thumping music in the sitting room.

'Who?'

'*Giselle*!' screamed the blonde woman, as if she expected to hear an answering cry.

'I think you know who Giselle is,' the constable said. 'You were with her earlier. Where is she?'

'Well, she's not here, is she?' Leo replied angrily. 'It's got nothing to do with me. Mr. Prescott's the guy you want.'

Mrs. Prescott gave an incredulous snort.

'This is Giselle's mum,' explained Constable Goodall, indicating the blonde woman and already beginning to wonder if some mistake had been made. 'She's been out of her mind with worry because Giselle didn't come home from school today at the usual time. We presume you saw her, or know something about her whereabouts, because a note from her to you was found and her teacher here had noticed you were working late. I understand you sometimes invite some of the children to use your computers.'

With a thrill of horror it dawned on Leo who Giselle was. A terrible scenario flashed before him. 'I don't know anything,' he said, remembering the condom on the little minx's head. He unlocked the sitting room door and switched off the wireless.

Her mother's fact contorted with distress. 'Tell me where she is,' she pleaded tearfully. 'Please just tell . . .'

'I'm sorry. I've no idea.'

Mrs. Prescott eyed his bare chest with suspicion and

loathing, her mouth like a pig's bottom, 'You . . . you skunk.'

Leo looked helplessly from the mother to Brown Owl to Ruth. As their eyes met, he suddenly had the illogical feeling that she had come with them to try and protect him as the cards began to stack against him in a hideous dossier of incriminating evidence.

Constable Goodall spoke again. 'I presume you won't have any objections, sir, if we take a look round – I've got a warrant by the way – and then I'd like to ask you some questions in private. It may help us build up a picture of her movements in the past few hours.'

'Certainly, I'll answer any questions you like but I keep on telling you I can't help you. I took no notice of her note, naturally. She was hanging about after the other children had gone but I checked that she wasn't waiting for me in the Yellow Room, and then I went home myself. Is this the usual way the police behave . . . breaking into the homes of members of the public in order to talk to them?'

The constable looked uncomfortable. 'You did say you were locked in, Mr. Derbyshire,' he reminded him severely, 'if you remember?'

'Yes. Nonetheless, I'll want compensating,' Leo retorted grimly. 'Well, go ahead, look where you like. I'll take you upstairs.' He turned back to the three women. 'Have you rung everybody you can think of? There's my telephone. Why not try again now and see if she's come home yet. Keep trying everybody.'

'Yes, why don't you ring home again?' Ruth agreed.

With a hopeless sigh, Mrs. Eden tried the number. 'It's engaged.'

They sat waiting in tense silence. It gave Ruth a weird sensation of surreal homesickness to be back in Leo's flat in these bizarre circumstances with the familiar mess of scattered papers and all Thomas's toys and books lying about. As Giselle's mother dialled again, she got up and wandered over to his desk. Curiously, she picked up a sheet of paper beside the computer to see what he was working on.

Some words caught her eye, her stomach lurched and she read on.

'. . . *It is fine to say that men should not desire young girls, (or boys), but the fact is, most normal men desire any attractive girl. If she happens to be fourteen instead of sixteen, his instinct doesn't change, only his sense of survival. It means . . .*'

She stuffed it quickly into her pocket as Giselle's mother gave a cry. 'She's home! Oh, thank God. Yes . . . yes . . . such a stupid thing to do . . . yes, was she . . . playing Monopoly? You tell her from me she's a really naughty girl and we've been worried stiff. Yes, all right. I'm coming now.'

She beamed at the others, shaking visibly now her daughter was safe. 'Can you beat that? She went to one of her school friends whose parents are away. I never thought of them, you know. I don't know why. Only the brother was at home and they've been playing Monopoly and she forgot all about the time. I'm so cross with Giselle. Her father says she's just walked in as if nothing had happened.'

Ruth smiled. 'What a relief.'

Brown Owl retained her trap door mouth. 'Yes,' she said, looking almost disappointed. She would have adored Leo to be arrested.

When they'd gone he went into the kitchen and made himself a cup of tea and some toast. He took his tray back into the sitting room and sat with it on his knee, staring into space, too shattered to make the necessary movements to eat and drink.

He felt weak from his narrow escape. What if Giselle had never been found? He wouldn't have stood a chance against the police and Mrs. Prescott. Would Ruth have stood up for him then?

She hadn't said a word. She'd come and gone and they had not spoken to each other. How could they go on damaging themselves like this and letting Thomas get caught in the middle. Perhaps he should try to give up the child, cut off and forget about him? He could make a fresh start with some new woman who was prepared to have a baby for him.

He took a sip of his tea and slopped some of it onto the tray, which showed a tranquil Cornish scene entitled *Polperro Sunset*. Why wasn't life ever like a Polperro sunset? Joy's husband Roly had made this raffia tray while he was in a loony bin having a breakdown. He'd seemed tough but Joy was tougher. Women were.

To have a place in society men have to earn their position. They have to gain respect by being brighter, stronger, or in some way more able than the next man. It starts at school, and as boys they soon discover their ranking.

Civilisation is largely a monument to men's sexual frustration. Great art is usually diverted passion. Women recognise this and make the mistake of thinking that great artists are passionate lovers.

Women are never going to change men. Any woman who thinks his love for her will change him is a fool. Men and women live in totally different worlds and will always do so. A bond far stronger than love is a common purpose. When there is no obvious objective in a relationship, the couple will start splitting up because love never solved anything. It is too consuming and too impractical to be applied beyond serving nature's purpose. Nature is not concerned with happiness but simply with the survival of the species. You can't rely on someone else coming along to make you happy. No one will.

18

She Said

He thinks he's God which makes rational
planning impossible. These delusions of grandeur
prevent him from operating on everybody else's
level. How can he look after children when he
can't look after himself?

'Did you see that woman ranting on about me in *The Guardian*
today? D'you know, fun doll, she's trying to make out I don't
know what I'm talking about?'

'What are you talking about?'

'I've written an article complaining about the heroines in
children's fiction.'

'You told me you never read any stories with Thomas.'

'No, I don't see much of that stuff myself because he and
I concentrate more on visual images, but I had a few points
to make about current female attitudes.

'By the way, my teaching is going from strength to strength.
I'm setting up a huge project with the council for handicapped
children. I've done three articles about my work and I'm gong
on television soon with a party of children from Thomas's
school to demonstrate what we're doing. *Chelsea Charlie* is
going into computer games now and onto laser discs. Kids
will be able to play football with him on the screen. They'll
be able to make up their own cartoons and colour them.'

'Leo, how marvellous! What a triumph you're being.'

'Didn't you think I would be? Yes, well, things are going
well, for me at the moment, apart from my difficulties with
Ruth. She's moving Thomas to another school.'

'So you won't have access to him?'

'Oh, I'll be teaching there soon. I've already written to the head.'

'You must drive Ruth absolutely bonkers.'

'That's the idea, but I think she is mad. I suggested we went together as a family for counselling and she's compiled a long diatribe about me which she's sending out all over the place. It's all in columns with headings. I'll read you a bit. Well, *Mental Deterioration* is the head of one column. *Unawareness. Poor memory. Can never remember what arrangements have been agreed.* Blah blah. *Confused. Unaware that Thomas is becoming more and more independent.* Another heading – *Grandiose Ideas. These delusions of grandeur often prevent him from operating on everybody else's level. He plans a secret system of computing for all Haringey schools. Has formal acknowledgement from Prime Minister which he shows to everyone. I find this disturbing.* Blah blah blah. *Battle of Power. Seems to thrive on conflict. Has no concept of reality. Thinks he's God which makes rational planning impossible. How can he look after children when he can't look after himself?* D'you think Ruth's in love with me?'

'I suppose she could be moving in a mysterious way.'

'Not as mysterious as my way. I'm going to take her to court. I've nearly finished my book on why men hate women, but I'll probably have to use a pseudonym. I must be very careful to preserve my saintly avuncular image as the author of *Chelsea Charlie*.'

19

He Said

'I don't know why you flew off the handle. I was afraid you'd take it the wrong way.

When *Why Men Hate Women* by Herrick D. Johnson was published, it created a stir. Everybody was reading it. Ruth Bly reviewed it in *Plain Speaking*. "Outrageously sexist," she wrote, "fizzing with prejudices. I yelped with rage when I wasn't howling with laughter."

'Roo, who is this woman-hater, Herrick D. Johnson?' Sweetie asked.

'I've no idea.'

'It's a very bad sign, I've always found, when someone puts an initial in the middle of their signature. Mail order con men do it, and the lower classes and Americans. Is he a Yank? I don't think I can read it, really, do you? I expect it's for hairdressers. Arnold Pope's been on to me about it. He wants to get in touch with Herrick Johnson to present the prizes at a charity fancy dress he's organising in the country.'

'Are you and Marigold going?'

'Ohh.' Sweetie made an appalled sound and rolled his eyes to heaven. 'Wild horses wouldn't get me to it. Marigold wants to go, of course. She wants to make up a party with my godson. Fancy dress ... good grief, we don't want to encourage any of that where Tony's concerned.' He laughed at the outlandishness of the prospect. 'What is Arnold thinking of?'

At that very moment Arnold Pope rang.

'Arnold, sorry, we're none the wiser here. We don't know

this Johnson chap so we can't help. I should write to him care of the publisher. They'll forward your invitation, I should have thought.'

'You'll be coming to my party with Marigold, I hope?' Arnold asked.

'Well, no, Arnold, thanks very much. Fancy dress . . . er, not quite my line. Got a lot on my plate at the moment.'

'Marigold said you'd be coming.'

'Did she . . . mm. 'Fraid not.'

'I hope you'll be able to make time for some swims with all your commitments,' Arnold observed smoothly. 'I've looked over the wall into your lovely garden. I didn't know you'd built a luxurious pool. You've been keeping very quiet about it! Must have taken a few buckets to fill that up with our present water ban. *Plain Speaking* keeps telling us how wicked it is to use our hose pipes.'

Sweetie jolted in his seat. 'No, well . . . yah, we did think it might be an idea to have a little pool.'

'Super,' Arnold agreed enthusiastically. 'Do the locals know yet? They'll be queueing up with their cozzies when they do.'

Sweetie ran his hand through his delectable white hair. 'Actually Arnold we'd rather decided that it might be better to try and keep its existence to ourselves.'

'Very wise of you. The last thing you want is the hoi polloi all over the garden when you're trying to have a Sunday afternoon snooze in the sun. D'you mind if I pop over occasionally? My swims don't take long. I'm in and out. Then we could have a dram and chew over one or two ideas.'

'En principe, Arnold. Let me ring . . .'

'I'm surprised you got planning permission, to tell you the truth,' Arnold Pope went on. 'It's so difficult to get anything new through in our little villages. And you've been so vigilant yourself, I gather, opposing extensions and so forth, and the proposed sports centre. I would have thought you might have

HELEN MUIR

met with a bit of opposition from some quarters . . . sour grapes, I mean?'

Cornered, Sweetie decided to brazen it out. While he spoke, he shook his fist. 'Why should I need planning permission to build a small pool in my own garden?'

Arnold pounced. 'Phew . . . that's a bit reckless, old chap. You'll have to keep it dark, that's my advice to you. I can see why you didn't hold the church fête this year. No, no, worry not. I won't breathe a word. I won't come prancing up your path in my bathing trunks.'

'Thanks. I'd be grateful if . . .'

'And Dodo and I still hope to see you at our fancy dress. Can I count on you for a few tickets? It's a good cause. Aids. They're a hundred quid each. Say four?'

'Four,' Sweetie said meekly. 'Well, that's it then,' he added in a different voice as he put the phone down. 'I'll have to move house.'

Joy was sitting in the sports shop with her feet up on the desk reading *Why Men Hate Women*. Even the depressing revelations in Leo's book about couples' rising expectations of marital happiness in theory, but worsening prospects of it in fact, failed to dampen her mood of general satisfaction.

She had just spoken to the court, arranging payment to another supplier who had sued the shop, and heard there were apparently no further debts outstanding for the time being. This meant she could relax without having to watch the windows for bailiffs and whisking to the door before they could get in and start seizing all the stock.

She had just got her writing out when Clive rang. She could tell it was a portentous call because it was unexpected. He sounded hesitant and a bit distant. He wanted to see her later, he said, because he'd been thinking about something rather important concerning them. He thought they ought to progress to the next stage in their relationship. They were only marking time if they went on as they were.

206

'What d'you mean?' Joy said.

'I'll tell you later,' he replied, his voice full of promise.

Usually Joy felt it was a matter of honour not to make gossipy phone calls from the failing shop but the temptation became too much. She couldn't work and she couldn't read. She put her book aside and rang Jill.

'I had to tell you,' she said, with a little squeak of mirth. 'I think Clive's going to ask me to marry him!'

'No!'

'I *think* so. I don't see what else it could be. He's sounding extremely serious and we're meeting on one of the non-meeting days. He never does that.'

'Well, could you?'

'Mm . . . on my terms . . . um well I nearly could. I mean we've gone along very peaceably for a long time. It's a habit and there's a lot to be said for that. I suppose we could define our rules quite clearly. I haven't thought about it yet but isn't it funny? It's rather pleasing to receive an old-fashioned proposal after all these years. How nice of Clive. I am fond of him. What a dear little soul he is.'

Filled with optimism and energy, and basking in the feeling of being so appreciated, she put the wireless on and started to tidy up the shop. It was an exceptionally quiet morning. There weren't many customers at the best of times but there were so many problems. It wasn't a restful place to work and the owner was often away. When he wasn't lecturing at the Business School, he was off round the world on his own account charging thousands of pounds to international companies for his advice on how to run a successful business.

She flicked a duster here and there, humming to the wireless. *Won't You Charleston With Me?* Suddenly, in her sensible skirt and clumping shoes, Joy took off round the shop, whirling and kicking and joining in with the few words she remembered from seeing *The Boyfriend* five times thirty years ago. *I could be happy with you*, she sang, charlestoning into the changing rooms to take a curtain call and out again to give an encore. Brown followed, intrigued, bumbling about her legs. She had to push him aside in order to deliver some final slow high kicks which dislodged a box of squash balls.

> *In our attic*
> *We'll be ecstatic*
> *As love-birds up in a tree*
> *All we want is a room in Bloomsburee*

The phone rang. It was Matthew.

'Darling,' she said, breathlessly. 'What would you and the others think if I got married again?'

There was a shocked silence. '. . . *married*?'

'Yes.'

'Not Clive?'

'Yes.'

'You want to marry Clive?'

'Well, I might. Only *might*. I thought you liked him.'

'Sure. But it's a bit different, isn't it, if he's going to be in our family for ever.'

'You don't think it's a good idea then?'

'I didn't say that, did I? It's up to you really,' he conceded reluctantly. 'Are you pregnant or something?'

Joy laughed happily. 'Don't be absurd, darling!'

'But how are you going to live with all them puns and him saying What's your poison, squire, and all that archaic stuff?'

'Does Clive-imo call you squire? I can't believe it. How extraordinary of him! But my goodness me, it's a lot more respectful than addressing everybody as "man", or whatever it is, in the Rastafarian manner. In the past you'd have been calling him "Sir".'

'Oh, mum, you know. I'm only saying you don't like things like the pencil knife and "Pleased to meet yer".'

'If I don't mind, why should you?'

'I thought you did mind. You went on and on about it to us.'

'Yes, well, we've got to step forward with the times, Matt. We're all saying toilet now.'

'Yeah.'

'Clive means very well, that's the point. But it's only a thought, you know. He . . . oh sorry, darling. Two customers. Got to go.'

Too late she saw the enormous van outside. The men were not customers. They were bailiffs. Brown growled softly as she reached instinctively for his collar.

They informed her they were from the Sheriff's Office, instructed by Bloomsbury County Court for recovery of goods to the value of fourteen hundred and forty-four pounds.'

'But what is this?' she demanded, astounded. 'I don't understand. I've just been speaking to the court. They told me there was nothing else outstanding.'

They shrugged and showed her their papers. It could have been another court, they said. They were acting on behalf of a company called *Swiftwear* which had gone on supplying tracksuits and sports shoes while the shop ran up an unpayable bill.

'Can you just hold on?' she pleaded. 'I'm sure I can do something.' But where could she ring? What could she do? The bank wouldn't help. The manager was poised for the kill himself.

'I'm going to try and contact the owner, Nick Morse. He might easily be back from Greece earlier than expected. Please hold on. Better still, could you come back and see him tomorrow?'

'Sorry, love.' They were polite but they were not friendly. She could tell it was too late to try and stall or cajole them. They were going to seize the shop's contents.

While she telephoned Nick's flat and the Business School, leaving urgent messages, the two men set to work. They were leafing impassively through the rails of anoraks, tracksuits and T-shirts, making notes of prices and little piles to take away.

'Why can't you wait?' Joy asked angrily. 'This is a man's livelihood, you know. You're making him bankrupt while he's away. You can't do that to him. It's outrageously unfair. He knows nothing about this fourteen hundred pounds and nor do I.'

They had already started carrying things out to their lorry when the phone rang.

'Oh, Nick, thank God,' she said, explaining the situation in a low desperate voice. 'Please come quickly. They're taking all our stuff.'

'Try and stall them,' he replied. 'I'm on my way from the airport. I'll be about forty-five minutes.'

'He's coming! Look, Nick Morse is coming,' she shouted, going out to the street. 'Please wait!' But the men took no notice of her.

Joy sat with Brown watching helplessly as the minutes went by. When would he come? What could Nick do? Her neck had gone stiff. She felt sick. While the men tramped in and out, steadily and implacably, the little shop was disappearing before her eyes.

Suddenly, to her relief, Nick Morse arrived. He drove deftly into a parking space in front of the bailiff's van and was out of the car in one swift athletic movement, calling a greeting to the men.

He looked unabashed, Joy thought, marvelling at the difference in their temperaments. While she was leaden with shock, almost beyond speech, there he was, still spruce from his flight, adrenalin flowing, revelling in a challenge. He smiled as one of the men passed him with a clutch of tennis racquets.

'D'you mind, mate,' he said genially, reaching out and taking them back. 'My assistant hasn't been paid yet. I'd like to give her one of these racquets in lieu.'

The man paused sullenly as Nick held them out. Joy took the one he was poking out towards her more obviously than the rest. It was the most expensive in the shop. She thanked him and placed it beside her ready to hand back to him later on.

Nick wasted no time. He went outside and stood talking with the men on the pavement. Minutes later he was in again, looking triumphant. 'They want five hundred quid for themselves. They say they'll just take what they've got in the van and leave us the rest. I've promised to hide it all so the shop looks empty from the street. Joy, where on earth can I get five hundred quid now the banks are closed?'

'They won't take cheques, will they?'

'No, it's got to be cash. Look, stay here, will you, and watch the men while I go and try to raise it.'

They went on loading while he was away. Now she couldn't even look at them. What foul bastards.

Three quarters of an hour later, Nick was back with three hundred. 'All I could get for you,' he told the two bailiffs apologetically. 'I can get you two hundred tomorrow.'

After a brief discussion outside, the men took it. They shut up the back off their van and drove away.

'I'm going to meet them tomorrow,' Nick explained to Joy. 'When I give them the rest of the money, they're going to let me know when and where my stuff will go up for sale. I can buy it back. Now, we've got to hide everything they've left.' He took off his jacket and started to haul things into a concealed alcove at the back of the shop. Joy felt too tired to move. She wanted to lie down and weep for a hundred years. Instead, she got up and started to help. There wasn't much left.

At the sight of Clive her gloom seemed to increase rather than diminish. He was in a most jaunty mood. Going over to Motspur Park for the evening, on top of everything else, hadn't been a good idea. Her limbs were aching and she felt he was barely listening to her description of the catastrophe at the shop.

'Well, of course, you saw that coming, didn't you?'

211

'I know, but what a sorrow, isn't it? And what crooks those men are. They must be making a fortune from all the bankruptcies.'

'Lucky for your friend they are crooks. At least he's salvaged some of his stuff.'

'Not much. The shop's done for. I haven't got a job now.'

'No, I suppose you'll need another little job to earn a few pennies.'

'Well, it's not as easy as that, you know. I've got to find somewhere that Brown can go, somewhere I can take my writing and something that I can actually stand. It's quite difficult.'

'Agreed. Nobody's going to want that dog, are they, really? I thought you were making a mistake when you took him on. Now, shall we go to the Taj Mahal? They can't do enough for me there.'

The trouble about Clive, Joy reflected resentfully, as they drove to the Indian restaurant, was that he couldn't cope with down moods. He only wanted her to be grinning and giggling. He wanted everything to be fun, most particularly to-night after his special telephone call. He was disappointed with her now because the atmosphere wasn't right and he couldn't give comfort.

The atmosphere grew worse instead of better.

'Hallo there! Good evening,' Clive boomed in his exuberant manly voice as they stepped into the restaurant. 'Over there, Joy. Our usual table in the corner. Buti knows the one I like, don't you Buti?'

'Noh, noh, noh. Take another table.'

'Can you take the lady's coat?'

'Noh, noh, sit over there.'

'We don't want to sit by the window. We'll go in my usual place.'

The waiter barred their way. 'Noh, noh. Go, go. Not here, please.'

'Very well, Buti,' Clive said, offended. 'But I must say I don't see why not.'

'Sorry, no service. Only those tables.' He indicated the front half of the room.

There was only one other couple eating. 'I expect they're not getting many people in here at the moment,' Joy whispered.

'They'll have even less if they're not careful.'

'So what's been going on with you?' Joy asked, while they looked at the menu.

'Nothing much,' he replied briskly. 'I've had a note from Marigold Belper.'

'Who's she?'

'You remember. She was at Leo's court case. We had a long talk about our war relics and got on rather well. She wrote to me via the imperial War Museum for some reason. Luckily they know who I am, so they forwarded it.

'What does she want?'

Clive looked pleased. 'She wants me to go to a fancy dress party.'

'A what?'

'Fancy dress party,' he repeated, suspiciously airily. 'It's a charity affair.'

Joy tensed. 'Well, am I invited?' she asked in a sharp voice.

Clive reacted to her tone. 'She doesn't mention you.'

'You mean that old woman in an alice band with beady eyes and bird legs? Are you going?'

'She might buy one of my guns. She could be enormously helpful with contacts.'

'Why mention it then, if I'm not going?'

'Of course, you can go if you want to,' Clive replied reasonably. 'It's just that we don't necessarily do everything together. It might not be one of our days.'

'But I introduced you,' Joy persisted incredulously. 'I sold my article to her husband.' When Clive ordered one portion of rice between them, she lost her temper.

They ate in strained silence after that, until Joy, feeling distinctly awkward, tried to break it.

'What were you going to say to me?'

He took a second helping of aloo peas and passed her the dish. 'Pardon?'

'You said you had something important to say to me . . . about our relationship?'

'Oh, not now.'

'Why?'

'I'm not in the mood. You may not want to do it anyway.'

'Try me.'

'No.'

'When will you tell me?'

'I don't know.'

'But I thought you were going to talk about it to-night. Go on. You made it sound urgent.'

He sighed as if she'd defeated him. 'I can tell you now but it's probably a mistake.'

She smiled expectantly.

'You know my friend Barry . . . you met him? We worked together.'

'Yes.'

'You remember Denise?'

'Mm . . . I do, the fun doll.'

'They've suggested we go on holiday together.'

'But I can't be doing with somebody who thinks George Herbert was a minor Victorian poet.'

'Yes, she was a bit batty in that respect, but you're not writing a biography of George Herbert, are you, so I don't know what you're worrying about.'

Joy laughed.

'There's no harm in spending some time with them, is there? I thought it might liven us up a bit. They've kept their relationship very much alive and Barry says that's the secret.'

She asked: 'What's the secret?' But even as she spoke she guessed what he meant.

'They swop partners occasionally.' He flicked it at her, looking foxy with a sort of truculent insouciance, as if it was the most natural thing in the world.

'If you want Denise, you have her.'

His face went blankly defensive as if she was overstepping the bounds of normal decent social intercourse. 'I was afraid you might take it the wrong way.'

'Clive, I'm just thunderstruck.' She could hear her voice, piping and unreal as if the conversation was a bad dream. 'If you want Denise, get on with it. You don't want me.'

'I do want you.'

'This is hardly a sign of it. You must be absolutely mad to think I'd get into an arrangement like that, and with that perky little tough of all people.'

'Look, it doesn't matter. Forget it. I like our friendship. It was only an idea.'

'You are a sod.'

'No, I'm not a sod. Why make such a fuss? Barry says it makes them more desirable to each other.'

She bent her head over her plate. She tried to speak but her mouth trembled. Tears dropped into her prawn curry.

'Joy,' he said, in a quiet curt voice. 'There's no need for all this. Please don't make a scene in here.' He pushed his plate away.

She sniffed and smoothed the wet away from under her eyes. She felt foolish and embarrassed with the waiter hovering and the other diners listening. Their murmured conversations had dwindled to silence. She looked up unfocusedly as the waiter moved to take their plates away.

'Thank you. That was lovely. I couldn't manage any more.'

Clive smiled, relieved. 'That's better. I don't know why you flew off the handle. We usually enjoy our days together. I like to see you, you know that. Don't spoil it.'

She stood up. 'Shut up, Clive. I don't want Aids. Neither do I want a perfect stranger sticking his tongue in my mouth and loosening my lower front teeth. And I don't want any more of you. I'm going home.'

'No, don't . . .'

'Just sod off.' She collected her coat and left the restaurant.

It took her over half an hour to walk back to Clive's house where her car was. She didn't know whether he passed her in his car or not. The lights were on in his flat but she didn't ring the bell. Some of her belongings were in there but she'd have to think about retrieving those another time.

She drove mechanically, in an exhausted shocked dream, trying to collect her agitated thoughts. She'd sensed he wanted Denise that day of the picnic. Now everything in her life had been wiped out in one day. Clive. Her job. Sometime she'd have to try and make a new beginning but she didn't see how she'd have the strength again to do it.

As she drove across Hammersmith Bridge, she thought of Leo. She could pass his house and it would be comforting to tell him what had happened. She glanced at the clock on the dashboard and saw the time. Too late for him. His narcolepsy would have struck him down. She drove on.

In fact, Leo was awake and up and in a far worse state of mind than Joy was. He was in torment.

He had received a note from Ruth informing him that Thomas was having problems. Leo was not to see him again unless he came to her house to do so. Visits were to last a maximum of two hours. He was never to entertain the boy on his own premises and he was not allowed to take him away on holidays.

The trouble was sparked off when Thomas came to spend the afternoon with him the day before. He'd asked Leo if they could go back after Christmas to the farm in Dorset where they'd stayed together in the spring.

'You'll have to ask your mother.'

'She said we could.'

'I don't think she can have meant that.'

'Yes. Yes, she did, dad. She did.'

'But look,' Leo said helplessly, showing him the list of access dates Ruth had granted him. 'These are the days Mummy says I can see you. There's nothing about having you after Christmas, I'm not even seeing you at Christmas.'

'Why can't I see you at Christmas? Why can't I come here?'

'Because Mummy wants you to be with her. She may be taking you to Aunt Melanie and the cousins.'

'Okay. I can stay with you after.'

'We'll have to see. Christmas is a long way off. But you know she doesn't let you stay with me very often.'

'She doesn't like the mess,' Thomas explained apologetically. 'And I haven't got a proper bedroom. You told me you were going to make me one.'

Leo smiled. 'I'm gradually tidying this place up. Didn't you notice the kitchen and all the new machines? I will make a bedroom for you.'

'Which room?' Thomas demanded eagerly. 'Oh please, dad, make the bedroom for me.'

They went upstairs and decided upon the room. It was filled with clutter but they stood there, happily planning the paint colour and where the bed should be. Then they went out and called at a furnishing shop and Thomas chose the carpet and the curtains and some shelves which would be put up when the room was ready.

'Every time I come, Leo, we can do a bit more to my bedroom,' Thomas said. He went home in a state of high excitement to tell his mother.

Then the letter arrived from Ruth cancelling all the arrangements. Leo opened a Court File.

20

She Said

Please don't ever call me fun doll again.

'Fun doll?'

'Please don't ever call me fun doll again.'

'All right, I won't but listen. I have to tell someone. I have a new computer . . . eight and a half thousand. It's sitting here winking at me.'

'What does this one do?'

'Complicated graphics. Multimedia presentations. It's got all the nobs and whistles, and it's exceptionally fast and powerful. It's like having a new love. You feel full of energy and the world is at rights again.'

'I'm too tired for a new love.'

'Yes, I've got one of Tom's friends here keeping me company. He's playing with my computers. I'm all right when he's here.'

'Are you all right?'

'I feel suicidal. The Social Services have put a report in to the court saying I am not to see Thomas. They say I'm high-handed.'

'It'll be all right in time.'

'Yes, but time is running out for me.'

21

The Consequence Was

They all met at Arnold Pope's fancy dress party.

The setting, early evening, late summer, in Arnold Pope's Oxfordshire garden was perfect for a fancy dress party. The mellow yellow stone house caught the setting sun as each guest took a glass of champagne and gravitated towards the pond where the Bonanzo Quartet was playing Beethoven. Muted conversation from the isolated little groups was loudly punctuated by the shrieks of children. Fairies in pink net with strapping legs, and flop-eared bunnies with voices like fog-horns, raced about chasing each other in and out of the shrubbery.

Joy had come morosely with Clive, and was regretting that she'd had to leave Brown with Jill. Her costume, which had cost her neither thought nor expense, was an unoriginal cross between Gypsy Petulengro and a tango dancer. Her flouncy tangerine dress, from the family dressing-up trunk, was widely tiered. She was wearing a gaudy bandana round her head and carrying a cigarette holder. Clive had commented at once on the passive cancer risk although they were out of doors. She was still very angry with him and she felt like a fat mad old bag.

Clive was dressed as King Charles I but nobody could have guessed this, she thought critically, because of his common nose and foxy gingerness. The nose had started to loom large in her mind and was making her terribly aggressive towards him. So much so that she had consulted a herbalist. The man, a charlatan, advised her that if she stopped drinking coffee, which she loved, she would stop barking at Clive. She'd stopped but it did not still her irritation. She'd been revolted by the nose on the way in the car. She was obsessed with it. She remembered it pointing like an excited dog's tail when he was laughing with Denise in an exuberant and flirtatious manner and eating up her picnic. When she spoke to him she had to look away. Looking away from him now, she suddenly saw Leo. She gave a delighted squawk.

'*Leo!*'

'Oh, hullo,' he said, taking the coincidence in his stride. 'Hi, Clive.'

'I didn't know you'd be here,' she said, her spirits lifting. 'What on earth are you coming as? You look like a poacher.'

Clive gave an exuberant manly laugh.

Leo laughed too, obviously quite pleased with the poacher image. He hadn't dressed up. In his snobbish insecure way, he'd dressed down. 'I'm the Man in the Street. The chap on the Clapham Omnibus.'

'I always imagined him wearing a bowler.'

'I don't possess a bowler hat. Anyway I didn't want to dress up because I've got to present the prizes. I don't want to look like a complete idiot.'

'Leo, how lovely!' she said, reaching for another glass of champagne as the tray went by. 'How nice that you've been asked to give the prizes. Are you going to choose the winners yourself? Can you choose us?'

'I expect there'll be a parade and judging.'

'Well, I have to say,' Joy went on, staring about. 'Some of these people have taken a lot of trouble. Look at that mermaid, for instance. She'll have spent hours and hours sticking that sequinned tail onto those green lurex tights.'

'I've seen at least three Mrs. Thatchers,' Clive said.

They stood where they could watch the other guests arriving as they sipped their drinks.

'There's Long John Silver. He's going to get cramp!'

'Over there, look. Nelson, d'you think, with the eye patch?'

'Is that a Franciscan monk or is it a turd?'

'How's Thomas?' Joy asked.

'He's forgotten my birthday,' Leo replied sadly. 'The first time ever.'

She answered quickly. 'That's family life, isn't it. Birthdays are always being forgotten. Thomas won't have any money and Ruth won't be giving him any for that.'

'I'm cutting myself off completely from now on. It's too painful.'

'You can't do that. You're the father.'

'I'm not needed.'

'You are needed.'

At that moment Arnold Pope, an Egyptian mameluke in a red fez, scurried across the grass with cries of amused welcome for a little group of new arrivals emerging onto the terrace.

Conroy Sweeting had made no effort because coming at all had put him in such a bad mood. He had come as himself. Nevertheless, his pink spotted bow tie and ice blue seersucker jacket looked like fancy dress. Marigold was wearing a hat with ear flaps, goggles, a long trailing scarf and jodhpurs. An early female explorer? Amy Johnson? An insect? Arnold Pope kissed her on both cheeks. 'My dear, most original!'

Tania Galway-Lamb came next and she did look original. She looked very peculiar indeed. Her smiling squashed face was partnered on this occasion with the body of an animal, a tiger skin leotard and fraying rope tail. She was a sphinx.

'Yes?' Arnold said, his voice lifting unnaturally.

'My godchild,' Sweetie explained solemnly with a strangely challenging stare. 'And Miss Ruth Bly, our *Plain Speaking* columnist.'

Pope smiled in sincere relief to see a wholesome, ordinary young woman stylishly dressed in a short cream dress and scarlet tights with red and green feathers at her neck. She was holding the hand of a small child in a space helmet.

'You look good enough to eat,' he said.

'I'm a salad sandwich,' she replied. 'But you can't eat Thomas.'

'Yum, yum,' Arnold bent over the child, gnashing some queer brownish teeth. 'I'll see how hungry I get!'

'You can't eat me!' Thomas shouted. He pulled away from his mother and darted off across the lawn.

Ruth went after him.

'There's my family,' Leo remarked in a wondering voice.

He was about to detach himself to go and talk to them when Mrs. Pope materialised in white as a voluptuous angel and called out to him. 'Mr. Derbyshire!' Wings bobbing, she came forward, holding out both hands. 'What an enormous pleasure for us. I'm Dodo Pope.'

'Hullo, Dodo.'

'I've only just heard you were here. It's a great thrill. My grandchildren adore *Chelsea Charlie*. We had no idea so many children would be coming today. I expect they'll all want your autograph. I was going to ask you if we could possibly persuade you to present a children's prize?'

Leo looked trapped. He began an embarrassed cryptic mumble. 'Well, no, I . . . er, not really, you see . . .'

'I know it's short notice but do please say you will? Just a few words. We've got Herrick D. Johnson giving the grownups' prize but he hasn't turned up yet.'

'Not that rat!' Ruth Bly said, in quite a loud voice, behind them.

'Oh, d'you know him?' Dodo turned eagerly. 'We're all dying to know what he's like. He sounds rather fierce. I know a lot of people loathe him. There's a clutch of enraged feminists here waiting to tear him to pieces!'

'Daddy, daddy . . . there's my dad!' Thomas flung himself at his father. 'Happy birthday, dad!'

Leo swung him into the air.

Ruth gave a cautious po-faced smile for Thomas's benefit. 'Many happy returns.'

'Many happy returns,' Dodo echoed. 'Now, if it's your

birthday, there is no excuse. You'll have to make a little speech for us.'

'At school I've made you a train out of a toothpaste carton,' Thomas declared proudly. 'Dad, is this your birthday party?'

They all laughed.

And when Mrs. Pope left them, Leo and Ruth had to talk for the child's sake. Thomas looked so pleased that they were both overwhelmed at what they'd done to him. But Ruth didn't dare look straight into Leo's eyes in case she began to forget how angry she was. He was mad but the old magical sexual glitter was working, as it always did, weakening her. It was fatal.

'So who are you meant to be in that cap?' she enquired, struggling to get a grip of herself. 'Are you a rat catcher? No, I expect you're God, aren't you?'

'Yes, I'm God.'

Ruth crouched down to help Thomas who had a stone in his shoe. When she stood up, she couldn't see. 'We'd better circulate.' She turned abruptly, her eyes full of tears and walked away.

Leo watched her go and find somebody else to talk to. She was mad and she'd destroyed him. Should he leave now? He didn't know what to do. Certainly one thing he realised he definitely could not do was admit to being Len Derbyshire *and* Herrick D. Johnson. It would be like being Dr. Jekyll and Mr. Hyde. And if he didn't care much what people at this party thought, what about Ruth and the social workers and the Court? They'd make sure he never saw Thomas ever again.

The controversial woman-hater would have to be unavoidably detained, that's all there was to it. He could easily bribe a waitress to announce a message from some outlandish place hundreds of miles away. As he looked about for the right person to do it, he suddenly bumped into Tania Galway-Lamb who was parading past him on winged feet in the tiger skin body stocking and exuding party spirit.

Neither spoke. His stomach lurched at the sight of the grinning lantern-jawed face but it suddenly gave him a preposterous idea.

'Tania!' he called, going after her.

In another part of the garden, Clive and Joy had joined the Sweetings. After mutual congratulation on the brilliance of their costumes, the two couples were exchanging a few polite remarks before Marigold and Clive disappeared to discuss some rare items from Clive's collection of ancient war weapons.

When his mother passed on, Clive was telling the little group (raising a religious theme to interest the editor of *Plain Speaking*), he'd been extremely shocked to find the crematorium automatically used the new prayerbook for their funeral services.

Sweetie nodded. 'I've heard that. How beastly for you.'

'But he doesn't believe in God,' Joy said.

Alone with Sweetie minutes later, she found herself intimidated. She marvelled that she'd dared to bark at him about her drinking article. He was so tall, so ducal, so dashingly superior.

'Aren't we meant to be on the move?' She flicked back her bandana tails, talking to keep the conversation going. 'Do we now parade round the edge of the lawn for the judging, d'you imagine?'

'Oh, I'm not doing that,' Sweetie replied. 'I'm not in fancy dress.'

She widened her eyes humorously, taking a bit of a risk. 'You do surprise me.' She looked him up and down, gesturing at the floppy pink bow tie and pale blue milkman's jacket. 'You look like a minstrel.'

He laughed too, throwing his head back and tumbling his beautiful snow-rinsed hair. 'Do I? In that case, a minstrel I shall be.' So they stayed together as the exotic queue shuffled slowly across the grass to the lively strains of the Bonzano

Quartet. Boxers, bathers, soldiers, belly dancers, Big Ben, Hitler, The Mad Hatter, Mother Teresa, Alan Whicker, a sunflower, a sandwich board, a hen . . .

'Conroy, I think you ought to have a piece in *Plain Speaking* about jockeys' excessive use of whips these days,' Joy urged. 'Racing's become a most disgusting spectacle.'

'No, no,' he replied dismissively. 'It looks much worse than it is on television.'

'It's got nothing to do with what I've seen on television. We know they're all exceeding their ten allotted hits per race because the jockeys are suspended one after the other. Suspension has become a way of life. They don't care. They should lose their prize money.'

'It doesn't hurt the horses, you know.'

'I know exactly what it does. I had a horse myself,' she said crossly. 'The point is, it never happened in the past. It's all part of our general descent into yobbery and greed. The brute wins in our society. He's our hero now, but he's got to be stopped.'

This was a subject more dear to Sweetie's heart. He stopped and turned to her and smiled. 'We have a little luncheon once a month at *Plain Speaking*,' he said sweetly. 'I wonder if you would care to come to our next one?'

'Ladies and gentlemen!' Arnold Pope clapped his hands for silence. 'Welcome to Greenlawns! I am tremendously grateful to you all for making the journey out here to Buscot today and for taking so much trouble to make our little country event such a spectacular success. With your support, we will have raised over fifteen thousand pounds for our charities this year, and I do hope those of you who can are going to stay on to hear more from the Bonzano Quartet later on. Chairs are set out by the lake and, if there is an overflow, perhaps people would be kind enough to spread out onto the far lawn beside the rhododendrons. Supper will be served in the house when the fancy dress contest is over.

'And now for the judging. A difficult task indeed because

of the unusually high standard of dazzling and original costumes. We have divided it into two sections. An adult section and a children's section. Mr. Len Derbyshire, author of *Chelsea Charlie*, and doyen of the children's fiction world, will give away our children's prize but, first, I am going to call upon Herrick D. Johnson, who has recently burst into print to tell us chaps what to think about the ladies! His book has been on the best seller lists for three weeks and he needs no introduction from me. I haven't read the book yet so I can't agree or disagree! So here to tell us who our fancy dress winner is, ladies and gentlemen . . . Herrick D. Johnson!'

The audience applauded. Many craned their necks curiously. A few gasped. Wreathed in bumper smiles, tail swinging, Tania Galway-Lamb stepped forward.

On a bench in the shrubbery, Amy Johnson was tête à tête with Charles I.

Clive had brought along one or two of his best battle trophies to impress Marigold Belper, anticipating a possible sale if she offered enough and without an inkling of the ingrained freebee mentality of the elderly scrounger. He was flattered to befriend a war correspondent from the national press. And she was still under the impression that he worked at the Imperial War Museum or she would not have given him the time of day. She was making herself agreeable now, paving the way for future favours. When Clive said, 'My arms await you!' she giggled like a girl.

'How is Peter Nugent?' she enquired, picking up one of the ancient guns. 'I hear he's taken early retirement from the Museum?'

Clive emitted a loud manly laugh. 'That's one way of putting it, Marigold. Isn't he in the nick?'

'Darling Peter? In prison? How? Why? What a terrible thing! So many people seem to be going there these days.'

'I think he's been accused of rape.'

'Peter was? I can't believe it.' She leaned towards Clive,

her beady eyes blinking earnestly between the flying helmet flaps. 'You know, I've spent hours alone with that man. I never had the slightest trouble from him. Well . . .' She shook her head helplessly and turned back to the rare pistol in her hand, 'Firearms never let one down, do they. Now tell me something about this one . . . Scotch, of course?'

'You're right. No guard round the trigger. It's meant to be one of five known examples. The company discontinued. One in the Visser Collection made fifteen thousand. Sotheby's have tried to tell me the barrel doesn't belong to the stock, but I don't accept that. It seems a likely marriage to me.'

'Oh my, Clive, what a perfectly beautiful little pepperbox . . . so elegantly engraved . . . d'you know I'm getting awfully hungry, aren't you?'

'I'll go and get us some food,' he offered immediately.

He zoomed towards the house on his nimble feet, eager to continue his secluded session with Marigold Belper and not leave his precious treasures for too long. Out of the corner of his eye he spotted Joy poised uncertainly on the terrace with no one to talk to. At the sight of him, she perked up, smiling with relief, but he deliberately kept staring ahead and went straight into the house to fill up two plates.

It grew dark as he sat on with Marigold. The strains of Haydn and Schubert from the Bonzano Quartet floated thinly over the hedge and lanterns hanging in the trees threw long shadows on the grass.

People sprawled with their drinks, their costumes falling apart. Wigs and shoes lay abandoned. When the classical programme ended, the quartet played jazz and slowly the drunken guests stood up to dance.

Leo looked for Ruth. He couldn't see her but there was his son. Thomas was over-excited now, darting hither and thither with another boy, making a nuisance of himself. Leo was glad they'd pretended to be a family for his sake. He was even glad he'd signed over half of his *Why Men Hate Women* royalties to Tania Galway-Lamb.

Tania had stopped signing autographs. She was sitting under the trees being harangued by a feminist who had taken exception to the book.

Bemused but unabashed, she slowly screwed up her face into a smile of excrutiating lasciviousness. 'Little scamp! I want to smack your wrist! *I like women*. I like to give them little hugs to keep them happy. Why not come and have dinner with me at my club, then I can give you lots of hugs? I know what you want,' she added, with a coyly deep-throated laugh. 'You want to rape me, don't you? Wanton little witch!'

'I think you're a wanker,' said the feminist.

Joy picked up another glass of wine although her head was already dizzy with drink. She'd been searching for Clive for ages because she wanted to go home. In the gloom across the garden she thought she saw Leo and Ruth dancing. She'd have liked to have danced with Clive but their dancing days were long since done. Where was the stupid swine? In the distance she heard a muffled crack.

In the shrubbery, Marigold and Clive were shooting. Boredom and alcohol had made them argumentative and they had ill-advisedly set up a target.

'Of course,' Marigold said, wishing she could get up to the house for a good look round, 'these little jobs were only for the hat or the sock . . . for travelling. Good fun for the collector but quite useless. You couldn't hit a door with one at four feet.'

'My dear girl,' Clive exclaimed, nettled. 'I most certainly beg to differ. You can be deadly accurate with a derringer.' He stood up and stuck his glass on the branch of a tree.

Belper fired and missed. Fired and hit the tree trunk. On her third attempt the glass shattered.

'What did I tell you?' he said.

He was fixing her glass into position when Joy sighted him.

Afterwards she went over and over what happened in her

mind. She saw Clive standing at the tree. She saw Marigold with the gun in her hand. She could have called out a warning when she saw Thomas and his friend come whooping along the hedge behind them but the sound froze in her throat. With a curious sensation of exhilarated detachment she stood still and watched.

Thomas cannoned into Marigold Belper, fell against the bench and broke his leg. Thrown off balance, the tipsy old woman pressed the trigger. In one of those tragic freak accidents that are never satisfactorily explained, the bullet went straight into the back of Clive's head and killed him.

22

And the World Said

Deary ... me ...!

When Thomas came out of hospital, his mother and father collected him together and Leo prepared a special celebration supper in his newly done-up kitchen. There was a white cloth on the table, a candle, napkins, enough knives and forks and an immaculately printed menu lying at each setting.

CAFÉ DE LEO CONTINENTALE

Starter	Pate – Tuna à Thomas
Main Course	Poullete Kiev avec frites et vegetables
Desert	Glace avec le tarte pomme ou melon ou Gateaux Ruth
Cheese	Votre choice
Wines	Vin de Maison Coke

Thomas's bedroom was all ready for him with a new pine bed and the blue carpet and curtains he had chosen. He was thrilled that his parents were talking to each other again.

'Now, wherever I am, I won't always be missing the other one,' he said.

He went off to bed without any trouble, anxious not to upset the harmonious atmosphere between Ruth and Leo. But, early in the morning, as it was beginning to get light, he got up and padded into Leo's room to make sure they were still together and it wasn't a dream.

He stood at the door watching them. They were making love.

Suddenly Leo's head turned and his eyes focused on his son. 'Tomtom!' he said horrified. 'How long have you been there?'

The boy jumped onto the bed and climbed down between his mother and father. 'Hallo, Tomtom,' Ruth said, smiling, and gave him a small satisfied kiss.

'Sleep well?' Leo asked. 'This is good, isn't it?'

'Yes, it is good,' Thomas agreed, not entirely reassured. 'But while you two were asleep your heads were banging together.'